IRON
CROSSED

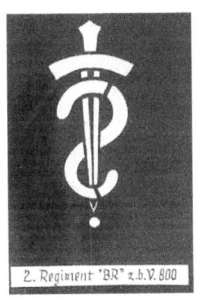

2. Regiment "BR" z.b.V. 800

Renata Rose
&
Phil Rose

Revised Edition Jan. 2018

ISBN-10: 0646975110

This book is dedicated to our parents Martin and Marlene Schlaefer. You shared with us the roads you walked, the wars you fought, the love you found and the struggles you faced in your new homeland. You taught us your values and you were always there for us no matter what. We owe you such a lot.

If only we could have just one more day with you both we would say, again: *thank you for everything – you were THE BEST!*

… the race is not to the swift
nor yet the battle to the strong.

…

But time and chance happeneth to them all.

(*Ecclesiastes* 9:11)

Chapter 1

1951 – *News!*

He picked his way carefully between the piles of rubble, the crushed bricks and splintered beams imperfectly shrouding the remnants of what once had been people's lives. A pale pink arm poked out, long separated from the rest of the doll. A bit of tap glinted in the grimy afternoon sun.

No houses in this street were still intact; gaps now where most had stood, or empty fire-blackened shells. Sure, in some areas of the city, homes had already been re-built and work was going on to banish the destruction of war. The *chuff-chuff* of the rubble-trains floated over to him from a jagged skyline of new buildings and cranes. Now and again you also caught the odd metallic squeak from the few remaining trams they had co-opted to help shift the piles of rubble. Here though … *still looks like a bomb's hit the place*.

He smiled grimly as that was of course exactly what had happened – *hundreds of bombs, thousands of bombs. Well, what did they expect, when the place was right next to a major submarine pen?* In this area it could have been yesterday, not five years ago, since the war ended.

He wiped the grime from his forehead. That was then; this was now. However was he going to tell her?

Do you want the good news first or the bad news? That would help lighten the mood.

Nope, that would make it sound frivolous. He could just hear her: "Is this another one of your silly jokes?" No. This news definitely was not frivolous.

This was going to upset her, he knew that; but there was no way around it. Hell this was making him more anxious than he had ever felt before a mission. He needed her to understand how important this was to them. *It meant control of their future!* The amazing thought stopped him in his tracks. Yes! That was it! Only since the war had finished had the possibility dawned on him that he actually had any control over what might to happen to him; which direction his life would take; and the right to make his own decisions.

1

He turned into their road and was confronted with its two rows of corrugated iron sheds. Each shed just two rooms. All toilet and washing was communal. You wanted privacy? – You got your water from the tap at the end of the sheds. You carried it back home one saucepan at a time, heated it, poured it into a tub, and washed yourself. Now what had that Yank said? *You wash up as far as possible, you wash down as far as possible ... and then you wash possible.* He smiled, the man's drawl still in his ears bringing back the American prisoner of war camp in Italy. He could still picture him. A really decent bloke who had treated him with respect; who had saved him from being beaten to death because of that supposed tattoo. Now what *was* his name? No. His face was still there; his name gone.

Share a few outside toilets between two hundred people and you get a really, really bad stench. As often happened, more memories were triggered: streams at dusk, clogged with rotting carcases. He pushed them aside. *I wonder if that'll ever change; if the memories will ever fade?* He stopped thinking smells and he stopped worrying about what to say as he neared the shed he shared with Leni and the two children.

Yes! *Control of our future.* That was the best way to think about it. That news was surely, no, definitely, more good than bad! Surely she would see that too. The excitement built with each step and Martin caught himself grinning at the nosey next-door neighbour for whom he on less auspicious days reserved his best scowl. The door offered its usual resistance, its tinny squeak cut short by his energetic shove.

"Leni? Leni, where are you? I've got some fantastic news! LENI!!"

the chuff-chuff of the rubble-trains

Rubble-train (left) and tram (right) combine to cart away post-war devastation.

Chapter 2

1935 – *Test*

I'm not so sure – look at what he's doing to peoples' rights."

"Well, you can say what you like about Hitler, but he's certainly got rid of the unemployment. You go to the city – to Leipzig – you don't see all those jobless people hanging around on the street corners anymore."

"Have to call him Führer now, don't forget!"

Hitler's apologist, Herr Bluhme, was the firm's *Zimmermeister*, the head carpenter who was currently the foreman.

The young Martin couldn't help noticing, despite his nerves, what a hulk of a man Bluhme was. Most noticeable was his neck – or lack of it. His shoulders and head just seemed to be one square unit. *That's what my Dad means when he talks about someone having lots of muscles.*

Herr Bluhme's face looked like someone had run over it with something very heavy starting at the forehead and rolling down. He had a downward turn not only to the sides of his mouth but also the eyes and cheeks: everything seemed to be sliding down towards his neck. He looked to Martin as if he didn't smile very often. In fact, Martin thought, he could not see any smile lines in that face at all. Herr Bluhme currently had a scowl on his face, as he argued the merits of the new German Chancellor with his workmates.

He turned his attention to the young lad standing in front of him, and his eyes squinted as he bellowed, the sound seeming to come from somewhere deep down. "Well young Schläfer – Martin isn't it? – your older brother says that you want to be a carpenter with us, is that correct?"

"*Jawohl*, Herr Bluhme!" A loud, firm voice, not wanting to betray his nervousness. The effects of Hitler's employment policy had not made themselves felt here in the German countryside as well as in the cities, and he had been searching for work for weeks and weeks. As both a member of the Nazi Party and its paramilitary arm the *Brownshirts*, Bluhme had been made a union rep and wielded a lot of influence at work. When Martin's elder brother Otto had asked,

4

Bluhme had done him the favour and agreed to interview Martin for an apprenticeship. Bluhme looked the would-be carpenter's apprentice up and down.

The youngest child in the family, Martin had turned fourteen in January 1935; and while he still had a boyish air about him, he could, when he wanted, exude a confidence and maturity beyond his years. Thus what Herr Bluhme saw was a tall, handsome, well-built young man. Strong jaw, nose beautifully proportioned to his face, deep green eyes with eyelashes that made most girls envious. Face framed by soft curly hair. All in all, he noted with approval, features typical of the ideal Aryan male.

Martin's father was a very small man: his party trick was to walk back and forth under the outstretched arm of his wife. He had always said, flexing the muscles on his short little arm, "Look my boy: THIS is what matters. Build strong muscles and you will be OK all your life." Martin understood why his father felt that way: hard manual work was the only life his father had ever known. Up at four every morning feeding and mucking-out the horses; home again at six for a hearty breakfast of bacon and eggs; then working all day until after nightfall with only short breaks for meals.

Heeding his father's advice, Martin had decided at a very young age it was easier to concentrate on building big muscles. School had never really been something he enjoyed. His school reports always said that he worked hard and had impeccable behaviour, but he felt he did just enough to pass, nothing more. He had to miss a lot of school anyway during the *Kartoffelferien* – the 'potato holidays' when he and other children were given official leave from school to help with the harvest. And often he had to be away just supervising the younger children whose mothers were working in the fields bringing in the turnips and sugarbeet.

So, at the age of fourteen there he was, waiting to be interviewed for a position as apprentice carpenter to the firm *Fricke*, who built most of the houses in and around his little home town of Wiederitzsch, near Leipzig, in the east of Germany.

"Well young Schläfer, if you want to work with us, you'll need to pass a test."

Martin nodded. *A test?* He hadn't expected that. *Let's hope it's got something to do with maths. I'm not too bad at maths.*

"*Bist Du schwindelfrei Martin*? Have you got a head for heights?" Bluhme nodded in the direction of the house currently under construction for the local vicar. Its sturdy wooden framework was completed, the little fir tree on top indicating the imminent *Richtfest* – the traditional topping-out ceremony. Martin understood the head foreman would soon pronounce his blessing from on high, hurling three glasses of red wine to the ground to protect house and inhabitants.

"See that? Get up onto the roof and walk along the *Firstbalken* – that's the plank between the two chimneys. It's there for the chimney sweep. It's six inches wide so you shouldn't have any problem. That's your test! I'm not going to employ an apprentice who shits himself when he gets up high. Are you up to it, or are you going to run home to mummy?"

"I am not scared of heights."

Internally he heaved a great sigh of relief; that test he knew he could ace. Like most boys growing up in the country he had spent a lot of his time balancing on things. He loved the old walls surrounding the town and climbing over the old bridges that were in disrepair. His friend and nephew Kurt, who was only eleven months younger than Martin, usually came along, and the two of them had spent a lot of their childhood just clambering over things and the higher the better.

Before Bluhme could say another word, Martin had climbed up to the attic, out of the window and onto the narrow ladder leading to the top of the high-raked roof designed to let the heavy winter snow slide easily off. He climbed higher and reached the beam spanning the two chimneys. He was feeling very cocky and pleased with himself when he lost his footing and fell. He managed to grab the beam with one arm, legs dangling in space. Swinging his body to get a purchase with his other hand, he stifled a scream when the beam's wooden splinters embedded themselves deep into his palm and fingers.

Looking down, he now realised how high up he really was – a fall would surely break his back, or worse. He swung one of his legs over the beam and missed, his fingers almost relinquishing their grip from the pain as the splinters went in even deeper. He caught his breath.

Another try, swinging his leg higher this time. Yes! Wrapping his leg firmly around, he heaved his body up and over the beam, now harming testicles as well as hands. He forced himself to stand upright, swaying a little on the beam until he steadied and found his balance again. He walked determinedly, not looking down until he reached the other end.

Shaken and not a little sick, he realised that if his reflexes had not been so good he would certainly have either died or been very severely injured. It now looked considerably further down to the ground than before. *Need to be much more careful in future. 'Cept there's probably not going to be a future, at least as a carpenter. I guess that's one job I've really messed-up!* He looked down apprehensively to see Bluhme's reaction.

But Herr Bluhme was busy talking to one of the other men on the site – perhaps again extolling the Chancellor's, sorry Führer's, virtues – and had not witnessed the near disaster. He looked up. "Look down at the ground Martin, look down! I can't tell whether you have a head for heights otherwise! OK, OK, that's fine: come on down." He gestured in an off-hand way.

"Come along with me to the office. I need to give you some papers to fill in. You need to take them to the Technical College. Tell them you'll be starting on the usual date. What's up? What are you shaking for? The height got to you after all, eh?"

Martin thought quickly, clenching his fists so that the blood from the splinters was not visible. "Nein, Herr Bluhme! Like I said, I'm not scared of heights. I was just nervous. I really wanted this job. And yes, my brother told me all apprenticeships start on the same day, always the first of April."

"Job, Martin? JOB?! This is not a *job*, Martin. Becoming an apprentice carpenter means you are embarking on a profession, and a highly respected one. Once you are qualified, you have a place in society and people's respect. People defer to us when we wear our journeyman's *Tracht* – our traditional uniform. It's not for show, you know. It means something. It represents a fine tradition going back many, many years. You know what the eight pearl buttons on the waistcoat stand for? The eight hours a day you will work. And the six buttons on the jacket mean six days a week. You'll wear that uniform with pride when you finish your apprenticeship and do your three years' journeying. It's a symbol of your proven ability and devotion to your Journeyman's Guild."

Sensing all this symbolism was being lost on Martin, Bluhme tried a new tack.

"Just think of it, Martin. You'll travel all over the country and have wonderful experiences in many different places a normal person would not hope to visit. All that time you mustn't go within fifty miles of your home town, so you won't return home for a long, long time! It will set you up for life, make a real man of you, *mein Junge*. A man of the world!"

The young Martin was indeed destined to travel, but not in the marvellous way Herr Bluhme had envisaged.

becoming an apprentice carpenter

Part of the yellowed first page of Martin's original apprenticeship agreement with the building firm *Fricke*, as signed by Martin and his father Max on the 1st April 1935. It stipulates a probation period of four weeks, to be included in his three-year apprenticeship if Martin is accepted. Sections 2 & 3 set out mutual obligations: the teacher is duty-bound not only to teach the apprentice the trade of carpentry, but to ensure he remains hard-working with good habits. The apprentice undertakes, among other things, not to give away secrets of the trade to outsiders. Martin's father is also obligated. In section 5 he is to provide not only the tools of the trade, but board, bed and linen, also seeing to the cleaning of the latter. Interestingly, the spaces for the amount of money involved – indicated by the script letters *RM* (for *Reichsmark*) – are left blank.

Chapter 3

1936 – Sniff

Martin would have liked to ask what his pay would be – there were blanks on the form where the amount should have been shown – but worried that it may seem ungrateful or even disrespectful. So he just politely thanked Herr Bluhme, left with the four pages, found a firm surface to write on, filled them in and that very afternoon took them straight to the Technical College office.

Although he had had to work on the farm for part of the day since he was very young, he was not accustomed to being on his feet all day, and the men on the site kept him running from one task to another. Consequently he found he wanted to get to bed early and fell into an exhausted, but deep sleep every night. But within a few weeks he was relieved to notice he was no longer falling asleep straight after dinner. And look! With each passing week he could feel those muscles growing as he got stronger and stronger. And, although one couldn't see that in the mirror, confidence grew with the muscles.

"No Martin that's a chisel. I wanted an awl." "No lad, this is the way you saw wood properly!" "Martin you have to watch out, people up there will just drop things. They won't care about you being underneath." Thus he learnt, spending his days getting tools for people, holding wood, sawing bits marked to various lengths, carrying things up ladders and things down ladders, and being appropriately cautious. Assigned as errand boy to a team of five qualified carpenters, it kept him really busy. He also felt he was learning a lot just through watching them work. Naturally curious, he never stopped asking questions and the men all answered willingly and patiently.

"Hans, where do you get your tools from?"

"Good question youngster. Where do you think? Na, I'll tell you. A real carpenter always makes his own tools. Ja, I know it states in your apprenticeship contract that your father will buy them, but a good carpenter – like us – well, we always make our own. So, it's time you started to learn how to do that. And then something just as important – how to look after them."

His first pay! He desperately wanted to look inside the little brown pay-packet. He had never had any of his own money – no-one in his desperately poor family had ever had money because his father was paid in food for his farm work, with no cash changing hands. But he did not want to appear too eager in front of the others. That would display his lack of maturity and inexperience with money. And also, deep down, he was a private person, not prone to share his feelings with anyone. So the packet was pocketed as nonchalantly as he could manage, to enjoy in private somewhere, once he got home.

He had earned the princely sum of 25 pennies per hour! Ten *Reichsmark* – ten marks for the week's work. Enough to buy the occasional beer and meal out, and of course the material he needed to make his own tools. The rest he would give to his mum. His parents had already told him they expected him to contribute at least half his wage, just as their other children before him had done when they started to work and still lived at home.

Martin's fiscal reticence did not go unnoticed by his team.

"Happy with your pay, Martin? They take out tax, pension and health insurance, but it'll get better each year, you know. When you qualify, you'll be netting about eighteen *Reichsmark* per week. Enough to spend on a girl-friend!"

Yeah... Martin's imagination had barely succeeded in uniting some unspecified but beautiful girl-friend with eighteen *Reichsmark* when the pleasant mental image was rudely interrupted by an amazing sniff.

Now, a normal sniff would not have intruded upon Martin's consciousness, preoccupied as it was with women and money. But this sniff was different. After several short attempts it embarked on a long, drawn out inhalation that seemed to collect more and more phlegm from the owner's throat and nose as it lengthened in time, culminating in one heavy revolting gulp. There was no mistaking that sniff. He found himself counting the usual five seconds of mucosal gymnastics before the final swallow.

Getting to know the sniff's owner had been painful. Alfred Stepke was four years older than Martin and was a newly qualified carpenter. Problem was, he let everyone know it. Problem was too, he had the looks to get away with his showing off. Blond hair, always carefully

11

combed back in the latest fashion; deep blue penetrating eyes. Strong jaw and a nose that looked like it had been broken more than once. Which it very well might have been, if the many stories Alfred told during the meal breaks about his female conquests could be believed. The older men just laughed it off; but Martin secretly envied him, wondering just what it was that enabled him to effortlessly pull *so* many good-looking women. They obviously were not deterred by his sniff: that was sure. On the rare occasions he produced a handkerchief he was careful to point out his name embroidered lovingly onto it by his latest conquest.

Alfred, for some reason, especially had Martin in his sights, and thought it fun to take every opportunity to provoke and annoy him. The harassment had become worse of late. Apart from Martin there had been no new apprentices at Fricke's in the last eighteen months and so it was Martin's role as the youngest to get the food at meal breaks. They were called *Brotzeit* – bread time – but there was a sensible amount of *Bier* involved too. Three times a day, he took orders from the five men on his team, bringing back the food and Bier from the local shop.

"What took you so long *this* time: how difficult *is* it to find the shop? You've got my change wrong again you dumb arsehole. And I didn't order this liver-sausage *Du Idiot*!"

Martin glared at Alfred. He'd given up arguing: "Alfred, you must have forgotten what you ordered" or "I write down how much you give me and your change is spot-on, mate." This time he really felt like adding to the distortion of that nose which clearly appealed to some women. Unusually for him, he felt himself losing it. His left hand shot out, grabbing Alfred around the throat. Ah, but Martin never lost it completely. A firm, painful squeeze. An equally controlled voice, quiet and menacing, addressed the startled Alfred from within a few inches of his face.

"Right. I've had a gutful of this stupid crap of yours. Just once more and I'll give you a thrashing you will never forget, understand? You'll be sniffing through your ears."

"Easy! Easy!" Alfred gurgled. Martin relaxed his grip. A little.

"So whatever is your problem Alfred? I've never done anything to you."

The hand came away.

"To be honest I was pissed off because you got this apprenticeship. I was there when you came for the interview. I saw you almost fall, cocky little bugger. I've been waiting for you to screw-up and hurt one of us. But, I guess I was wrong; maybe you did deserve the apprenticeship after all. Anyway, Martin, all apprentices get given a hard time – it's traditional. But you are half-way through yours now. There haven't been any disasters, and it looks like you're a good bloke. Look, I'm sorry."

Martin accepted his hand.

Tentatively at first, and without realising, it the two young men gradually grew to like each other. By the time Martin finished his apprenticeship he counted Alfred as one of his closest friends, more than a work-mate. They shared a similar sense of humour encumbered by an acute sense of responsibility. Martin even grew to tolerate his sniff.

deep down, he was a private person

Martin in mid-apprenticeship, age 16.

paid in food for his farm work

No mechanisation here. Martin's dad Max, hand on horn, directs the ploughing against a monotonous Saxony landscape in the mid 1920s.

Chapter 4

1936 – *Two pounds of sausages*

Use your feet more, Martin. That's right! Keep your distance. KEEP YOUR DISTANCE. Let him come to you. *Richtig*! Right! Fight smart. Work the angles. Yes! Yes! Much better. OK lads, that's enough for today. You're all coming on well."

"Must say that right hook of yours is coming on nicely Martin. Last one really took the wind out of me." They climbed out of the ring, sweating despite the cold.

Martin grinned through the sweat. "You weren't so bad yourself mate."

"How about we go grab a meal and some booze."

"Sounds like an excellent idea, Paul. Something liquid always goes down well after a bit of hard sparring."

Martin had started boxing in his last year at school, when it had been introduced as part of the *health and fitness* culture promoted by the Third Reich – fit youngsters will make good soldiers, you see. He enjoyed it so much that he joined the local club, and when he was not on the building site, divided most of his spare time between the ring and reading. He was pleased to discover that it was making him even fitter, which was at least partly responsible for recent successes in a number of local boxing competitions. Trouble was, he didn't like hurting anyone, and really felt bad when he knocked someone out. This did obviously not bode well for a professional career, but he found that the small prize money helped to make him feel a little better about the pain he had inflicted. And boxing also increased his (already not insignificant) self-esteem. Interesting: people seemed to respect you more when they found out you boxed. Or perhaps it was just fear.

Not by nature gregarious, Martin nevertheless still enjoyed the camaraderie of the other club members. They were often good for a belly laugh about something or other, usually related to sex, and usually over a beer. He found it good to laugh along with them, even though he did not always understand the details of the joke.

His sparring-mate Paul Brenner was different from the others, though – he was an *intellectual*. He was attending Leipzig University, studying to become a veterinary surgeon. Tall and slim, he'd look at you with his gentle brown eyes before his long reach landed the punch. He always looked as if he needed a good meal. But Martin knew that in fact he ate like a horse. His private speculation was that Paul burnt up lots of energy with his intellectual activity and his constant fidgeting, because he just never kept still. His legs would bounce and his feet would tap and his fingers would beat out a rhythm and he was always excited about something new he had learnt. Especially if it concerned horses, his great love. It was nice that he seemed always to want to share this knowledge with his friend Martin, who did not always find details about horse anatomy or feeding techniques particularly interesting, but was always happy to lend an ear in the spirit of friendship. But Paul also shared knowledge of other things – historical, political, scientific – and Martin, being of an inquisitive nature, liked that.

The brown colour of Paul's hair still showed through his military style short haircut, and, for some reason neither he nor Martin could fathom, women wanted to mother him. Whenever the two of them went out together Paul would get the older ladies smiling at him while Martin was the younger ones' target. They consequently made a good team when it came to attracting women, an activity they practiced whenever they could.

They had actually been at the same school together but Martin had been in the class above Paul and as the elder boy had pretty much ignored him. Their fathers worked on different farms, but as usual in a small village people know quite a bit about the other families and were always interested in what was happening with or to whom. Both families had seven children and both fathers worked on farms so the young men, when their lives *did* finally cross, had a few things in common apart from boxing and women. They laughed a lot when they were together, sometimes over the silliest things. Martin enjoyed sharing the jokes he heard from the men at work with Paul. What seemed to make Paul laugh the most was Martin's ability to tell the story with a poker face, such that Paul was not aware that a joke was being told until the punch-line.

Stand-up wash, clean clothes and on their bikes. From Wiederitzsch it was about twenty minutes hard cycling to Leipzig, to the nearest good food, drink and women. On the way they decided to head, once again, for *Lilli's*, Martin's favourite. The owner had named the restaurant after his daughter.

"Why do you reckon *Lilli's* is so good?

"Well for me it's the atmosphere, it's *sehr gemütlich* - nice and cosy. It feels a bit like home, only with a better fire, and decent music. And the smell of the food."

They parked their bikes in the lane and went inside.

"What do you fancy?"

"I'll have the blond one over there in the corner."

"No, to eat, idiot."

"Oh, okay. *Eisbein*, sauerkraut and dumplings, obviously. The pork knuckle meat simply falls off the bone and I love the way they spread the gravy all over the dumplings here. What about you?"

"Mmm, sounds good. I'll have the same." They called over the waitress and ordered their meals along with a beer each. Then they turned their attention to the important business.

"What about those two over there, veerry cute, don't you think? I fancy the brunette. I think the blond fancies you. She can't keep her eyes off you."

"I know, I told you I fancied the blonde. C'mon, let's ask if we can join them."

They both strolled over to the girls, trying to look sophisticated and nonchalant. Martin showed-off his freshly-won muscles to their best advantage. Paul gave them the benefit of his gentle smile.

"May we have the pleasure of joining you?" Paul addressed the blonde with the appropriate politeness. "My name is Paul and my friend here is Martin."

The brunette looked Martin straight in the eyes. "Pleased to meet you, I'm Hannalora. But you can call me Hanni."

Martin thought she looked lovely: pretty oval face, lips full and pink. Her eyes were soft and grey, and her hand, as he took it, felt strangely silky. Having seen how gentlemen kissed ladies' hands he was eager to try it out. He bent over in as gallant a fashion as he was able and made contact. Whoa! That degree of physicality was a bit much for our young male virgin. A definite stirring in the groin. Not bargained for. Oh, no, down boy! Not now! Better sit down before she sees it.

"Yes, join us by all means."

Equally enthusiastic about meeting two nice sooo well-behaved young men, both girls replied at the same time; and as all four laughed at the simultaneous response, Martin quickly installed himself next to Hanni. Paul took his place next to Erika.

Well, they got on famously! The later it got the more they laughed and chatted. Egged-on by the fantastic mood and not a little schnapps, Paul just *had* to tell that awful joke. Martin, who had heard it so many times, knew what was coming from the first few words. He cringed. But too late.

"So, there is this hick farmer who's up in town for the first time with his wife and child. He needs to go to the toilet but can't find one. There's a tree there though, and as this farmer already has a paper bag with him, he does his business behind the tree in that.

Repressed giggling from the girls. Paul took that as encouragement.

Along comes a copper. Seeing the man has just pulled up his pants he says for a laugh "what's in the bag?"

"Two pounds of sausages" says the farmer, thinking quickly.

The copper says "right mate, that's a two Reichsmark fine" and writes him a ticket. "There's no way that's two pounds of sausage!"

The farmer shells out the two Marks. When he gets back to his village he warns everyone: "For heaven's sake don't go to Leipzig - if you don't shit exactly two pounds they'll fine you."

The girls doubled up. Martin, who had joined in with a chuckle to be polite, was relieved the joke had not destroyed the mood. Heavens, it had actually improved it! Another round was called for.

11.30 came and the girls said they had to go home. Martin and Paul were allowed to walk them to the bus-stop. Martin, emboldened by the way Hanni had taken his arm, put his arms around her and even started to nibble her ear.

"I like you very much. May I see you again?"

This performed in mid-nibble. Hanni leaned against him and sighed. "Thank you for the compliment, Martin, but I've already got a boyfriend. He's away this weekend. I think you are really nice, but I have made a commitment to him."

Bugger. Would have been nice to be able to see her again, get to know her a bit better. Oh well.

"Well, he's a very lucky bloke. If anything happens between you two, here is my address." He wrote on the beer mat carefully pocketed for precisely this purpose. She would not use it, but, hell, he could always hope. "Well, at least let me give you at kiss, I've been eyeing that lovely mouth all evening!"

Sweet-talking Martin got his reward. It was long and sensual, and had about the same arousing effect on him as the brief earlier contact. The bus came. The girls disappeared.

"Gee, that Erika was something, eh. I am going to see *her* again!"

"You lucky bastard. Hanni said she'd already got someone, so I guess that's the last I'll be seeing of her, more's the pity. She was really nice. But, all in all that was a pretty good night. Though if you tell that farmer joke one more time I'm going to throttle you. It's so crude!"

"I thought it went down rather well." Paul saw that his friend was actually serious. "OK, mate, no more farmers shitting in Leipzig."

They got on their bikes, left the city lights, and pedalled off into the dark, quiet countryside on their ride home.

stand-up wash

Street ablutions after work. Left to right: Martin, Paul, Alfred.

Chapter 5

1938 – *Letter*

The note from Otto's battered old accordion swelled as if it would rattle the few empty beer-glasses left on the table. At the crescendo, faces turned in expectancy towards Martin's Dad.

"OK Dad, you're the oldest, you start us off!"

Alfred, invited to the party together with his sniff and latest girlfriend, looked at Paul with a glance that said *what was this about*? He quickly found out, as a strong tenor's voice belying its owner's size drowned the accordion:

"Ooooooh My hat it has threeeeeeee corners ..."

"Come on mum, your turn. You can do it!"

Not so strong, this new voice, but confident and polished from lots of practice:

"Yes! Threeeeeee corners has my hat ..."

Martin's upraised hand stopped the brief applause to allow for his equally melodious continuation:

"If it hasn't got threeeeeee corners, then... "

Everyone knew you had to have a pause here before the punch-line. Then they all managed to join in at the top of their voice:

"IT'S NOT MY BLOODY HAT!"

As usual, the well-honed family performance was followed by much slapping of backs, slopping of beer, and general laughter.

"Come on Martin, drink up! It's your celebration, another beer! No, another schnapps! Everyone, fill up! Let's drink to Martin's successful graduation as a qualified carpenter."

"That's kind of you Alfred, but you know we've got to work tomorrow and we've already had a fair bit, enough to give us a decent hangover."

Martin's nephew Kurt was not going to turn down the chance of more drink though. "I'll have some schnapps. Martin's too, if he's not going to have any more."

The admonition was affectionate but firm. "You've got to work tomorrow the same as me, Kurt. Perhaps you shouldn't drink any more. We've been at it for four hours already, you know."

But Kurt never saw the need for that kind of temperance in life. It had always been like that. Perhaps that was why he was so damn BIG. Same height as Martin but twice the weight; considered far too fat by everyone except his family, who ignored his expanding girth, and continued to spoil him. For farmers this meant giving him as much potatoes and pork as he wanted, and then some. Martin had also been complicit in this, often letting Kurt have his share of treats. Preferring the quiet life, he quickly learnt that it was easier than having Kurt throw a tantrum, usually together with a whole lot of potatoes, which he often did if he could not get his own way. Now, though, Martin had started to worry about Kurt's lack of discipline and restraint. If anything he now showed even less inclination to heed others' orders or advice.

Living in the same house, Martin and Kurt had grown up together, and were pretty much inseparable, more like brothers than nephew and uncle. Kurt was born just eleven months after Martin and had been breast-fed by his grandmother because Frieda, Martin's oldest sister, always had to be away working in the fields and did not have enough milk. Martin's mum had had plenty, so it seemed logical to them that she nurse both boys.

It was only when Martin started on the building site, and Kurt started his apprenticeship as a cook (what else?), that they both went their separate ways and made new friends.

"Why are you always trying to spoil my fun, Martin?"

Ever the peace-maker, Paul looked to head-off any bad feeling creeping into the gathering. "Come on Kurt, Martin only has your best interests at heart. Anyway you've done a marvellous job getting all this food ready. Sure helps, working in a kitchen, eh?" But Kurt's morose tone did not disappear.

"No Paul, I didn't contribute. Grandma did all the preparations. Nothing's too much for her baby you know."

"Well, Frau Schläfer I must say this is the best feast I have ever seen! You women are fantastic, the way you can prepare wonderful food like this!"

"Well, *we* women thank you for the compliment, Paul, but actually I did it all on my own." This with a pointed glance towards Kurt's mother Frieda, from whom people assumed Kurt had inherited not a little of his laziness. Having twice put his diplomatic foot into it, Paul fell back on his last hope of preserving the mood.

"How about another song from your family's repertoire? Otto. What about …?"

But a loud knock interrupted Otto's accordion almost before it had started. Strange, at this hour. Couldn't be anyone close, as they were all there in the family home for the celebration. Martin's dad came back holding a letter. "For you, Martin. Looks official."

Perplexed, Martin took the envelope with its Imperial Eagle stamp.

"*Reichsadlerstempel,* Martin? What's Hitler writing to you for?"

"Let's see … A train ticket… and … I am to report to the *Westwall*. What's the *Westwall*? And why would they want *me* there?"

Seeing that no-one from the farming community was going to offer an answer, Paul broke the silence. "The Western Fortifications, Martin. It's the old Siegfried line, from the war. There's a lot of talk at university about what Hitler's up to over there. He says he's building it to protect us from invasion from the French, but a lot of people think that actually it's to stop them attacking us when we invade in the East. Hitler's being sensible – doesn't want a war on two fronts. It's absolutely enormous. They say it will go for over 500 kilometers between us and the Franzman. Hitler is recruiting hundreds of thousands of men to work on it. He has apparently given it priority over all other work. They need carpenters and you're one. Well, like everyone you don't have much of a choice – you've got to go unless you want trouble for yourself and your family."

Martin believed that his life would settle into a comfortable routine once he was qualified: he was earning good money, enjoying his friendship with his mates, and meeting a steady stream of potential girlfriends.

This was of course a naïve thought, given the momentous changes in Germany's internal and external relationships. German troops had marched into the Rhineland, reclaiming territory that they said had been taken from them by the Versailles treaty after the first world war. Austria too had now been made part of the Greater German Reich whether it wanted to or not. Hitler's fascist state had long since emerged in the concentration camps for political dissent, the Nuremburg race laws that deprived Jews of most of their rights, and the ban on all except the National Socialist party.

Like most of his generation in the countryside Martin's naivety was a combination of indifference and indoctrination. It was simply hammered into the school children running round in a circle singing patriotic songs – and cane strokes encouraged the patriotism of any child not singing with sufficient enthusiasm – that The Fatherland came unquestioningly first, last, and in between, with no room for the individual. And its due was *Pflicht* – DUTY! Already the 12 year-old boys understood well that the most wonderful thing that could happen to them was to die as a hero for their *Vaterland*.

But Martin's response was not motivated so much by indoctrination as youth's adventurous spirit.

"Why wouldn't I want to go, Paul? I am OK with going. I've never been out of Leipzig. Be good to see somewhere else and who knows what we could get up to there – might have some fun. Hang on tho' – you say *war*? *war on two fronts*? What war?"

"Come on Martin. Surely you don't believe what the Führer is saying about peaceful coexistence? Anyone who's actually read what he wrote in *Mein Kampf* can see that he's not going to achieve his goals without war. Sure our marching into Austria was peaceful but sooner or later … ."

"Mum, why the tears? That's just Paul's ideas. There won't be another war."

The soft affectionate face of the old photos was still there, but she was now big and cuddly, with a huge bosom and straggly grey hair.

Her normally sparkling green eyes, which Martin inherited, welled with tears in response to his bear-hug. "Martin, it's not the prospect of war … " More sobs. "… you're still my baby, despite your muscles. I've given birth to thirteen children, only seven have lived, and you are the youngest – only seventeen! I just don't want you to leave home yet."

"Come on, grandma, cheer up!" Kurt came to the rescue. "*I* haven't got a letter. *I'll* still be at home. I know, show us that party trick of yours with grandpa. No cheating now, arm out straight!"

Wiping her tears with one hand, she held her arm out horizontally for her husband to walk under. "Come on then my giant!"

He dutifully and proudly walked under her outstretched arm, and then back again, for all the world like executing a complex dance step. This was no limbo dancing though, as Martin's dad was considerably shorter than his mum, and it only required a little bending at the knees for him to pass underneath. It was easy to see from the way they looked at each other during this long-established weird family rite, attracting much applause, they were still very much in love.

"Mum, I'll be fine. I'll be using what I have learnt, and I'll learn some more, and I think it will be really interesting. I don't know anything about the Siegfried line." He gave her a hug and blew raspberries into the soft part of her neck. Tickled by his lips, her smiling eyes scrunched up.

"Just promise you'll look after yourself. You'll need to take lots of warm clothes and underwear. I'll start on the ironing."

"No mum, no. My tools are the only important things to take. A single change of clothes will do, otherwise there'll be too much to carry."

"Martin's right, Ma. It'll be a good experience for him. He'll learn more about work, perhaps earn more money. He'll be fine Ma, he'll be fine."

Later that evening, when the guests had gone, his dad took him aside, out of earshot of his mum. "Martin, Hitler has worked wonders for Germany these past years. They say he has given us security and hope for the future. That he is making Germany great again. Some say he is a great man too. But. But." A quick glance to make sure no-one was listening. "But, I've heard what his *Brownshirts* do to people who

25

don't toe the line. They appear out of nowhere with military precision and beat 'em up. With military precision. Someone has trained them. People even get killed. And no-one does anything about it. Take my advice Martin and always keep your thoughts to yourself. You know you are safe within the four walls of our family home but you must never say anything against Hitler or the government while you are at the Westwall, OK? Or anywhere. There are people everywhere who will report you, and then who knows what will happen to you. And think of what that would do to your Ma. Remember now."

The next day at work everyone was talking about the letters summoning them to their six months' obligatory *Reichsarbeitsdienst* – State Labour Service. Alfred had found his waiting for him when he arrived home after the party. It did not take long in a small village for the word to get around. It looked like at least three hundred men from the village were heading westwards to work on the Wall – a miniscule part of the 300 State Labour Service units deployed to work there before the war.

Neither Paul nor Kurt received a letter, though. Being a student, Paul had no trade that would make him useful; and Kurt still needed to finish his apprenticeship. Martin promised to keep in touch with them both, and tried to spend as much time with them as he could. While he was excited by the prospect of new experiences, he was also a bit apprehensive, sensing it might be the end of his rather carefree existence. Not being with family and friends would also be a big change for him.

He had only been given a few days' notice along with his train ticket. He knew saying goodbye to his nephew Kurt would be the hardest, because they had been so close when they were younger. Kurt was also a bit upset at not getting a letter. "You lucky bastard Martin. Wish I was going. I hope you don't finish the work there too quick, then maybe I'll get asked to go too. Make sure you write every week and tell me what it's like and what you have to do and why and what the people are like and…"

"OK OK, Kurt, I promise to write and tell you everything, especially the fantastic grub they'll be giving us." A brotherly hug.

"I'm coming with you to the station."

"NO, Kurt. I've told Mum and Dad and everyone that I don't want people at the train station. Mum'll cry and it's easier for me to say goodbye here, before I go."

"That's not fair." Kurt pouted.

Martin just shook his head. *Will he ever grow up and do as he's told?*

considerably shorter than his mum

Martin's mum and her 'giant' husband outside their home *circa* 1928. The young man on the left with the defiant stance is Martin.

Chapter 6

1938 – *Westwall*

Leipzig was in the East, the Westwall in the West. It took 12 hours on the train to get there. Martin and Alfred travelled together with two other men – Jacob and another Martin – who they were friendly with from the firm *Fricke*. Martin and Alfred had a lot of time to get to know them a little better. They played cards – skat mostly – read, talked to each other and slept.

"I wonder who paid for all our tickets – must have cost a bomb."

"One of my brothers works for German Rail," said Jacob. "According to him they've set up something called the Vehicle Group Management Unit West. They've used the railway lines built to the western front in the war to shift all the workers and materials to the Siegfried line. The buses too. The government's paying. Nice of them, for once."

"Don't know about nice – I bet the government doesn't have a say in the matter! They say Hitler's given priority over everything else to getting the Westwall completed. He's fanatical about it. They even requisitioned the postal service to get the letters out."

Wonder what's so important about getting the Westwall completed. Perhaps they are still afraid of a French attack to recover the Rhineland. Then Martin remembered Paul's words about a war on two fronts. His dad's words of warning came to him at the same time. He kept his worries to himself.

On arrival at Saarbrücken they were met by a man who introduced himself as Hubert Petersen. He looked tired and dirty and did not seem to be enthusiastic about meeting Martin and the others from the village.

"How come they told us to get off at Saarbrücken? There's no Westwall here, is there?"

"The Westwall's everywhere mate! Just follow me. It's about half an hour's walk. I'm your welcoming committee to show you where you will be working, eating and sleeping. And trust me, you won't be doing much else".

So off they set, carrying their few belongings with them. It did indeed take about thirty minutes to get there. The first thing that came into view was a very high fence of some kind stretching as far as the eye could see. It seemed to be draped with material that reminded them of the hessian they used for potato sacks back home.

"Obviously they do not want anyone to see what's going on here," Martin said to Alfred.

Hubert overheard. "Spot on. It's top secret work we're doing here, and they don't want the Froggies to see what we are up to."

Once beyond the fence they stopped and took in the view. Martin was reminded of an enormous human ant nest. There were men everywhere. They were scrambling in all directions in-between enormous cement blocks shaped like pyramids. Row upon row of them, all side by side like soldiers, with pointy tops all gleaming and white from the freshly dried cement. He could see the formwork for new rows waiting for the cement so they could be added to those already there. Hubert followed their astonished gaze. "You know what they are?"

One of the older men in the group piped-up, "Of course – tank-traps. No-one's going to drive a tank through those in a hurry."

"We call 'em *dragon teeth.* Actually they come in several sizes, some as big as you, so perhaps there are different dragons. One of your jobs'll probably be constructing the formwork for them."

It was getting late and Martin and Alfred were starting to feel hungry. They normally had dinner a bit earlier than this, the march to the site and being shown around had taken time. "So where's the barracks and where do we eat?"

"You've got to build your barracks first, mate," said Hubert. "Some of the lucky ones who got here earlier are being billeted, but you'll be in tents. The good news is that you'll always have a warm bed 'cos you share it with the shift worker you're alternating with. Work goes on twenty-four hours a day, seven days a week. Bad news is most of 'em have lice."

Martin, who thanks to his family's ablutionary habits had not had much acquaintance with lice, and did not like the idea of them, was about to remonstrate, but remembered his dad's advice and thought better of it.

"As far as grub is concerned, we use a voucher system – you take them to private restaurants or private houses and exchange them for the meal. You can get cigs and sweets at designated canteens. Any other questions?"

"Just how many bloody barracks have we got to build then?"

"We've been told that there are about five hundred thousand men but word has it that up to a million've been recruited since the Führer decided to increase the scale of the building program. He is convinced that it is an essential defence against possible invasion."

They were shown their tent and issued their food vouchers. They then had the long walk back into town and a restaurant where they digested a good meal and the enormous task ahead.

Back in their tent it seemed they had barely got their heads down when reveille sounded at 4 a.m. and everyone was out of bed, into the mess hall and then introduced to their foreman. He was tough, with an aura of authority, and Martin felt approvingly that he would not take any nonsense from anyone. *I guess when you are in charge of so many blokes you have to be tough.*

"Listen up!" The foreman glared at Alfred. "For God's sake stop that bloody sniffing. You lot will be doing the formwork for the bunkers – once you've built the barracks. You can see from these plans the bunker walls and ceilings are one-and-a-half metres thick. That means the cement they'll be pouring into your formwork every single day will be something you will always remember. They've calculated we're going to be using close on three-and-a-half million cubic metres of the stuff."

That took a bit of time to sink in; it was so far out of the realm of anything they had done before. Martin and Alfred found, however, the initial surprise at the sheer magnitude of the enterprise soon gave way to monotony.

The barracks were completed surprisingly quickly, and to Martin's and Alfred's relief they then both got their own bunks not far from the new dining mess they had also built. Then the work started in earnest – on the bunkers.

The Westwall was an unbelievably intricate set of fortifications of more than 1000 self-contained yet interconnecting gun emplacements – every five kilometres a bunker – stretching over 600 kilometres from

Kleve on the border with the Netherlands in the north as far as the town of Weil am Rheine on the border of Switzerland in the south. And it had depth as well as length, also extending 30 kilometres into Germany. Each gun emplacement was part of a multi-storeyed bunker with escalators between the floors containing air and electricity generators, quarters for the defenders and resident rifle-squads (15 beds in five tiers of three), and well-equipped kitchens serviced by good cooks to feed them all. All levels spoke to each other through tubes. Underground tunnels allowed quick communication by train between each bunker. Entrances were gas-proofed and guarded by machine-guns.

The situation was indeed as Paul had explained on the day Martin received the letter ordering him to the Westwall. Hitler had planned these fortifications from as early as 1936 when he had marched unopposed back into the Rhineland, whose western border would carry much of the fortifications. In anticipation of his invasion of Poland he had escalated its construction. 18,000 bunkers had been built so far. Another 10,000 were to be completed by October 1938. In that way he could be ready for any French attack from the west when he invaded in the east in 1939.

Reveille sounded at 4 a.m. every day, and they worked usually between 10 and 12 hours. Seven days a week. They had one day off every two or three weeks; the rest of the time it was just plain slog. They all soon fell into a constant state of exhaustion. The men were divided into groups of 500 in each camp. Martin never really got to know most of the other men in his camp, apart from those he worked closest with. Everyone was too busy, or too exhausted, to spend much time socialising. They worked, slept, ate, thought about women, and worked some more.

"Alfred, I've just been to see the foreman. You know, these working conditions of ours are beginning to worry me. Today, when that idiot with the electric saw slipped and half cut his leg off, I just had to go and say something."

"Just about everything here is an accident waiting to happen. What did you say?"

"I said the way we're expected to get that 60-ton armour plating for the bunker walls into place is ridiculous. We never had it that bad on the site back home. I said every day I expected to see someone killed. I don't know what I'd do if someone copped it right in front of me. You know what he said? To keep quiet for my own good. That he'd raised the same issues with his boss and been told to pull his head in. There is a job to do for the *Vaterland* and Hitler wants it done without any questions."

"Yeah. I heard they said the same to the blokes who went to complain about not getting paid on time, or not getting paid at all. Keep quiet or you'll end up in one of those concentration camps, a hell of a lot worse than here."

"Remember they told us we'd be working here for three months? Now we find out we have to do another three. It seems they forgot to tell us that six months is the average time for each bloke. Best thing is probably to stay on automatic mode and be extra careful. There's no point in doing anything other than getting on with the job we've got to do. Perhaps having such a strong wall of defence between Germany and France means that there won't be any invasion and I'll soon be able to get back to Leipzig and get on with my life. This hasn't turned out to be what I expected. It certainly isn't the Germany I know."

a very high fence of some kind stretching as far as the eye could see

Erecting a hessian screen to obscure the work extending the Westwall fortifications.
[reproduced with permission from the *Bundesarchiv*].

the Westwall's everywhere mate!

The 600 kilometre extent of the Third Reich's Westwall/Siegfried line on Germany's western border. The town of Saarbrücken, where Martin got off the train to start his Westwall work, can be seen in the south of the darkly shaded Saar region (SAARGEBIET). [Source: Wikipedia > Westwall]

we call 'em dragon teeth

One of the many post-war shots of dragon teeth – the little dragon probably – on the web.

he could see the formwork for new rows waiting for the cement

Formwork for the smaller dragon teeth being put into place before concrete pouring. [reproduced with permission from the *Bundesarchiv*].

Chapter 7

1938 – *Kanal*

Martin looked at the letter instructing him to go to Brunsbüttelkoog to work on the Kaiser Wilhelm Kanal. Assuming from previous experience that many would have received the same orders, he quickly found Alfred and asked him if he had also got his letter.

"Bruns-what-where?" Alfred asked.

"Brunsbüttelkoog. I suppose it's near the Kanal, and that's way up north near Denmark they say."

"Well, yeah, I've got a letter too, but it's not the same as yours. It's from the Army. I've been called up. It's the *Wehrmacht* for me."

So they were to be parted. They had spent almost every working day together for four years, and had both grown up a bit since their first testosterone-fuelled confrontation after Martin's apprenticeship test. Martin knew he would miss Alfred, sniff and all. *Especially* the sniff. It was, after all, a kind of ever-present link with home. Most of the time Alfred was an optimist. Martin was aware that he had tendencies towards pessimism – who wouldn't in those times? And he was glad to have Alfred cheering him up with his more positive outlook.

This positive outlook invariably involved Alfred's description of his ideal woman. It would make Martin laugh because every day the description changed from tall to short, thin to curvy, blond to redhead, intelligent to sporty. Each time the description changed, they laughed and agreed that Alfred would be happy with any girl as long as she had breasts and wore a skirt.

Promises were made; they would write regularly and also keep in touch through their families. It had made their new, tough experiences easier having someone to share things with – someone they knew well, who would listen to all comments without judgement. This was, in those times, a luxury. Most Germans had to be very careful of what they said and to whom. Everyone had a story to tell of someone who had done or said the wrong thing and had not been heard of since the SS came to 'question' them.

Martin got his few things together at the end of the week. The Westwall was in the west; Brunsbüttelkoog in the north. A long way to the north – the bus trip would take about six hours.

Martin got on the bus and looked around. There was no-one to play cards with or even talk to and after chatting a bit with the driver he managed to pass the time catching up on some sleep or just gazing out the window vaguely wondering what lay ahead of him this time. They arrived very early in the morning, just as the sun was coming up. Waking up to the vast expanse of water appearing on his left out of the heavy mist he called out to the driver to drop him off.

"I thought you wanted the Kanal? That's the river Elbe mate. The Kanal's just a bit further up. It flows into the Elbe. Cuts pretty much through the centre of the town."

He got off into the mid-December North Sea air, fresh and tangy. *Fresh my arse; more like freezing*. But he warmed up a bit in the brisk walk to where he had to report. Even in the mist, Brunsbüttelkoog was dominated by the Kanal. He could not help stopping and taking it all in, once again in awe of an engineering feat; this time one that had created this waterway between two seas.

"Yes, it's impressive, isn't it? But not as impressive as what we sometimes see going through it these days."

A voice had materialised at his side, from an avuncular type smoking a pipe. He looked quite old to Martin, but then anyone over 30 did.

"You are in for a treat, my lad. Just wait a couple of minutes and … there! What did I tell you!"

He nodded in the direction Martin was obviously expected to look. In the middle of the Kanal a tug was puffing its way out of the mist. Not sure just what there was about a tugboat to get so excited about, Martin withheld comment. And then, the prow of the biggest ship Martin had ever seen bisected the mist, followed rather quickly (because she was making quite a few knots) by a massive turret sporting three 11-inch guns, each easily as thick as a man.

"Quite a sight, isn't she? That's one of our newest and finest: the *Graf Spee*. I think the English call her a pocket-battleship, but she is really a battlecruiser. Same armament as a battleship but less armour, which means more speed. So she can outrun the more powerful ships and catch the less." A pause. "Must have extremely large pockets, those English."

Martin watched in awe as the rest of what he himself would have been happy to call a battleship ploughed majestically by, her light grey superstructure sloping gracefully from the high narrow bridge to the aft turret, likewise sporting three 11-inch guns. A huge wash hit the Kanal embankment from her bow wave. Martin had seen big things before, at the Westwall, but they had neither been moving nor majestic. If Paul had been there he would have gone on about the immorality of war in producing killing machines of such beauty. *Pity the poor bastards on the receiving end of those guns.*

That was how he met his new supervisor Reinhold Schmall. Reinhold was very much a family man; he often spoke about his children and his wife, whom he jokingly called "Your Highness". He smiled a lot and had a gentle fatherly way of explaining things to Martin.

The Kanal had originally been built to connect the North Sea with the Baltic and thus shorten the sea journey around Denmark. But with impending hostilities the shorter journey would become even more important. Hitler understood that in the event of war it would be vital to cut-off supply to England from across the Atlantic. U-boots would help to destroy the convoys from America but the German navy's ships like the *Graf Spee* were also to be part of this so-called commerce-raiding, sinking many thousands of tons of shipping carrying their valuable cargo of food and war materiel towards England. For these really big ships there was only one way out into the Atlantic from their bases in the Baltic to the east of Denmark: up and around the Jutland peninsula. The Kanal, however, linking the port of Kiel in the east with the North Sea port of Brunsbüttelkoog offered a second, quicker exit. Hitler had ordered it widened and improved.

Reinhold knew a lot about the 61-mile-long waterway as he had been working on it ever since it was first widened in 1917 to allow larger vessels through. He called it the Kiel Kanal. He was always happy to talk about what had effectively been his life's work. Martin listened intently to be polite. He could see it meant a lot to Reinhold that his knowledge of the facts was appreciated. He too called it the Kiel Kanal.

There were currently about two hundred men working on the Kanal, Reinhold explained. Their goal was to put larger sluices in some parts and replace weathered or damaged sluices in others. Everything had to run smoothly so the newer ships like the *Bismarck* would be able to use the canal as soon as possible to gain quicker access to the Atlantic. Martin was part of a gang that had to manually cut large pylons supplied from surrounding wood-mills which were then rammed into the eight metres deep water with a three-ton hammer. The pylons were to create a wall; they did this by lashing them with big leather straps and then putting bolts through them once they were firmly lashed. Then the pylons were cut off at the same level. Before all this could happen, though, the men had to work on a method of protecting the banks from high wave-wash. They had to use different mixes of concrete and sand depending on whether the bank was above or below water; stronger for above the water to protect against the strength of the wave wash and exposure to the elements.

This was all new to Martin, but he learnt the methods with his customary thoroughness. That wasn't the only thing he learnt. Three tons is quite some hammer. Before mechanisation finally arrived their only pile-driving method was for a group of them to haul it into the air and then let go. There were a lot of songs they used to maintain a rhythm, pretty much all of them lewd and crude, with many verses. Perhaps this helped the men to remember them.

It was dangerous work, but unlike the Westwall, Reinhold was very safety conscious and kept reminding the men about the safety rules. Like the Westwall, however, they worked hard – initially six days a week then seven, putting in 10 to 12 hours each day.

Martin had been working like this for some 15 months when he reported to Reinhold's office for work one morning at the beginning of September 1939. Instead of sending him out with instructions for the day's work, Reinhold gathered all the men together in his hut.

"Most of you don't have wireless I know, so I thought I should tell you. I was listening to the broadcast of the Führer's speech to the Reichstag yesterday. It seems the German army has invaded Poland. They started it. He said those damn Polacks attacked one of our border stations, and that they have been mistreating German women and children, and that it was time to act. So yes, we have invaded Poland."

The general level of exhaustion meant that it took some time for the men to process the news. Most took the information at face value. A few wiser ones realised there was so much propaganda in the media these days it was impossible to sort the fact from the fiction. Martin was trying to work out what it all meant for him and his friends when Fritz broke the silence.

"So Poland's been invaded. So what? The Poles won't be able to do anything about it. They've only got cavalry against our Panzers, for God's sake."

"War, Fritz. That's what's so what. The British and the French have said they would defend Poland if it was attacked. Now we will soon see whether they will put their money where their mouth is. Let's hope they see sense and don't intervene."

Three days later the answer came. England and France declared war on Germany for its invasion of Poland.

****

"An OLD old WOman who's GOT a HUMP ..."

With each word the pile-driver rose slowly in the air. Martin, underneath, strapping the pylons tightly together before they were bolted, was wondering what all this war news would mean and not concentrating on what he was doing.

He lost his grip and slipped between two pylons. He must have hit his head when he fell and was fished out and taken by boat, unconscious and bleeding, to the nearest doctor. He was lucky; nothing had been broken, and the men, seeing him loose his footing, had not let go of the pile-driver at the customary end of the next line. But he was pretty bruised and shaken-up. He would be very sore for some time. The fright and bruising had an up-side: he would need at least a week off sick, and was issued a leave pass.

Work on the Kaiser Wilhelm Kanal circa 1939

Top: Machinery for elevating the pile-driver (Martin is second from right).
Bottom: Shoring-up the banks. The elevating machinery seen in the top picture is in the background.

one of our newest and finest

Pocket-battleship *Admiral Graf Spee* on the Kaiser Wilhelm Kanal. [source: Internet]

Chapter 8

February 1941 – *Call-up*

'Y ou are to report for duty at *Wehrmacht* training camp Hamburg-Harburg.' It came, as he knew it would: the call-up letter. The third letter that would mark another uncontrollable change in his life. He too was now off to the Army.

A month after his 20th birthday, Martin duly arrived in Hamburg. He was assigned to the *2nd Pionier-Ersatz-Bataillon 20* – a battalion training engineers to replace those already dead or wounded. He reported for duty at the main office. The man behind the desk ticked his name off a list and officiously told him to go to the barracks with the words 'administration office'. He would be issued his uniform and equipment there.

Martin located the barracks mostly by the long queue standing in front of it. He took his place and waited. Once inside, everyone was interested in the procedure enacted in front of them at a long trellis table.

First came a washing-powder carton, large but empty. Martin's was *Persil* (it *washed whiter than white* he noted). This was for their clothing once they had received their uniforms. For they retained none of their original clothes – shoes, underwear, hat, tie, shirt – all were replaced by army equipment. They wrote their home address on the washing-powder carton; that's where their clothes would be sent. The only items they were to keep were personal: toiletries, watch, wallet.

The *Wehrmacht* training in Harburg was to last eight weeks. They knew straight away it was going to be very tough, even for Martin who was fit and relatively hardened from his Westwall and Kanal work. Some men found it hard to cope with the brutal regime. But they had to as there was no place for weaklings, who simply disappeared, no-one knew where.

The men soon found out there were two types of training. One, which they referred to by its commonest commands – *Marsch! Marsch! Hinlegen!!* – was self-explanatory: March! March! Hit the ground! The other was more focussed on their role as army engineers. One of the principles of training in the German army was a demand for maximum realism. All the difficulties associated with war were part of their training so that nothing could come as a surprise to them in battle. Martin and his group of trainees were given large amounts of ammunition of all kinds including grenades. Reduced charges to be sure, but they would still blow your arm off if you didn't handle them properly.

"We do on occasion incur loss of lives in training. This is because you recruits are learning how to become experts in the handling of explosives – real explosives. Those that die in training mean fewer losses in battle. I am telling you this so that you will be careful and pay attention to the instruction your trainers give you. Those that don't will find themselves scattered in little bits across the training ground."

The men were exhausted at the end of each day: physically from all the hard work; mentally from having to concentrate to avoid blowing themselves, and their mates, up. After eight weeks Martin was chosen along with thirty others to be sent down south to Rosenheim am Inne, a Bavarian town about 30 miles south-east of Munich. "Special training" they said (although it was hard to see how anything could be more specialised than what they were doing already). Rosenheim, as its name said, was situated on the river Inn and they were to be instructed in how to control water-craft in strong currents.

The Inn's powerful current wasn't the only novelty the south of Germany presented to the men, like Martin, from more northerly parts. On their first parade-ground appearance, they expected to be ordered *in den Knieen rührt euch!* indicating they were to stand at ease but only by bending the knees. Instead they all nearly doubled-up with laughter when they heard their Bavarian sergeant incongruously bellow out *Fiessl am Plotzl!* To their northern ears that sounded like 'keep your little feet on the little spot!' Their ill-disciplined response earned them an extra hour's parade-ground marching.

Being with a group of men all day meant that you got to know each other quickly. Of the 12 men in his group, five were experienced life-savers, two were engineers with a good knowledge of bridge building and five were carpenters who had worked on various aspects of bridge or canal work, especially the intricate locking systems of the canals. Along with more generic army skills, their training on the river taught them to control, manoeuvre and repair all kinds of water-craft like boats, pontoons, rafts and dinghies. With oars if possible; without if you had to.

Again, because he was already fit and strong it was not too hard for Martin but some of the men found it really tough, especially the two engineers who had spent much of their time behind desks. The cold was everywhere. You could not escape it. The team would spend most of their days wading through icy water or crawling through cold mud, negotiating fences and other obstacles. At the end of the day they would get into the shower fully dressed. Not out of modesty! It was the only way to get all the mud and dirt off their clothes before stripping. It was the only way to get their clothes really clean again. And of course the showers, too, were cold.

Martin was emerging from the showers one evening, shivering but reasonably clean, and starting to dry himself vigorously in an attempt to warm up.

"You carpenters are all soft. Not like us intellectuals. Wait until you get out fighting in the snow – then you'll really know what cold is. You need to be a *thinker* to be able to appreciate that kind of cold."

Though it was the last place on earth he expected to hear it, he recognised Paul's voice immediately. Told to put his university studies on hold, it turned out that Paul had been conscripted about twelve months earlier into the same Pioneer Battalion as Martin. But he looked different now. Older, care-worn, battle-hardened. The company had already lost many men and were back at training camp for replacements.

"You've already seen active duty. What on earth do you need more training for?"

"They think we need to sharpen our skills, and they also want us to share our experiences with the new recruits, though I reckon it's actually better they *don't* hear what they're in for. I wrote to you quite a few times to tell you about things but I guess I never got any replies cos our division was always under way. Or perhaps the censor decided what I wrote was too graphic."

Martin realised he didn't know what they were in for either, and perhaps he didn't want to know, so he kept quiet.

Three weeks into the training Martin's foot became very swollen – the same leg that he had injured in his fall on the Kanal. The doctor ordered a day's rest and the swelling went down. But it returned as soon as he resumed training. So, off to hospital again for a few days to try and get the swelling permanently down. While he was there he got a visit from Paul.

"There's some bad news. Your group was doing some practice runs in the river last night with another team. They were lining-up some pontoons so a bridge could be built for the division's men and vehicles to cross. Something went wrong and two pontoons collided. Some men got thrown overboard in the collision. Six got lost. They weren't recovered."

"Who for Christ's sake?"

Paul told him the names of the six who had drowned.

"Jesus, four of them were the best swimmers in the troop, accredited life-savers! We were mates. We all started training together. Two of them were a bit older than me with wives and kids. They were both so proud of their babies, they kept photos of them in their wallets, they loved to tell us all the little things they did and said. How could that happen with all our training?

"Word has it that they didn't follow protocol. They think the current was too strong and when one got into trouble the others followed trying to help without remembering to secure themselves first."

Martin found it hard to come to grips with the fact that such good swimmers could be so easily lost. This was the first time he had been confronted with the death of people near him. It really shook him up and it was weeks before he stopped having nightmares about the drownings and thinking about how it could have been avoided. He also felt lucky that his swollen foot had meant that he was not there. He then felt guilty that he had been lucky.

a month after his 20th birthday

Hamburg-Harburg recruits class of 1941 spick and span and serious in their dress tunics with peaked caps. Martin is fourth from left.

Marsch! Marsch! Hinlegen!

A group of young trainee soldiers at Hamburg-Harburg, this time in field uniform with steel helmet, demonstrate their newly acquired ability to *hit the ground*.

Martin and his group of trainees

A group of distressingly young Hamburg-Harburg recruits. Martin crouches bottom right, obviously sharing in the general ebullience. This may have something to do with their location in front of what looks like a *Bavaria St. Pauli Brewery* in Hamburg. The group poses, typically, with some of the brewery's serving staff. Many of these young men, perhaps most of them, would not survive the war.

Chapter 9

April 1941 – *Fight*

Paul walked over. "How's your boxing? Still got it in you? How would you feel about me setting up a fight? There's a bloke in my unit called Peter Schlecht and he never stops bragging to anyone who'll listen how fantastic he is in the ring. I reckon there's a bit of extra money to be made here. I've seen him go a few rounds and you could beat him easy – his mouth moves more than his fists."

"I feel fine, my leg is good. The doctors have no idea what caused the swelling. My training's back to normal. You've seen that yourself in the last few days Paul. Know what? I like the idea, it'd be a challenge. I've not been in the ring for a long time though – not since I left home ... but yeah, I think it's a good idea. It'll break the monotony of training. And it'll keep me warm! OK, you set it up. We can start putting in some sparring work after dinner every night. Let's hope this Schlecht bloke is as bad as his name means. But he'd have to be bad to be as bad as you."

The build-up to the fight took several weeks. They put in as many training sessions as they could in preparation. Paul went around taking bets from anyone who was interested and Martin worried with the odds Paul was giving how they would ever pay if he lost. Peter's friends also spent a lot of time spreading the word about the fight so that on the day the tension was high.

The army training camp gym already had a boxing ring. Martin could feel his heart rate up as Paul, his second, held the ropes for him to climb in. But otherwise he was surprised to note how calm he felt. Peter Schlecht was already in his corner, standing next to an even meaner-looking second who Martin did not recognise. One of the army trainers who had offered to act as referee was now beckoning them both into the centre of the ring.

"OK, no hitting below the belt, protect yourselves at all times ..."

"Yeah yeah we know all that ... let's get on with it."

Peter pranced around. Martin preferred just to stay light and balanced, but when he moved quickly he really did move quickly. He easily slipped Peter's first clumsy straight right, ripping his left low and hard into Peter's ribs. Peter's "oooofff" and the crowd's roar seemed to happen simultaneously.

It got better. With every punch that he couldn't land Peter got angrier, unable to find an opening. Martin, pleased to see his defensive and evasion skills had also not deserted him, was content to keep his face covered and await the next opportunity. Which of course came.

"Go Peter!!" Distracted by a yell from the crowd, not necessarily from one of his supporters, Peter's attention shifted for just a fraction and his face paid the price, distorting grotesquely under the impact of a really hard right. He staggered and went down on his knees. Martin's blow had landed right on the nerve, the spot all fighters look for on their opponent's chin. You can make a giant's knees crumple if you connect with it hard enough. Martin had, but his experience already told him the blow did not have enough force for a knock-out. No matter – his opponent was on his knees and the referee was counting, *eins! zwei! drei!* Shaking the sweat from his head Peter clambered up slowly onto his haunches, with the bell putting an end to further proceedings.

"I think my left hand's busted, it hurts like buggery, I can hardly move it."

"Well keep your left for light jabbing, Martin, and keep away from him till you can get in a solid right. That's what you'd do normally anyway. The right's your power punch. You're doing great: you've already knocked him down, you've got the psychological advantage."

The roar from the crowd was now deafening, they loved the sight of blood and to see a strong man on his knees made them scream louder and louder. "Get up you pussy! Take it like a man! Kill him!"

"See I knew he was all talk, you can take him easily now. He's making the same mistakes I always made – signalling his punches. Just pretend you're sparring with me and you'll nail it easy."

"Alright for you to talk. He still knows his stuff, Paul. I can't hit him with ideas. He's not going to be a pushover."

But ideas *were* useful. By the middle of round four Peter's punches, although still powerful, had become slow and signalled: he would drop his hands just before he threw a jab. It was a good fight plan. Peter would get a straight right in the face before his fists got anywhere near Martin. The cuts on his forehead widened and the blood started to get in his eyes. Even when he forced Martin against the ropes and whaled away ferociously with huge left and right rips to the body, Martin kept his hands up high and took a lot of the punishment, and Peter's blood, on his forearms and gloves.

"Give it to him! Knock him out! Go, go, go!" The crowd did not seem to care who was getting the punishment as long as someone was being thrashed. It seemed, too, the crowd's roar spurred the fighters on; it was somehow contagious.

"His body punches are really killing me."

"It's OK; it's OK. You're all over him like a fat kid on a cookie!! Just keep doing what you're doing."

Fifth round and the body punches were indeed starting to take their toll. Martin knew he had to finish it off this round or he would get seriously hurt. But Martin's punches had also taken their toll, and Peter started to gas out, his hands getting lower and lower. They circled each other several times in the centre of the ring making a few ineffectual jabs at the air. The crowd started to cat-call and whistle. They wanted the brawl to continue! They wanted more blood!

But Peter too knew that his resources were near an end. It was now or never and he rushed in with his head, and guard, down. Martin exploded. Left! right! left! right hook! All on the button, the adrenalin dulling the pain from his left hand. The crowd, now getting their blood, screamed even louder. Martin took a quick step back and for once put all his weight into a huge right uppercut. Peter's head snapped back and he went down, lying motionless on the bloodied floor of the ring.

The noise was deafening. You couldn't hear the referee count him out. Peter, who was only just opening his eyes, certainly couldn't. Paul was ecstatic. His friend had won, and won well. He had given that oaf Peter a thrashing and they had made a lot of money into the bargain. And Martin had taken all the beating. Hey - what's not to be pleased about? He gave Martin a big bear-hug. Martin, wincing, also felt very pleased with himself: the bruises didn't hurt so much if you were a winner.

Martin's left hand turned out not to be broken, and his victory started a run of fights. He went a number of rounds with men who, as is always the case, were keen to prove that they were better than he was. They weren't. He quickly developed a reputation as a boxer. As he fought fairly, he also won respect. He became a favourite with the crowd who were betting more and more on him.

Paul was very happy; as Martin's self-appointed manager he was making a lot of money from the betting. None of it was legal, though, so he had to be careful.

But in the end Martin tired of the constant stream of men who wanted to prove they could beat him, and his heart was no longer in it. His brief but successful fighting career ended with a challenge from a real brute of a man from one of the other groups.

"Jesus Paul he's a walking mountain! He's only got to land one punch and I've had it."

"C'mon Martin. I know he *looks* big but look how well we've done so far. We've beaten everyone we've fought. We can win this one too."

"*We*, Paul? In the end, Paul, you know, no matter how good you are, there's always someone better than you. OK, I'll fight him but this will be the last. I'm getting tired of it all."

"OK, probably a good thing. I'm not sure how much longer we can keep the extra cash a secret anyway."

It was clear to Martin from the outset that his opponent was not only a hulk but a professional hulk. Paul had not asked enough questions: turned out he was the Bavarian middle-weight champ. Of course people had kept quiet about this to make some money. Martin managed to stay out of danger for a while, but took a strong right towards the end of the second round just above his left eye. Paul was able to stem the flow of the blood with a liberal amount of Vaseline, but he was not the world's best cut-man: Martin's defence was so good that he hadn't really had much practice from previous fights.

"You can still do it Martin – only need to land one of your right hooks. Don't give up yet, you have had cuts before. Some, anyway."

"No, mate. This bloke's more than a class above me. I think this time I've bitten off more than I can chew."

"Well, no problem Martin. I'll just throw in the towel."

"Absolutely not. People have bet their wages on me. I can't just give up without a fight."

Sure enough, Martin started to take a fearful hiding. It was all he could do to avoid being knocked out. He was starting to think that being knocked-out might actually be a better option than the thrashing he was getting when … *Eight! Nine! Out!!* the referee's words slipped slowly into his groggy consciousness. *Ah … yes! I'm being counted-out… I think.* He became gradually aware of the sound of the crowd. He was bent over on his knees, his head on one side against the canvas. He could feel the corner of his mouth pressed firmly against it. He was dribbling onto it. Blood and saliva. It didn't smell nice. He opened one eye.

"Martin! Martin! You OK Martin?"

"Yeah... I … Yeah. OK. Jus' gimme a minute."

"Na Saupreis. Kõst di fei guat wehra bloss boxa kõst net! Na, krepierd bist a net. Höft 'm Buam a bissl."

"Woss he say? I wish those Bavarians'd speak German."

"He said 'you can defend yourself pretty well, you bloody Northerner. Trouble is, you can't box'. But he says you aren't dead either, and he asked them to help you up. Nice bloke really. For a Bavarian."

There was no convalescence for Martin of course. He had to keep working along with everyone else. But each time it hurt when he moved he reflected on his relief that his reputation had finally been overthrown and he could get back to normal. No more harassment from men always trying to use him as proof of their prowess, their manhood.

Paul, on the other hand, missed the excitement and secretly bemoaned the loss of money Martin's defeat had brought them. They had just about lost all that they had made from the previous fights. Well, that *Martin* had made. He rationalised the outcome by saying that there was not much to spend it on at the moment anyway. And they would not now be caught with their illegal gains.

Chapter 10

May 1941 – *Obscene bridge building*

I've volunteered you lazy lot to build a bridge."

Their training over, they had returned north, to Hamburg. Everyone was expecting to be deployed at a moment's notice but for some reason nothing happened.

Lieutenant Hardt sensed that his men would lose their edge if they weren't kept busy. They were getting restless and probably bored; and they had started squabbling lately over little things. A solution had offered itself in the form of a bridge in a village outside of Hamburg. It had been destroyed by recent flooding. The villagers had no able-bodied men as they were all away fighting or helping clear away bomb damage. Hardt was a plumber and resourceful. Having heard over a beer of the bridge's destruction he volunteered his men to re-build it. That would keep them busy and be a good opportunity for his team to learn some new skills. The balanced nature of the undertaking appealed to him. They had been taught to blow up bridges. Now they could try building them.

They had to handle a 2500-pound hammer to drive the timber piles supporting the bridge into their foundations. Projecting his resourcefulness onto fifteen men of his team, he called them together and explained that the fall of the hammer needed to be strictly regulated to avoid injury to the piles.

"You've got to rig it to a hoist with ropes so you can elevate it sufficiently high for the impact. The blow has got to cause the pile to compress and rebound."

Herr Leutnant Hardt, Sir! What's that in normal German?"

"That will make it travel like a wave through the pile, driving it deep into the ground. They need to penetrate deeply otherwise the soil under the foundation could get washed away."

"Where are we going to get the piles?"

"Normally they should be steel or concrete, but you'll have to use timber. We'll cut piles from the local forest. You've all been taught during training how to fell a tree correctly so you shouldn't have any problems. We'll need twelve I reckon given its size but for God's sake make sure that they're big enough to hold the load of the bridge *and* the weight of any possible traffic. And it's not just pissy wooden farm-carts we're talking about – there will be tanks going over too. Fischer, you'll supervise the placement of the piles and the operation of the pile-driver."

Lance Corporal Stephan Fischer was the smallest man in the group. He made up for his lack of size with a big attitude and a big mouth, not, unfortunately, matched by ability.

It took five days to choose the piles and cut them to size. It wasn't just a matter of correct dimensions. They also had to be sure that each one had no insect damage and was a nice hardwood that would weather well.

On the first attempt the pile-driver smashed obliquely into the pile and the ropes broke – Fischer hadn't positioned it correctly. It hit the water with a huge splash that drenched them all.

The men swore. Hardt was furious.

"Does anyone actually have any idea whatsoever of how to do this properly?"

"*Jawohl Herr Leutnant*! Absolutely, Lieutenant! I worked for 18 months on the Kiel Kanal doing exactly this kind of work."

"Martin, You idiot. Why didn't you step forward at the outset?"

"*Herr Leutnant* didn't ask."

"Well take over now then, before someone gets hurt."

Martin's main technical contribution was the singing. He got the men to grab the ropes. He would start them off with an old favourite from the Kanal. Martin started singing; they all started heaving.

> *Ein altes Weib, was bucklig is',*
> An OLD old woman who HAS a hump,

The pile-driver gave a jerk and left the ground.

> *Das fögelt man von der Seite.*
> You FUCK her from the SIDE.

It started to move slowly upwards.

Und wenn es dann noch Kinder kriegt,
when PEOple HEARD she'd GOT a KID,

The weight climbed higher still.

Dann wundern sich die Leute!
The PEOple were surPRISED!

On *PRISED* they all let go and down it came crashing into the pile. A cheer went up and the men took up the ropes again for another bit of rhythmic crudeness and climax.

When all the verses were sung – and there were a lot – Martin introduced new songs learnt over a long period on the Kiel Kanal, each with a strong rhythm dictating each heave and enough crudeness to keep everyone happy.

When the men stopped for a smoke they went down to the river's edge, where their pile-driving and singing had attracted groups of women from the village. They all stood around laughing and chatting, obviously finding the lewd rude songs entertaining.

A bridge of course is a lot more than piles sticking out of the river, and it took them another three weeks before the superstructure was completed to allow traffic to cross in safety. Martin's expertise came into use again as a carpenter.

Eventually the bridge was built and it was time to move on again.

"OK men, we have two days of marching ahead of us. Eighty kilometres from here we will be taking part in some war games to hone the skills you have learnt before we let you all loose on the real war."

The end of the first day of marching saw them arrive at another river. Everyone was looking forward to a swim. The weather had been lovely and warm for May and their march had made them all hot and tired. The river looked inviting.

Stephan Fischer was into the river before anyone else even had their clothes off. Martin saw him disappear under the water and waited for him to come up again, anticipating where he would appear. But Stephan did not surface.

"*Hilfe*, help! man drowning! *HILFE*!"

Recalling the mistake from the previous drowning incident, Martin was not about to ignore protocol this time. He grabbed some rope, tied it around his waist, and threw the other end to *Leutnant* Hardt. He dove in, swimming as fast as he could to the spot where he had seen Stephan go under. He felt himself being pulled by the current and could see and feel a whirlpool generated at the bend of the river, trying to suck him in as it had Stephan. He realised there was no point in continuing the search: the vortex was too strong. He signalled to the men on shore and with relief felt the pull on his life-line as he was hauled back in. It took all his strength as well as those of the men pulling to prevent him from getting sucked in too.

It took nine days before the body was found. It had surfaced, grim and bloated, several kilometres from the bend. Experiencing death again so soon after the first men drowned affected all the men badly. Once again Martin was in shock. He could not sleep. Every time he closed his eyes he would see Stephan going under.

Chapter 11

June 1941 – *Elite*

I am looking for volunteers for the Brandenburg Division. You won't have heard of them, or the heap of Iron Crosses First Class they've won already. Why? Because what they do is very hush-hush. They are a special ops elite commando group – that's what the *z.b.V.* means after their name: *zur besonderer Verwendung* – for special purposes. They go in first, quietly, *before* the main army, securing bridges and roads and airports and preparing the way for the main assaults. Who do you think laid the foundations for our successful blitzkrieg in Poland? Who do you think was there *before* the army went in? Brandenburgers. Sometimes we go in with boats, sometimes with gliders, sometimes we parachute in. Sometimes we infiltrate behind enemy lines in the mud, just on our elbows and knees."

"Sounds like a real suicide squad, Herr *Oberleutnant*!"

Some of the men tittered. The young recruiting lieutenant's face remained impassive. Ignoring the comment he went on:

"Anyone who speaks another language is especially welcome. That is the best way to gain acceptance if you are in a foreign country, the best way to encourage insurrection, the best way to fool the enemy. So, we want you and will make elite commandos out of you – out of those of you, that is, who possess the courage and skill and initiative and fitness. Who know how to fight alone. Who are Real. Men."

"Herr *Oberleutnant*. I've been in a spot of trouble with the police. Does that disqualify me? Erh … I've done a bit of time. In prison I mean.

"I know what you mean. Look: we are not the Salvation Army. If you are good enough for us you are good enough. We only want volunteers, remember. You have ten minutes to think about it. Dismissed!"

The young lieutenant had deliberately not responded to the 'suicide squad' comment, as it was actually pretty close to the mark. The secret nature of the Brandenburgers' undercover work brought with it a very high casualty rate: one in two did not return. That was actually the reason for the recruitment drive – to replace others who had already been killed in the line of duty.

Their origin, as a secret organisation, is still not very clear. But at least one of its roots can be traced back to a concept of Admiral Canaris, head of the German Army Secret Service, or *Abwehr*, to recruit overseas Germans with a special knowledge of their domicile who could furnish the *Abwehr* with intelligence on anything of relevance in future conflicts. Another, more interesting root is that Canaris and some of his political and military colleagues felt it would be a good thing to have trustworthy troops in case a coup became necessary against Hitler. Somehow the concept of a secret service troop became militarised. Its location, by chance, was in a barracks in Brandenburg, where, from October 1939 troops were trained exclusively for special undercover operations that could be carried out quickly and successfully in any theatre of war, anywhere, and with anything.

Martin and Paul were among sixty other men in the camp who came back to volunteer as would-be Brandenburgers. Who is to say why exactly they volunteered? Maybe it was the rashness of youth, the promise of excitement, the possibility of proving yourself A. Real. Man.

The young lieutenant addressed them again. "Welcome back. Hmm. No ranking officers among you, I see. Perhaps they are too comfy here swilling it back in the barracks. So, let's make a start. At ease! Sit down if you wish."

Most of them sat down. They watched the young lieutenant closely, eyeing his *Iron Cross First Class*. You didn't get to wear *that* without having been seriously in the middle of it.

"Some of you here – perhaps most – will not make it through the training which is hard and uncompromising. Also, if you decide after hearing what I have to say that the Brandenburgers is not for you after all, you are free to withdraw your kind offer to volunteer. But. Every single one of you here will Keep. Their. Mouth. Tight. Shut. about what I am going to say. Is. That. Understood?"

"*Jawohl*, Herr *Oberleutnant*!!"

"So. Listen up. We are advancing towards a strategic dam. The enemy is in control of it. He has laid explosives all over it. He will blow it up in seconds if he spots anything untoward. If the dam goes, all the surrounding countryside, two divisions of our troops and vital equipment downstream: they'll all be destroyed. There will be no water for our army or for the civilians upstream either. And you'll drown too. Now what do you propose we do?"

"We can't allow the dam to be blown up, Herr *Oberleutnant*!"

"I see. So we just forbid it?! Come on men, THINK, for heaven's sake!!!"

"We cannot do a frontal assault; otherwise the enemy will see us and blow the dam. So, we send out a small detachment …"

"Better. But they will be seen too. Well..?

"Erh, the small detachment must be in camouflage?"

"Good. You're getting warmer."

"I know! *Herr Oberleutnant*, I know! They must wear *warm* camouflage!!"

This time a ghost of a smile played on the young lieutenant's face.

"Maybe we could cover ourselves with leaves and twigs, *Herr Oberleutnant*?"

"I see. Like in *Macbeth*? No. This is open countryside. The enemy has cleared it precisely so they can spot anything. And a whole forest is not going to come conveniently galloping up, tweeting birds and all, so you can just put it on. No. There are no leaves, twigs or bushes."

Silence.

"*Herr Oberleutnant*! We could put on enemy uniforms?? We march right up to the dam singing a marching song in their language and disarm them. Bingo."

"Ah. Someone who has the remnants of a brain between their ears. The singing is not necessary, but helps. *Jawohl*! Excellent. That is it, precisely."

"But isn't wearing the enemy's uniform against some kind of regulations? And if you get caught with one on won't they shoot you?"

"Yes, and yes. It contravenes the Haig war conventions. But our whole purpose is deception. We don't play by the rules. Do you think the English will be sticking to their famous "fair play" in this war? Get real. They are the trickiest of them all. You will also hear from some quarters that you are defiling the spirit of the German Army and the concept of army discipline by not always wearing our glorious German uniform. Such comments you will ignore. They do not help."

"But *Herr Oberleutnant*. Surely uniforms are precisely for telling friend from foe. How can we avoid getting shot by our own army?"

"Equally bad – how can *you* be sure the enemy you're shooting at is not another Brandenburger group in enemy uniform? How can *they* be sure you are not the enemy despite your disguise? We use passwords. But yes you are right, and it has happened. Disguised Brandenburgers have shot other disguised Brandenburgers. And the German army has shot Brandenburgers they thought were Russians. Like I said this is no tea-party. You may still excuse yourselves, remember."

Eleven men now thought better of the deal and withdrew. The remaining volunteers were then given tests, both physical and intellectual. This weeded the original 60 down to sixteen, with Martin and Paul among them.

Training for the commandos was conducted at two schools, one in Düren and one in Brandenburg. Martin and Paul were both sent to Brandenburg.

Already very fit, they were made yet fitter. But most of the training involved developing skills followed by intensive testing. They were trained in guerrilla warfare. They had to learn tracking and navigation, moving silently through low grass, parachuting, diving, skiing, handling kayaks. They were taught sabotage skills – how to create explosives from potash, flour and sugar and how to detonate them. They learnt how to survive in close-quarter combat, how to kill silently. They learnt all about German and foreign weapons, they learnt marksmanship. They learnt about radio communications, intelligence gathering, basics of foreign languages, and the study of foreign armed forces, their equipment, and orders of battle. Parachute training was carried out at the Luftwaffe parachute school at Spandau. They were taught especially to use unorthodox methods to achieve their mission goals. Their ability to improvise in dangerous situations was tested. In short they were expected to be highly skilled soldiers trained for any terrain, any mission, any circumstances.

Their training took more than five months. When it was complete, they received their sleeve insignia and a short lecture from their trainer.

"You men are probably wondering what the dagger and question mark stand for. It's incognito activities in battle – that's hush-hush activities to you."

Martin, Paul and Alfred were assigned to the 16th Company of the Brandenburgers, in Düren. More importantly they also got two weeks' leave, and it would be at least that long before the company they were to join returned to base. They would then be replacements for men lost either in the Balkans or on the French front.

Two weeks off after all that intensive training - this was too good to be true! Martin had not had any leave for two years, since he was injured in his fall on the Kiel Kanal. Both he and Paul had hoped to be able to go home but the authorities had suggested that it would be best to stay near camp just in case the situation changed. For once the authorities were right, though not quite in the way they intended.

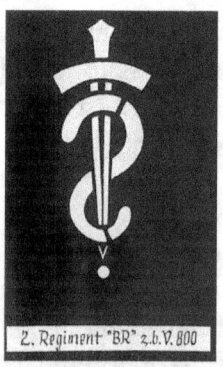

2. Regiment "BR" z.b.V. 800

dagger and question-mark

One of the Brandenburgers' insignia. The z.b.V. means 'for special purposes'.

Chapter 12

June 1941 – *Elli*

First priority, as always: beer and food. Hey! Just like old times! Into town to find a good restaurant, preferably one with music too. They had not walked far when the sounds of music and the smell of food, in that order, enticingly announced the presence of what they were looking for. In they went. Like Martin and Paul, a lot of men in uniform were standing around, and they were pleased to see a lot of girls and even more pleased to see they looked like they were having a good time.

The décor was inviting: subdued lighting and warm russet tones. The wall-paper of deep orange and brown hues was interspersed with little gold flowers. A thick carpet added to the feeling of opulence. Despite the uniforms, you could almost forget the war in here. But not quite. A plaintive song about a young German soldier on watch wafted over to them – a song called *Lili Marleen*, which had just shot from obscurity to become a great hit after being broadcast by the German Forces station in recently occupied Belgrade. Activating certain gastric juices on the way, the ambience took Martin back to his favourite *Lilli's* in Leipzig. How long, long ago that all seemed now.

They found a table near the dance floor and sat down, happy to relax. The air was full of smoke. Martin and Paul lit cigarettes and studied the menu.

"What's it going to be tonight then?"

"What else? I'm going for your favourite, *Eisbein*. Their pig's trotters sound pretty good, sauerkraut with red cabbage and dumplings, what do you reckon?"

"Yup. Their red cabbage sounds just like what my Mum makes, with fatty bacon and apple and grated raw potato. Bring it on."

They gobbled the food down, almost inhaling rather than eating. It was so delicious, and such a change from the mush they had been getting. They were sitting back feeling nice and full, watching the dancers and generally surveying the crowd, when Martin caught the eyes – the smiling eyes – of a woman whose strong, interesting face immediately connected with him.

"Think I'll just go over and talk to that woman with the black hair."

"She's been giving you the eye since the sauerkraut. Careful though – you know about older women – they'll have you for breakfast."

"That's kind of what I was hoping for."

"Go! I'm still undecided between the blond and the redhead."

"I thought you were still penning your undying love to Erika?"

"So I am, Martin, so I am. Doesn't mean I can't have a dance and talk to other women."

Martin was always a bit nervous talking to a strange, OLDER, woman but was encouraged by her smile. "Good evening, *Genädige Frau*. I'm Martin. May I join you?"

"You certainly may. But you can dispense with the 'Madam'. My name is Elli."

Oh God! A deep and husky voice to match the sea-blue eyes. *Should I kiss her hand?* And what a shape (he hadn't been able to see *that* from across the dance-floor). *Look at those breasts!* Her breasts pulled his eyes southwards from her mouth, her waist dragged them further, and her legs continued dragging … .

"Well soldier, are you going to spend the night just ogling me?"

"I apologise for my bad manners. But you know you are really difficult not to stare at."

"Oh so that's *my* fault is it? Now, will your full stomach interfere with your dancing? How long is it since you and your friend had a decent meal? I saw how quickly you demolished the house speciality."

"Well army food keeps you alive but that is about all."

He took her hand and led her to the dance floor. She slid into his arms and it felt to Martin as if she fitted into his body like glove to hand. (Aware of every part of her touching him, he didn't waste much time striving for a better metaphor.) How she felt! How she smelt! He found it difficult to speak. Touching her back and her shoulder and her neck made him very, very, excited!

She obviously noticed. "How old are you?" Surprised at the question he answered anyway. "Twenty-one."

"Martin, I am 35. I have not only a daughter but a husband who has been unfaithful to me. I waited over two years for his return and then got a letter from him saying he is in love with someone else. He met her while on leave, he wrote."

She paused. "That is, he WAS in love with someone else - I heard this morning that he had been killed. So, I am feeling really fragile at the moment. Fragile but not cowed – I need to know that I can still be loved. If he could find someone else, so can I! That's why I decided to come here tonight. But what I am really trying to say, Martin, is I think I am too old for such a young buck like you – I'm almost twice as old as you!

"What's age got to do with anything? I can help you forget your husband. Just let me try." *A stroke of brilliance. You are on form tonight lad.*

"I have noticed how keen you are already." She gave his groin a little shove with her knee. "Are you a virgin Martin?"

He felt the colour rise in his face but did not take his eyes off her. "Yes. But you can teach me." *Another stroke of brilliance. Must be the sauerkraut.*

"Hmm. I believe I *can* teach you. Teaching was my profession before the war. And *you* can help *me* forget my husband. Bid your friend goodnight. We can go to my place. My daughter is staying with her girlfriend tonight. She's developed a bond with her girlfriend's father. She really does not have good memories of her Dad, he has been gone for so long now. And now he's not coming back."

Martin walked over to Paul only slightly encumbered by his erection. He didn't need to explain.

"Must be your lucky night mate, make the most of it – don't forget we only have two weeks' leave."

Martin helped Elli into her jacket and took her arm escorting her from the club in a way he had seen in the movies. Her place was about thirty minutes' walk, which gave them a chance to learn a little about each other, though Martin found it difficult to concentrate in anticipation of what he assumed, or rather hoped, was about to happen. *How can we be swapping information like this knowing what's coming!*

Elli drove ambulances for the war effort and her daughter went to school in the village. Circumstances were difficult, as the majority of teachers, like her, were away at war. So the parents who were available took turns at teaching the children. She, like Martin, had just come on leave – that is when she had found out about her husband. Martin responded by recounting about his family, the Westwall and the Kiel Kanal, the boxing and the drownings.

"Here we are!"

Her little flat was above the local bakery, on the third floor. Well, it was more like a converted attic than a flat: small but very tidy, and tastefully decorated, for Ellie was very house-proud. It would have fitted into any time period. A classic style, after all, does not age. Pretty curtains decorating the few small windows were ill-equipped to provide the blackout that was to become essential when the Allies started strategic bombing in earnest. Beige-coloured walls, pretty floral cushions on a bed which served as a lounge during the day. All this would have reminded him of his mother's room; but such details of décor were pretty much lost on Martin apart from the location of the bed. Which trigged his first move. Grabbing Elli he started to kiss her hungrily.

She, however, gently pushed him away. "Whoa, *laaaaangsam* Martin! Slooooowly. I want to teach you how to please me. If you are a good learner I know it will also make you happy. Nothing is more pleasurable than making love. I will give you knowledge about a woman's body and how it works and the skills to bring any woman to incredible heights of sensual pleasure. I will give you the confidence and power to please any woman."

Martin, whose brain was struggling to believe what his ears were telling him, could only stammer. "Er... er... that sounds fantastic! Wh... wh... what are we waiting for? Start the first lesson. Just show me what to do."

She laughed, amused at the earnest eagerness sounding through her voice.

"I sound a bit like a school teacher. Sorry, habit. I just want it to be wonderful for you knowing it is your first time. Just do as I say and I know we will both be happy."

Martin had had much experience in carrying out instructions, and was able to follow Elli's, only with a lot more enthusiasm than normal. He obeyed to the letter, kissing her neck and her throat and the small of her back. It worked! She was moaning! He felt the tension mounting.

They were now undressed.

"Now, *gemeinsam baden*: we are going to share a bath together. Helping each other to get clean can be soooo much fun. And while the bath is filling up we will also share a glass of schnapps. Special schnapps. *Goldschläger Schnapps*, with little flakes of real gold in it. It's my husband's. He won't miss it now."

Gold flakes or no gold flakes, Martin groaned inwardly, not sure how much longer he could hold out against the effect of this sloooow schnapps-enhanced initiation. But he was determined not to spoil it for Elli, so, against the background noise of the bath filling up he focussed on her breasts. (His experience with breasts had stopped with his breast-feeding at three, so he did not find this difficult.)

"No, Martin, they are to be handled more gently. Tease the nipples, kiss them softly, suck them gently and watch their reaction. If they like the way you kiss them they will tell you."

Jawohl, Miss Elli. Am I being a good student?

He tasted the nipples and sucked them gently then a little harder. Her body reacted as he hoped it would. They got in the bath together and she washed him. As soon as she touched him he could hold it in no longer and came, shuddering all over.

"It is OK Martin. We have plenty of time to pleasure each other tonight."

A small bath imposes certain restrictions on full body contact but they managed to manoeuvre into a more favourable position.

God what a fantastic body. You can feel all the muscles when he moves. Can't wait to get him inside me.

Martin washed her back, her arms, her crutch. They dried each other and she led him to her bed.

"Martin, I know I am sounding like a teacher again but I am going to show you how to unlock the passion in a woman. If you do it right you will make us both happy. She lay on the bed and opened her legs a little. "Now, just gently part my lips." This confused Martin, who could clearly see her lips were already apart because she was talking to him. Ellie took his hand and led it to the spot. "There. We like it slow!

Much slower than men! Play with it gently, softly, wet it, tickle it, tease it and… "

Martin stopped any more words by exploring her mouth with his tongue. Elli hungrily kissed him back.

He listened and followed her instructions, improvising with a few of his own ideas. The feedback was obviously encouraging, and her sighs and moans excited him even more. During the several times they made love that night he learnt the satisfying discipline of holding his climax until he knew she was ready.

Not surprisingly, after that night of induction Martin spent nearly every moment of his two weeks' leave with Elli. Often it meant spending time with her 12-year-old daughter as well. Andrea was already a real Aryan beauty - glossy gold hair falling in soft curls almost to her waist – so different from the dark black of her Mum's. Her eyes were blue like Elli's and her body was like a young colt, all long legs and gangly. But Martin quickly saw that Andrea was a problem. She was clearly jealous and did not like sharing her Mum with him. Spoilt, she wanted her own way all the time, and, Martin saw, she usually got it. He tried hard to make the time with the two of them fun and not get too upset when he saw Elli being hurt by some cruel remark from her daughter directed towards him.

He took them out for meals, lunch on the weekend, dinner two or three times both weeks. They went for walks after school and twice to the movies together. When he was not taking them out, he dutifully played cards with Andrea while Elli got their dinner ready. He had only been back to camp once to inform them where he was staying. To Paul, his message was that he was deep in love and not to expect him back before two weeks.

Martin could no longer imagine life without Elli. He had already made up his mind to ask her to marry him before he left on his mission with the Brandenburgers. He knew she worried about their age difference but he was confident he could make her happy: hadn't he proven that over the last two weeks? The last day before he was due to leave, they were all sitting in the small kitchen having dinner. Elli was about to take Andrea to her friend again, so she and Martin could be on their own.

"Uncle Martin, are you going to marry my Mum?"

What a question from a 12-year-old! It took him by surprise and instead of telling her it was none of her business he replied.

"Well, yes, Andrea, I am certainly thinking about it."

"*Thinking* about it!! There are lots of men who would like to spend two weeks with my Mum. She told me you would ask her before you leave and you still haven't. What is wrong with you, why is it taking you so long? Don't you know that she needs you to marry her before you go away so that if something happens to you, like if you get killed, she'll get your pension after the war."

Elli tried to laugh it off, as if Andrea had said something funny. Martin just sat there not quite sure what to say. What had just happened? *Why didn't Elli step in and tell Andrea to mind her own business?* She was just a child; did Elli agree with her? Had they spoken about him and a future together? He had not missed the looks they constantly exchanged and the way they laughed together enjoying their own private jokes, often about things that seemed really silly to him. He had thought that with time he could become important in both their lives but he realised now that he would always feel excluded from their close bond.

Mumbling something inconsequential to Andrea, he turned to Elli.

"I must return to camp. Tomorrow's mission is being briefed. I did not want to upset you by telling you earlier, but it is not possible for me to stay any longer."

Elli heard the upset in the formality of his words. But she also knew that he was young and emotional and it was no good trying to explain further. She had taught him well and she had loved every minute of it. This young man had indeed made her forget her husband for the past two weeks and it had been wonderful. If only he was a bit older, he would have understood. Andrea had just been listening to her friends. It was always a topic of conversation in the war: what happened when men did not come back. Sure, some of Andrea's friends had mothers who had married men with the sole intention of getting financial assistance. But, when it came down to it, if Martin could get upset so easily there was indeed no future for them. He left her with a restrained kiss and hug.

Martin felt strangely both numb and gutted, but afterwards a part of him came to realise he had been incredibly lucky to meet Elli. Yes,

yes. He really had thought that he had found someone he could love for the rest of his life. She was such an amazing woman, but he knew her daughter would always take first place in her life. It would not have worked, he rationalised. Now he had to focus on the job at hand. Ah well. Back to the real world. Back to the Brandenburgers.

Well, we know first love always leaves some kind of special impression. But Elli was never, ever, to cede her first place in Martin's affections.

"I promise I will write."

Elli knew he would not.

Chapter 13

July 1941 – *Size <u>does</u> matter*

"Schläfer, you lazy bastard. Where's my morning coffee?"

He knew that voice! Or rather the sniffs bracketing it. Sure enough, looking up from his bunk he saw Alfred Stepke grinning all over that handsome face of his. In Brandenburger uniform.

"Ja ja, I know. You're going to beat the crap out of me if I try to bully you one more time. Nevertheless it is good to see you are still alive!"

Martin jumped up from his bunk and did something totally out of character, hugging Alfred and thumping him on the back. He pointed to the dagger and question mark insignia on Alfred's sleeve.

"How the hell did you end up with us?"

"Actually been with them for some time – we've just got back. You are the new lot supposed to replace our fallen comrades. And yes, it's good to see you too. Where's Paul? You wrote a long time ago that he volunteered for the Brandenburgers too."

"He's probably reading something about horse anatomy, let's go disturb him."

Paul was just as happy to see Alfred and gave him the same reception. He also wanted to know what Alfred had been up to, but then his curiosity turned to Martin's love-life. "So what's all this about you being in love with a wonderful woman? It was that one in the restaurant was it? Elli? Looked like you were hitting it off. Suppose that's how you have been spending these last two weeks – hitting it off." He couldn't help starting to intone the old Elli-ditty:

> *'Alles Scheisse, Deine Elli.'*
> *Schrieb sie mir im letzten Brief.*
> *Denn es blieb nicht ohne Folge*
> *Als ich neulich bei ihr schlief!*
>
> *'Total fuck-up! Much Love, Elli.'*
> *Went the letter's final line –*

Seems the result of our encounter,
Will emerge in nine months' time!

Well, come on, tell us, was it good, was she hot, did she give you head?"

"Paul, my brother-in-law once gave me some good advice. He said '*so was geniesst man und schweigt*' – 'that sort of thing one enjoys and keeps to oneself'. I have always believed a man should not need to boast about his conquests or share personal details with anyone. I respect Elli and I fell in love with her and I would rather just keep my memories and our activities to myself."

Paul blushed. "Yeah you're right, none of my business. Won't ask again."

"No problem. So how did your two weeks go? Heard any good jokes?"

"Come to mention it, I did hear one about a farmer who went to the city and couldn't find a place to crap."

"No! Not that one. Spare me please! Ok I suppose we need to get ready for the 7k march that Sergeant-arsehole-major Schaffer's got planned for us."

"God knows why he's pissed off, but the more pissed off he is the more goosestepping he'll make us do. Last time it was on a freshly ploughed field for heaven's sake. Three hundred meters *Achtungsmarsch,* then normal marching, then another three hundred meters goosestep. He's a sadist. I could hardly walk the next day."

"Yeah I hate it too. Goosestepping is supposed to make your legs stronger, but you know my legs can't take much ever since they got swollen in the river."

****

At the end of the marching, *Stabsfeldwebel* Schaffer called them to attention.

"*Stillgestanden*!! Attention!! Quiet! Listen up! Weekend leave is cancelled. The company is leaving on Monday for secret deployment on the Russian front. Not everyone, though – your corporals have been instructed to select the best. I may have seemed a bit tough on you all today, the exercise was intended to show me who's got it in them."

Martin's name was among those who were to report for the elite commando unit's next mission. He was relieved to hear that both Alfred and Paul were to be with him on this his first real mission. In fact it turned out that all sixteen men who were part of the original volunteers for the Brandenburg unit were accepted. He had become friends with them all. It was now July 1941.

Within two days they were ordered to get ready to leave, their precise destination a secret. They got onto a train in the early evening, found places to sit, and travelled through the night. They were awoken in the early morning by their commander's voice telling them to get out. Martin sniffed. He knew that smell. "We're somewhere on the coast."

Alfred stuck his head out the window. "Where the hell's Königsberg? Paul, you know? You're the clever one."

"Never heard of Königsberg?! It's a major historical and cultural centre of our glorious Greater German Reich – the philosopher Kant lived here. But its main claim to fame at the moment is as one of our Baltic naval bases."

They unloaded at Königsberg and continued with *Mottmarch* – motorised transport – in a long convoy of open trucks. They were taken to Riga, stopped for something that they were told was coffee but resembled another liquid, stretched their legs, and then continued to Pernau.

They were surprised at the enthusiastic reception they got from the locals: the people were happy to see the German uniforms; they even offered the soldiers rooms in their houses. Both Riga and Pernau were in Estonia, which had been occupied by the Soviet Union in 1940, when the non-aggression pact with Germany Hitler had astutely conceived was still in force. When, not long after, Hitler broke the pact and invaded the Soviet Union, Germans had been told that part of this *Operation Barbarossa* was to liberate the Estonian people from their Bolshevik Soviet oppressors who had instigated mass political arrests, deportations, and executions. The Estonians' hearty welcome seemed to confirm this.

The Brandenburgers were immediately put to work, instructed to prepare some fishing boats for their mission. The first thing was to reinforce the bows with tarpaulin.

"I wonder when they're going to tell us what it's all about."

"Well you don't need to be a genius to work out it's got something to do with these boats. I suspect we're preparing them for a rougher time than they usually get so that they don't get swamped and fill up with water. Uh-oh, what's *this*?!"

They looked up to see a long convoy of trucks just arriving, each one towing a trailer. On the trailers were strapped the wings and fuselage of gigantic Messerschmitt 321 large capacity transport gliders.

"Man, just look at the size of those planes. Now THAT would be something for us! I wonder if they're part of our mission."

"What else would they be for, Alfred? They're gliders actually. I remember talking to this bloke in the hospital bed next to me when I had my swollen leg during the training. He'd been building them. He called them *Gigant*s. They are giant-sized for a reason. They can carry over fifteen tons of heavy equipment. Just think, that's at least a couple of four-ton trucks and 88-mill flak with ammunition and gun crew. Getting them off the ground is not easy. They have to use rockets under the wings, *and* a troika of three separate planes to tow them up."

"So you reckon they're for us? I certainly hope not. You'd be a sitting duck in something that big and slow. Those DFS 230 gliders we trained on were much smaller." Grinning, Paul added "But I forgot. We all know size doesn't matter. Oh sorry, Martin. I forgot I shouldn't talk about those sorts of things."

"That's alright Paul: when you are my size it doesn't matter."

The next day they found out the details. Each company was divided into three units: groups of 12 to 14 men, each with a leader and a second in command. Martin and his unit were summoned to a meeting with the others in one of the local houses. They were briefed by their commander *Hauptmann* Benesch, suggesting that the operation was of considerable importance.

"Men. At ease. You will as yet know nothing of the background to this operation. So, I will now tell you why you are here."

The invasion of Estonia is part of our plan to get complete control of the Baltic, and that in its turn is an important part of our plan to conquer the Bolsheviks. Our Führer successfully launched Operation Barbarossa, as you know, in June this year."

The men were nodding. Most of them knew or had heard this on the grapevine. But that was the past. They wondered what was coming next.

"Estonia has not been as easy as we at first thought. It's been a long and complicated campaign, and we have not been able to defeat the Bolsheviks as quickly as originally planned. We have had to move to a new operation codenamed *Beowolf 2*. Now this is where the Brandenburgers come into the picture."

The captain's finger indicated the 50 or so men in the room.

"Under the direction of Lieutenant Commander Cellarius you will carry out a glider operation against the Soviet fortifications on the island Ösel. There are Soviet long-range 20-centimetre naval guns on Ösel sinking all our ships. Intelligence says there are three of them. Regiment 16 Brandenburg is to neutralize them – depress the barrels and blow up the mechanism. You have all had the training for this work. Well, you are Brandenburgers and everyone knows Brandenburgers can do anything! The first group will be flown in by the 6th Glider Squadron before dawn tomorrow, the 14th September. You will go in five of the 6th Air Landing Squadron DFS 230 gliders."

At this point, images of the sitting-duck Giant Glider fresh in their minds, the three breathed a sigh of relief.

"Our two spies amongst the Russkis have been instructed to signal if it is safe to land. The second group will go as re-enforcements by sea. There will follow four Me 321 large capacity *Gigant* gliders carrying supplies a few days later."

So they would be going in the smaller DFS gliders they had trained in after all. *At any rate, we won't be as big a target as the Gigants. Size does matter after all.*

"Any questions?"

Alfred stood to attention. "*Hauptmann* Benesch! Captain, with your permission: Once we have spiked the guns – how do we get out?"

"You will be taken-off Ösel by the fishing boats you have been reinforcing. That part of the operation is under the command of *Oberfeldwebel* Grabe." Martin, who had known Grabe from his first Brandenburger days in Düren, was pleased to hear this. Grabe was a *Zwölfender* – a career soldier. He had been in the small 100,000 man army the Versailles Treaty had allowed Germany after the war. You could count on him!

He continued with some more details specific to the separate groups and then handed over to their group commander *Unteroffizier* Haag. Martin felt some relief when he heard that Haag would be their *Gruppenführer*, as he had been told only the day before by some of the other men in his unit that Haag was a decent bloke. More importantly, though, word had it that he knew his stuff and could be trusted to get them out in one piece.

They got more detailed instructions from Haag on how he wanted the team to work together. "OK. Back to finishing-off the support boats. Do them well: they're your life-line for getting off the island. You can then all have the rest of the afternoon off. I suggest you refrain from going into town for grog and use the time to try and get some sleep."

He paused, clearly mulling something over.

"That suggestion is actually an order. Now, I know you have been instructed in the Brandenburgers to act on your own initiative and to even disobey orders if you think it will accomplish the task. But this is about maximizing your chances of coming back. An exhausted soldier is a dead soldier. So this time *ist der letzte Befehl heilig* – the last order *is* sacrosanct, understood? Assembly is at twenty-two hundred, take-off at twenty-three."

Bundesarchiv, Bild 101I-567-1519-18
Foto: Stöcker | 1943

those DFS 230 gliders we trained on

A DFS 230 glider. *DFS* stands for **D**eutsche **F**orschungsinstitut für **S**egelflug (*German Glider Research Institute*). [Source: Bundesarchiv, Bild 101I-567-1519-18/Stöcker/CC-by-SA 3.0]

the first thing was to reinforce the bows

Fishing boats awaiting deployment to Ösel.

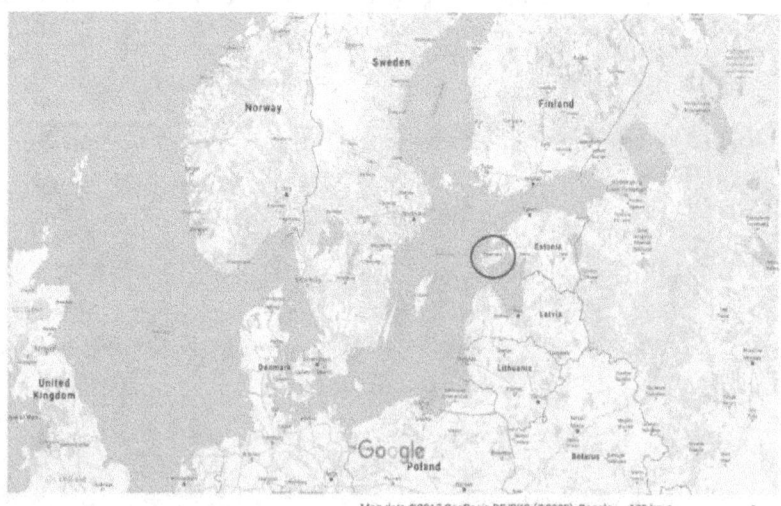

Soviet fortifications on the island Ösel

Google Map showing location of the Estonian island Ösel in the Baltic (in oval).

Chapter 14

July 1941 – *Fiasco*

The moonlight picked out the silvery corrugated fuselages of the five Junkers 52 aircraft, each with their ghostly glider in tow. It was deathly quiet at the end of their forty-meter towrope. Just the faint rumble from the triple engines of their Junkers tug in front and the swishing of wind against the taut steel of the tow-rope. The glider's cramped interior was lit up by the moon shining through its large cockpit, revealing pilot, a useless skywards-pointing machine gun, ten tightly-packed men, and their equipment. Peering out through the small window of the lead glider, Martin hoped the Russians below were concentrating on enjoying their earthly vodka and not spending too much time contemplating the heavens.

He caught himself feeling below his seat. His fingers met the cold steel of the container crammed full with explosives they would use to blow up the enemy naval guns. Everyone was sitting on one. It only needed one stray round from enemy fire below and the whole glider would go up in a ball of fire. He tried to think positive, to lighten the growing apprehension. Hadn't their Soviet spies told them there was only a handful of Russians guarding the guns? Wasn't the main body of soldiers at their base a long way away on the other side of the island? And nowhere near the guns they were to disable, eh? *Yeah, it'll be a piece of cake and we'll be home for lunch.* It was also somehow reassuring that his closest mates were with him up there in the freezing night. He quietly wished himself *Break a Leg*. Then, just for additional luck, he turned to his neighbour, Willi Krause. He thought a lot of Willi, he was a decent bloke. "*'s wird schon schiefgehen Willi! Hals- und Beinbruch*!"

"Ja, thanks Martin. Sure to be a total disaster! Hope you break a leg too! Several in fact."

The plan was for their Junkers tug to circle the island once to check their support boats were in place; and then the pilot would descend to about 400 meters and let his glider go. Then it was up to the glider pilot to locate his predetermined landing area and bring his glider in. The pilot saw, as did the men cramped near the windows, the pre-arranged signals from their spies below. The flashing made them feel all was going to plan, all would go well.

A feeling that dissipated quickly when they felt the glider banking for a second time, and realised the Junkers pilot was starting to circle the island again. "He probably can't see any support boats" the glider pilot shouted by way of explanation. "We can't go in without them – they're our only means of escape from the island."

Well, I guess he's got to do it – we've got to be able to get out of the place – but it's a big mistake. Vodka or no vodka, Blind Ivan will see us going over and if they haven't the first time they sure as hell will the second. Oh shit he's going round again!

On the third time round the pilot must have finally spotted the support boats, mustn't he, because the red light in the cockpit was flashing imminent detachment, and before they knew it the glider was released and they could feel their lonely descent slicing through the silence of the night. The other four Junkers followed suit, abandoning their gliders one by one.

The shooting started almost immediately, breaking the silence: savage machine-gun fire keeping up throughout their glider's approach, its bumpy landing and when it came to a standstill some 800 meters short of the planned landing site. Martin saw the pilot slumped over his control column and wondered how he could have managed to land it dead. At least two others had been hit. Even before the glider had shuddered to a halt Alfred, who was closest to its only door, thrust it open.

"Go! Go! Go!"

They didn't need *Gruppenführer* Haag's screaming. It was just like the sergeant had said during preparation. "OK. That's enough practice. You'll find you get out of the glider quick enough when you're being shot at."

The men scrambled out and hurtled towards anything that might afford some cover. Martin made it, together with Willi and a couple of others, into a natural ditch near a clump of trees and bushes.

They could see the Russians' location from the flash of their machine-guns. They were still some way away and their fire was no longer very well directed.

The gliders' silhouette would've made us easy targets. We're lucky to be still in one piece, especially with those wretched explosives packed neatly beneath our arses. Hopefully now the bastards can't see us and we're not quite such sitting ducks.

Willi apparently thought the same. He had been instructed to take pictures of the action, and pulled himself up onto his elbows, camera in his hands. He pressed the button, then slumped sideways with a bullet through his shoulder, into his heart. Nothing to be done. Dead on the spot.

The sound of planes above the machine-gun fire. Anxious faces looked up from Willi's motionless body. *Jesus, not Sturmoviks too? We're done for. No, thank God, they're ours coming back Must have seen the gun fire as they turned for base.*

The men heard the scream of the bombs followed by the jolt as they exploded. It scared them even more if that was possible. Then, in the aftermath, everything went quiet as the German *Luftwaffe* planes turned away. They guessed the bombing had done its job and taken out the Russian machine-guns.

From somewhere close by they heard the voice of Adam Meyer the first-aid officer.

"Is there anybody there to help me get the wounded out of the gliders?"

"Adam, this is Martin. I'm over here in a ditch." Half afraid the enemy would hear his voice. "I'll come."

"Let's try and get them to safer ground behind those trees on your right."

Martin could just make out Adam's trees silhouetted against the sky about twenty metres away.

"Even if their MG has been taken out we are still too close to the Russians here. And over there is more cover for me to work on the wounded. We know they don't recognise the Red Cross so there's no point in hoping that'll help. Let's just hope they can't see us in the dark, if they haven't been killed by our planes."

Well, we don't recognise their Red Cross either.

"We'll take your glider first, it's the closest. You ready? Come on then."

Martin took his belt off and wrapped his pistol in it: no point in taking it – it would be an encumbrance and you couldn't protect yourself anyway. Adam took off towards their glider with Martin following. Halfway Martin spotted the first casualty. Not knowing whether he was still alive, he managed to get some kind of a fireman's hold and struggled back with him to the safety of the trees. Dumping him unceremoniously, he took a couple of gasps of air and straightaway headed back. He almost fell over Paul. Him too he heaved onto his shoulders.

Paul was mumbling something that sounded like "Ich lieb' Dich Erika". *Well, at least you're alive.*

On his way back Martin saw more wounded. He put Paul down as gently as he could manage. "Back in a minute, gotta go get Frantz, he's still in the glider. Looks like he's copped it too."

It must have been at least four or five times that he covered the fifty perilous meters to rescue someone, though he was not counting. Having learnt long ago to function in automatic mode, he wasn't thinking at all. Finally, unable to see any more motionless forms out there, he collapsed flat on his back, staring up at the stars above the trees, gulping in air. Adam, who had been busy retrieving men from in and around the other gliders, was already attending to the wounded.

The thought finally entered Martin's head as he lay there that none of the injured had screamed, or made any noise at all in fact, when he was carrying them. He wondered if that was because they knew it would have attracted attention. Adam gave another answer.

"I'm afraid a couple have had it. Three others are luckier – *Heimatschüsse* – thanks to their injuries they'll be sent home. War is over for them. *IF* we can get them back, that is. Somehow we'll have to find commander Haag to report the names of the dead and wounded. Perhaps he's with the others, wherever they are. Your mate Paul is less lucky – he'll definitely be coming back. He copped one in the knee – just a graze – but he must have got concussion when he fell."

War's well-established triage principles dictated that those with the non-life threatening injuries were set aside with those who had no hope of recovery, the latter hopefully with some morphine to ease their death. So Paul was ignored with a "Well, he's not going to die from a grazed knee."

Things stayed quiet for the few remaining hours of darkness. The Russians hadn't started shooting again. With some apprehension, Martin watched the light improve as the sun started to rise. He became aware of the dawn chorus. *What amazing colours. How can the birds be singing? It's wrong. My friends have been killed. My friends have been injured. They shouldn't be singing. It's wrong.* He smelt the sea air, that lovely salty tang he could almost taste. It reminded him, of course, of the Kiel Kanal. *What I wouldn't give to be there now.*

Well, at least it was good to know Paul wasn't seriously injured. Not injured at all really, given how badly the rest of them had fared. Since he wasn't among the dead or injured, Alfred was probably OK too, somewhere. He'd seen him scramble out and head for cover, so he might have made it alive.

"Martin, you're covered in blood. Sure you haven't been hit? Let's have a look."

"No need. I'm fine. Must have come from the others. Shhh what's that?"

Something moving over to the left. Looked like some others who had made it out alive and been lucky enough to find a natural hollow to wait things out.

With dawn-break the shooting started again. The intensity seemed even greater: probably a detachment or reinforcements from the camp they knew to be on the other side of the island. That did not look, or sound, good. But yet again the Airforce provided them some welcome respite. They heard them before they saw them: this time three *Stuka* dive-bombers. With surprising accuracy, Martin thought, two bombed the Russians, one dropped something on them – a small canister. Bouncing near their glider it came to a halt several yards to the left of its shattered nose. Before they could retrieve it themselves Martin saw movement at ground level from just behind the wing. The movement materialised into Alfred, who must have run from his hollow to the glider. Sweeping the canister up, he headed doubled-over towards their trees, tumbling in. Remaining crouched, he looked around at the bodies.

"Martin, good to see you. Guess we're the lucky ones. Looks like our *Luftwaffe* buddies just dropped us a present. Let's have a look. He unscrewed the canister. OK. They say they're going to parachute some dinghies down for us. We've been ordered to make it out in them."

"What about those eighteen support boats – the ones we had to reinforce? Not to mention the pioneers with their heavy weapons who were to attack the coastal batteries and take us home?"

"Schön wär's Martin! Wouldn't that be nice! No sign of 'em. Message says support's been aborted. Weather, probably. We've got to clear out of here, but we have to tell the others."

"If there ARE any. Anyone else get out with you?"

"Gruppenführer Haag. I was the first out of the glider and he was second. We both fell into the ditch together. Our runner Dieter landed on top of us. For someone who doesn't weigh much he was mighty heavy. I need to report back to Haag first."

With that Alfred zigzagged back to the ditch and Haag. It was not long before he did the return trip.

"Gruppenführer Haag has volunteered you to try and locate the others".

"What about Dieter? *He*'s our runner."

"Our Dieter has bad feet."

"That's a really useful thing for a runner."

Deciding that the best direction to head in was away from the Russians, Martin took off from the trees running like crazy. He tried zigzagging when he could: it was difficult when you were running bent over. It was now daylight and he could easily be seen. An easy target. Terrified, he felt the rush of air as bullets whizzed past, heard the thump in the ground as others landed in the dirt. *At least I can hear them. They say you don't hear the one that gets you.*

the glider's cramped interior

Sitting arrangements inside a DFS 230 glider.
This one doesn't have explosives under the seats though.

Chapter 15

July 1941 – *Escape*

Luckily it didn't take him long to find the others. Their gliders had landed in a group slightly more to the north.

"What are you doing here Martin? Where's Dieter? "Is the runner dead?"

"No, he's just got bad feet."

A raised eyebrow was the only response. Once he regained his breath, Martin was able to pass on the orders about aborting the mission and making it out on dinghies that were going to be dropped to them.

Every half hour the German planes flew in bombing the Russians to keep them at bay. Some planes dropped inflatable dinghies on their side of the island.

Many of the dinghies were shot apart by Russian fire, but they managed to recover five intact. These were inflated and the wounded put into them ready for their escape. For the Brandenburgers it was a matter of honour not to leave comrades behind. But they could not take the dead back – there would be enough difficulties rescuing the living, given the small number of boats. They hated to leave their dead behind but knew they had no option.

The commander in charge went from group to group until everyone knew the evacuation plan. "We will drag the dinghies with the wounded in them to the shore during the night and make our escape just before dawn. Our intelligence is that the beach on this side of the island is heavily mined, so they will have to be located and deactivated. Three men will be going in ahead of us to do this and clear a path wide enough to drag the dinghies through safely. Schläfer, Stepke, Wolf, you've been trained for this, so you are the minesweepers."

Oh shit. But at least I didn't see Otto make any mistakes during mine training. We may just be able to avoid being blown to bits.

"As soon as the sun goes down and there is enough cover from the dark, head to the beach."

The three got together to plan their approach.

"We don't know what kind of land mines they've deployed on the beach so we don't know whether they are the kind that can be deactivated or whether they're the ones that are so sensitive they cannot be interfered with. Or both. God knows what we'll do if it's the second kind."

"Well, just mark them and people'll have to try to find a way around them."

"OK, so it's important to first find out what kind of mines they are before we all start trying to clear the beach. Let's hope Ivan's been consistent and sown the beach with the same, de-fusible kind. How about I go first to try and identify what sort of land-mine we're dealing with, then we can take it from there. If they're de-fusible we can then advance as a row on our stomachs stabbing into the sand sideways with our bayonets, just as we were taught."

The two men nodded in agreement with Martin. Alfred reminded them, "Remember, once we have deactivated a mine we still have to mark its location, so that people can crawl around it rather than over it – just to be on the safe side."

I can't see how any of this has a safe side. "OK we can do that with white cloth on sticks or something like that. Got any white cloth? No matter. We can prepare that somehow while we wait for dark. Underwear perhaps. Then the men following will know exactly where it is safe to crawl on their way to the water."

As the light started to fade with the setting sun Martin, Alfred and Otto set off crawling on their stomachs through the long grass in the direction of the sea. Immediately the guns from the men they had just left started firing as they diverted the attention of the Russians off them. They waited a while until the gunfire was heavy and slowly started crawling again.

Once they were in the wooded area where they were able to stand up, they continued moving in the direction of the beach. They walked for some time and the foliage and trees got denser, making it easy to hide.

They had been making their way through the undergrowth saying nothing and trying to make as little noise as possible. Suddenly out of nowhere they were confronted with a small patrol of Russian soldiers.

They were now in a particularly densely forested area and had not heard their approach, but there they were, unmistakable in their long brown coats.

It was a shock to all; you could see the astonishment on their faces. The night was torn apart in front of them, everyone was shooting at once as a reflex action. But the Brandenburgers reacted quicker. Two of the Russians went down straight away; one with a bullet in the middle of his forehead and the other hit in the chest. Neither made any noise as they collapsed. One was wounded – they couldn't see where - and disappeared into the bushes. There was no option for the rest but hand-to-hand fighting. Not a sensible option, given the amount of close combat training the Brandenburgers had undergone. They screamed as they ran towards the three Germans.

Within seconds they were at it, guns were no longer any use. Side-stepping a bayonet thrust, Martin drove his bayonet into the body of his assailant, deep. He went down screaming. Too busy trying to extract the bayonet, it never occurred to Martin that this was the first person he had killed. He turned to help Alfred who was grappling with another Russian, thrusting his bayonet through his side. He went down too. Otto was standing staring at the man he had bayoneted through the throat and the big pool of blood around his head.

They could see a trail of blood from the wounded Russian who had tried to crawl away. They followed it and found him dead. They stood there shaking, looking at him. Between the three of them they had just killed six men.

"Here, take one of these – help calm the nerves". Otto offered his cigarettes.

"Are you mad, that'll get us killed real quick. The smell can carry miles in this terrain and they might also be able to see the glow from a long way away. Put them away for God's sake. They might not have heard the shooting with all the other firing, but these Ivans will be missed for sure before long.

The chastised Otto quickly stuffed the cigarettes back in his pocket; he knew he shouldn't have had them.

They pushed on, after trying to hide the bodies. After about twenty minutes careful trekking they could hear the sea, and five more minutes brought them to the beach. There they rested. As soon as they thought it was dark enough, the three of them crawled onto the sand. Now, with the sand only inches from his face, Martin thought that the sea didn't smell quite as inviting as it had in his time on the Kanal. He started stabbing the sand obliquely, and so so carefully, with his bayonet. The sand adhered to the still wet blood.

It didn't take long. "I've got something hard here." The others stopped moving.

"Which kind is it?" whispered Otto.

"Dunno yet. Definitely one of Ivan's anti-personnel mines, tho', so the intelligence lads were right. Feels like it could be either a PMD-6 or PMD-7. I can feel the wooden box with its hinged lid and the slot cut into it, just like they showed us. Remember - anyone standing on the lid moves the retaining pin. Striker hits the detonator and boom! Up we all go. I'll try and disarm the activation mechanism by unscrewing the fuse from the explosive charge and unscrewing the detonator from the fuse. That won't make it harmless – the explosives are still there – but it's our best shot. Here we go."

Martin stopped talking and focussed. He could feel the sweat running into his eyes. It was a cold night, so he knew it was caused by his fear; he could also feel it trickling down his armpits, trickling into the small of his back. He had to keep blinking so he could get a clear view of the mechanism. He first concentrated on unscrewing the fuse. He gently ever so gently turned the fuse, decoupling it from the explosive charge. It felt as if he was turning for hours but was in fact just a few seconds. Yes! Got you, you bastard!

Martin paused and took some deep breaths trying to calm his nerves, just as they had taught him. He waited for his hands to quieten again. *Now for the detonator.* Gently, ever so gently, he began to unscrew the detonator from the fuse. It stuck. He tried just a tiny little bit harder. He could feel the muscles in his arms and wrists straining to open it without jiggling it by force. It came away. Yes! *So it can be done.* The two others heard a long, long breath of enormous relief. He placed a bit of white cloth on a stick next to the disabled mine so anyone following could see its location. He turned round to them and smiled.

Alfred and Otto, who had been holding their breath with Martin, returned his smile, inwardly smiling not a bit.

They had told them time and again in their training with live munitions. *The first one is always the most nerve-wracking. But you cannot, must not, let-up on your concentration. Remember 'every mine is a new mine - every mine is a different mine'. You start from scratch with each one, treat each one on its merits.*

Alfred muttered by way of encouragement. "OK, now we know it can be done, let's see how many of these beach babies we can put to sleep."

They all started slowly moving toward the sea, stabbing the sand gently with the oblique bayonet so as not to put any pressure on those little wooden boxes hiding in the sand like some silent enemy just waiting for a chance to kill them. Otto got the next one, then another; then it was Alfred's turn. Slowly, a small forest of white flags grew in the sand behind them, indicating where it was safe to crawl. Nothing more was said. The only noise came from the pounding of the waves and, they thought, their hearts.

It took all night to cover an area three metres wide and about 15 metres long. It seemed a lot, lot further. They were greatly relieved when they finally got to the water's edge just as the pre-dawn light started to change the sky.

"Shouldn't we look further out? The tide looks pretty much in to me, and perhaps Ivan's mined to the low tide watermark."

"No, I don't think so. I don't think they'd expect anyone to get to the water's edge over all those mines – look at all the flags behind us. We'll have to hope that the dinghies don't touch the sand when we push off, and anyway we haven't got any more time – look."

They followed Martin's gaze and saw others of the group starting to emerge from the undergrowth at the edge of the beach, dragging dinghies with the injured.

Five four-man dinghies. Thirty survivors - almost half the men had been lost.

"Listen up! The injured obviously stay in the dinghy. The rest will take turns in being in the water." Haag's voice yelled out so that every man on the beach could hear. But another voice screamed above him.

"If anyone tries to get on my dinghy I will shoot them. I will allow one other person on to paddle and that is Rudi, anyone else I will shoot if they try to get on board."

Martin recognised the voice of Rainer Sauer, a First Lieutenant in charge of one of the other units.

Maybe the guy had lost his nerve? The current situation left no time to discuss Sauer's mental state. And in any case you didn't argue with a Luger in the hands of someone who was mentally unstable. So now they only had four dinghies to go round and 28 men. Seven men in a four-man boat. Three would have to swim alongside each dinghy.

"OK. If the injured can paddle with their hands they will. We'll have to chance it with four per dinghy. Just chuck everything overboard you don't need: packs, rations, guns, helmets, everything. No, wait, keep the helmets for bailing. Those in the water will have to help propel the thing. We have no paddles so use your hands to row and most dinghies have one spade that can be used as a rudder."

The current that had prevented the sea landing of the fishing boats was now driving them back to shore. The water was cold when they first got in, but Martin and Alfred, who had been told to take a dip first, were surprised to find that their body temperature quickly adjusted, and that they didn't notice it after a few minutes. Adam joined them.

"Shouldn't you be in the dinghies to look after the wounded?"

"An extra body would sink 'em – you can see they're taking in tons of water as it is. In any case they are getting further and further apart and I can't keep on swimming from one to another."

Soon the logistic problem of getting the dinghies away from shore became the least of their worries. There was a crack of gunfire and then another one, and the sea erupted as bullets hit the waves. Those in the dinghies ducked down as much as they could, as if the rubber walls might give them some protection, and the men in the water started kicking their legs even harder, pushing the boats ahead of them.

Martin felt bullets whiz past him. Some fizzed into the water next to his head. It was quickly getting brighter and it was obvious that the Russians had a good view of the dinghies and their cargo. He knew they were bound to be hit.

He no sooner had the thought when he noticed that the dinghy to his right was now half submerged – whether from bullets or from overload or both – and although the men in it were still bailing with helmets it was no longer any use. They felt helpless as they moved further away from the hapless dinghy which could now hardly be seen. Martin thought of Max Kaufmann, who he knew was with it.

"Martin, you know I am terrified of all this stuff, especially with water – I've always been shit-scared of water." He had confided in Martin during one of the later Brandenburger training sessions.

"Why the hell volunteer for such dangerous work if you're so terrified?"

"I guess I want my family to be proud of me, to show them I can conquer my fears. Daft, isn't it?"

Yes Max, daft.

As the distance between them widened, Martin thought he could see the dinghy going under, just too late for the air support he could hear coming in.

Well, at least they took some fire off us. Wish it had been Sauer's boat.

He became aware that the bullets had stopped. Perhaps they were now out of range; perhaps the air attack had taken the Russians' attention. He felt his hair being pulled up and realised he had been drifting asleep in what now felt like lovely warm water.

"Come on in Martin, you've had enough bathing for a little while."

A replacement slipped over the side as hands heaved Martin in. The cold jolted him awake, the icy wind penetrating his sodden clothes. Within a few minutes, they had to pull in Alfred too, who was also falling asleep in the water. But they had no time to focus on the cold, as they had to take over the paddling.

They were alone. No other dinghy was in sight, all either dispersed by wind or current.

five more minutes brought them to the beach

Google Map of Ösel island and the Estonian mainland, showing the location of Pärnu (in the south east corner) where the gliders took off. Martin escaped from somewhere on the eastern or south-eastern shore of the island. The mini-island of Muhu (which is linked by a causeway with Ösel), and the locations of Kübassaare and the main town Kuressaare are also shown for comparison with the map Martin drew below.

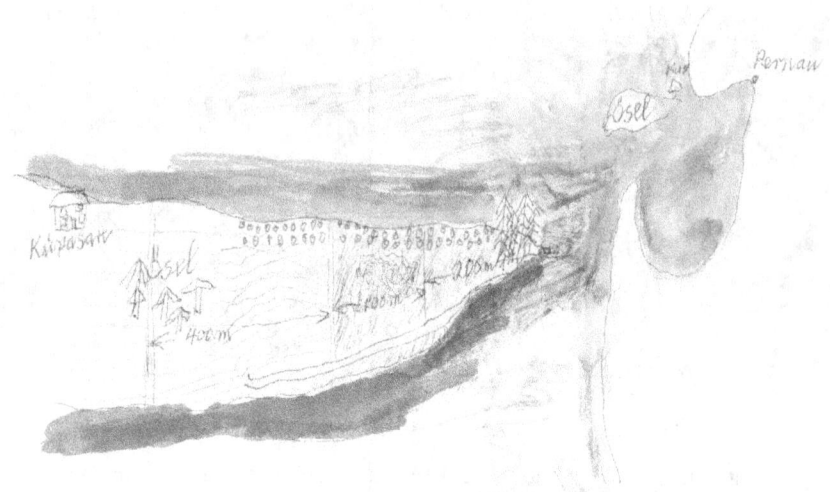

that the beach on this side of the island is heavily mined

An explanatory map of the Ösel terrain drawn by Martin when recounting the Brandenburgers' assault on the island. It appears to consist of two parts. On the right he has shown, relative to Pernau (Estonian: Pärnu), the location of Ösel and its mini-island Moon (Estonian: Muhu). You can see these places in the *Google* map in the previous figure.

The much larger scale map center and left shows, with little circles which he coloured red, the location of the Russian mines. He has also indicated some trees and a place he has called *Küpasare*, where he has drawn a house. The name *Küpasare* most likely identifies Kübassaare, and this in turn would identify the larger scale map as being the Kübassaare peninsula, which is marked in the previous *Google* map and is supposed to have had a coastal battery. (This means Martin's large-scale map should probably be rotated 90 degrees clockwise.) We don't know the significance of the meter measurements, other than indicating in detail the extent of the different terrains.

Astonishingly, Martin sketched this map *from memory some 65 years after the event*. It took him about five minutes, once he had found his coloured pencils and texta.

Chapter 16

August 1941 – *Head Count*

Y ou will be kept in the Pernau *Lazarett* for three days' observation. Your military hospital stay is necessary to determine whether you have received any lung infection from your prolonged exposure to the cold water."

Martin was too weak to do anything except smile at the medical orderly, and was amused to find himself helped onto a stretcher and transported onto land and into the hospital for the obligatory observations. But he didn't complain.

His dinghy had been the first to be recovered. During the course of several days, more survivors were brought in, picked up by fishing boats directed by *Arado* spotter seaplanes. A final head count showed they were still missing one dinghy. The debriefing revealed that the missing men were all probably those on the dinghy Martin had last seen with Max Kaufman, taking water badly. It was decided to have one last look for them, and an *Arado* took off late in the afternoon. It never returned. They radioed that they had spotted some survivors on the beach waving furiously and that they were going in to pick them up. The transmission ended abruptly. Another plane was sent out, at first light, and very much to everyone's surprise returned with human cargo. But only two, and much the worse for wear.

Max recounted what had happened to him and his group. "When the bullets started to fly, our dinghy got hit and started to sink pretty quick, and our group commander ordered us to try and get the wounded back to shore. So we started to paddle back. Of course we could see the Russians waiting for us on the shore, but at least they stopped firing. They yelled at us to get out of the dinghy. Our group commander couldn't get out because he had been hit badly in the legs. We tried to help him but they drove us away with their rifles and told us to leave him alone. One of the bastards put a gun to his head and shot him. They took us prisoner and marched us off without our boots. They kept asking questions about our mission, but we didn't give them any information, just swore at them. In the end they got really pissed off and must have lost patience. They tied our hands behind our backs with wire and lined us up against an old fence. We all knew that the end had come. I closed my eyes. I heard the guns go off. I felt nothing but fell down along with the others, and lay there trying not to breath. I had no idea what had happened, only that somehow I wasn't dead. I was really scared, expecting that someone would check to make sure we were all dead and finish me off. But they just marched off laughing and talking and smoking. I kept stock still until I couldn't hear them anymore; and then some. Then I heard some clever-arse whisper "Is everyone dead?"

No-one laughed.

"It was Alex, Alex Brandt. I whispered back, "I'm OK. They didn't shoot me." There wasn't a sound from anyone else. We waited, but just as we thought the bastards were far enough away for us to move they turned around and came back. For the second time that day I thought we were goners. But all they did was cut the wires off our hands, pocketed them, and left. After that you can bet we didn't budge – not for a very, very long time."

"So what do you reckon happened?"

"The only thing we could come up with was that the group of Ivans had our two spies in it - the same ones that flashed that it was safe to land our gliders. And they had aimed away from us when they lined us up for execution. All of a sudden we heard groaning and rushed over to Walther … Walter Fleisher, we had thought he was dead. He'd got it in the stomach and lost so much blood it was hard to imagine how he was still alive."

"But why would they have come back after shooting you the first time?"

"Perhaps they had second thoughts about what would happen if the Germans should ever find their men had been executed like that, with their hands tied behind their backs. It could have repercussions for the Russians, who knows? Anyway, we decided to try to make it back towards the side of the island where we had tried to escape from earlier in the dinghies; our only hope was that home base would miss us and send out a rescue team. Which is what happened. But Walther couldn't walk. Couldn't even get onto his feet. He told us to leave him, and just give him a gun for protection, in case more Ivans came looking. So we carried him to a tree and left him under it with a gun we got from a dead Russian who must have been killed earlier in the air strike. It wasn't long after we left him that we heard a single shot. We didn't go back.

"We walked for some time and found a haystack to hide in until morning. First we heard it and then saw it: one of our *Arado* seaplanes flying overhead; we took our shirts off and waved madly. They dropped a message with some rations, guns and ammo and instructions that if it was safe they would attempt to land and pick us up."

"God, that was risky – the Russians would have seen the plane too, surely."

Max's voice started to tremble. "Yeah. We hadn't seen any Russians since leaving Walther. Even when we stood in the open there was no sign of them. The seaplane landed. We ran across the beach and into the water. Then shots rang out and we saw the pilot slump forward. A couple more shots must have hit the petrol tanks and the front of the plane just seemed to explode. We couldn't see the navigator, or anything, for the smoke.

"We threw ourselves flat into the water. Somehow I got hit in the toe, but otherwise they missed us. Using the smoke for cover we managed to get round the other side of the plane and get the self-inflatable dinghy out. The navigator was dead. There was even more smoke when the whole plane went up and we were able to use that to make it back with the dinghy to the shelter we had only just left. We waited till night-fall, inflated the dinghy, and started paddling. Early the next day we saw another of our *Arado*s. It was circling at such a high altitude that we thought they would never be able to spot us. So we poured that green dye into the sea to highlight our position. We were well away from the shore by then and they were able to pick us up without anyone else getting killed. I guess we were pretty lucky."

****

Ösel had been a complete disaster. The enemy guns they had to dismantle were still intact and there were huge losses. Of the 55 men who embarked, only 23 made it back. Of Martin's glider group only five returned of the initial eleven. Alfred, Paul and Martin were once again among the lucky ones. Paul's wound healed quickly. When they finally returned to Düren, they handed their weapons over to the second half-company for cleaning and were given three weeks' leave.

On the 29th of September the German *Luftwaffe* shot down a Soviet courier airplane close to the positions held by the 96 *Infantriedivision* in Estonia. In the wreckage they found a Soviet despatch addressed to the Soviet High Command in Leningrad. It outlined the Soviet positions on the Estonian Islands and requested that all remaining Soviet forces on Ösel be withdrawn by rescue ships. Their plea for help was never heard because the last remaining pockets of Soviet resistance on Ösel's southern edge had been overcome by the *Wehrmacht* by the 5th of October. In all, 4,000 Soviet prisoners were captured from the Islands. Martin and the survivors of the initial raid wondered about the futility of being sent there in the first place, and why the Russians had executed their mates instead of taking them prisoner.

****

Two days after they were released from hospital, Martin and Max were relaxing in the barracks trying to avoid thinking of what had happened or what was to come. They looked up, and quickly stood to attention as they saw commanding officer Heine approaching.

"At ease. Schläfer, I am delighted to inform you that in the name of the Führer you have been awarded the *Iron Cross Second Class* for your bravery during operation Ösel."

"Well done Martin," Max thumped him on the back. "I heard the pilot that picked us up safely in the end got the IC2 for bravery too."

"I have even better news. To keep the IC2 company you have in addition been awarded the *Iron Cross First Class*. IC1 – that one is for seeing the whites of their eyes. Congratulations for the second time, Schläfer."

Martin's didn't want a fuss made of his awards, although it was unusual to get both Iron Crosses at once. But inside he was thrilled to bits. Max grinned. "Well, to be honest I think you deserve that and more for what you did. Everyone was talking about how brave you were, getting the blokes to safety after getting shot at during landing, and then securing the beach. You know you'll have to have a photo taken for your mum and dad. They will be so proud!"

"And when you think of that bastard Rainer and how he refused to share his dinghy with anyone else."

"They say that when Rainer got back our commanding officer gave him some of his own medicine. Took out his gun and said, 'You should be shot for cowardice, if it wasn't for your bloody high-up Nazi friends.' Rainer near shat himself."

Although he escaped punishment for his cowardice, the others developed more subtle ways of making sure Rainer did not forget he had lost their respect as a German officer. His presence would invariably be accompanied by the taunting – sometimes hummed, sometimes sung out loud – of a little rhyming ditty the men knew he hated:

> *Ach! wie Schade. Ach! wie Schade:*
> *Deutschland hat nur Marmelade!*
> *England hat noch Speck und Schinken,*
> *Frankreich hat noch Wein zu trinken.*
> *Ach! wie Schade. Ach! wie Schade:*
> *Deutschland hat nur Marmelade!*

> *What a sham! Oh what a sham:*
> *All that Germany's got is jam!*
> *England's still got bacon and ham,*
> *The French have wine to fill a dam.*
> *What a sham! Oh what a sham:*
> *All that Germany's got is jam!*

you'll have to have a photo taken for your mum and dad

Martin, still only 20, sports both Iron Crosses. *First class* was worn on the left breast; *second class* is the ribbon under the top button.

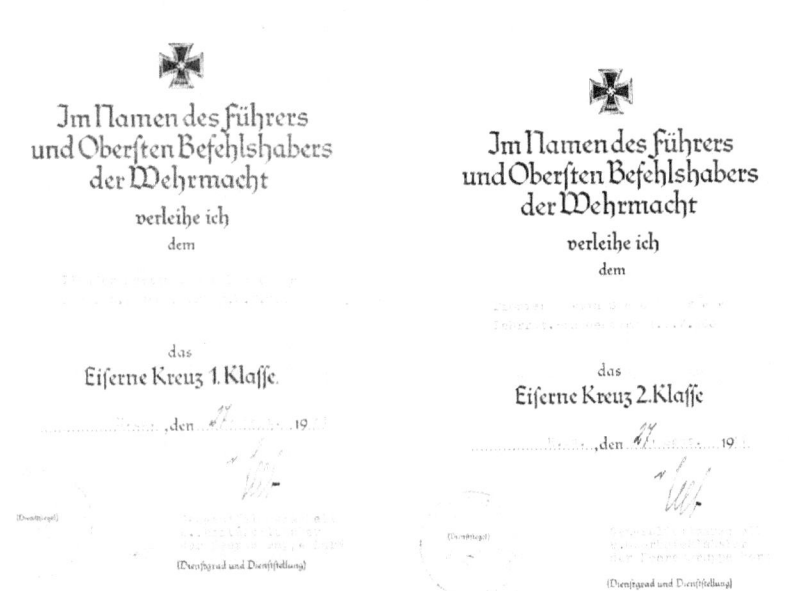

in the name of the Führer

The original certificates of award of Martin's Iron Cross First and Second Class dated 27th September 1941. They read (in part): *In the Name of the Führer and Supreme Commander of the Armed Services I award Pioneer Martin Schläfer of the Brandenburg Special Operations Training Regiment the Iron Cross First (Second) Class.*

Chapter 17

October 1941 – *Deserter*

Puzzled, Martin looked at the official telegram: '*Pionier* Schläfer is to report immediately to Wehrmacht headquarters in Baden bei Wien'.

Whatever do they want with me down in Austria? None of the others've said anything about going there.

On arrival in Baden, Martin went straight to army headquarters and presented his telegram. The orderly looked at it, picked up the phone, and as he was shown into a room to wait, Martin heard him ask for the *Schutzstaffel* before they shut the door. Everyone knew nothing good ever came from dealings with the SS. The war was already making Martin more and more apprehensive about authority, but this name made him really fearful, although he had no idea what they could want with him. After twenty minutes, two SS officers arrived, one of them tall and skinny with exophthalmic eyes and terrible skin. Martin found it difficult to take his eyes off the SS eagle on his sleeve and his SS Senior Lieutenant ranking of *Obersturmführer*. He sprang to attention.

"You have a nephew?"

"*Jawohl Herr Obersturmführer!*"

"Where is he?"

"I do not know the current whereabouts of my nephew, *Herr Obersturmführer!*"

"What DO you know about him?"

"I'm sorry, I do not quite understand what *Herr Obersturmführer* means."

"Are you an idiot, Schläfer? What is there to understand! Tell us about him!"

"Kurt, my nephew, was conscripted into Military Service some time ago, *Herr Obersturmführer*. I know this because he wrote to me about his *Wehrdienst*. I am serving with the Brandenburg Commandos and our unit has just returned from our first mission. I have not heard anything about, or from, Kurt for some time, *Herr Obersturmführer*.

May I respectfully inquire of *Herrn Obersturmführer* if my nephew is OK?"

"After three months as a soldier your nephew was reported AWOL. On his first one-day leave he made contact with a woman. His fellow soldiers say she was waiting for him after he eyed her off during a parade. He stayed with her for a week, violating his leave orders by six days. He took her to the movies."

"But surely that is not against the law?" Martin immediately bit his lip. You didn't joke with the SS.

"You realise I can have you shot for impertinence. This is a case of *Fahnenflucht* – desertion. Your iron crosses count for nothing with us if you are involved with a deserter."

At the word *deserter* Martin went cold all over. *Jesus what has he done now the idiot. Desertion – they put you up against a wall for that.*

"Your nephew was seen linking arms with the woman. Regulations strictly forbid a man in army uniform to have this sort of contact with a woman in public. Women and uniforms do not go together. The army police had been looking for him since he had not reported for duty. They spotted him, asked for his papers and arrested him. The only thing that saved him from more drastic punishment was the high opinion of his superior officers. He was jailed for three months in the military prison at Torgau. Upon release he was sent with no further training to the front. He was wounded early and hospitalised in Warsaw."

So he's still alive. What's coming next? They wouldn't be filling me in on the details if there wasn't more.

"While in hospital the degenerate fell in love with a Polish girl. A sub-human Polish slut, you understand. They should have shot him the first time."

Martin knew there was no answer to this, so wisely held his tongue, wondering where this was heading. What *had* Kurt done this time? He felt sick. Kurt was like a younger brother to Martin. He was always a bit head-strong but falling in love with a woman was not a crime, and so what if she was Polish? *We've known lots of nice Poles.* But of course, Martin knew only too well what the SS officer was ranting about: *Rassenschande* – the crime of racial defilement. According to National Socialist ideology all relationships between

Untermenschen – subhumans – and Aryans violated their sacred principle of Aryan *racial purity*. It was one of the worst crimes you could be accused of ... Martin's thoughts were interrupted.

"The Polish slut worked as a cleaner in the hospital. Your nephew was once again sent to prison for two weeks. Upon release the idiot went straight back to her, returning to camp just after curfew. His roommate told him the police had been looking for him. He told us that Kurt decided he had had enough, packed his kit, left the compound and went to stay with his whore. That is his death sentence. So, I repeat: where is he now?"

"I am very sorry, *Herr Obersturmführer*, but I really do not know. As I just explained, there is no way for me to know – I have been in training and on a mission fighting the Bolsheviks in Estonia"

"You can be assured we will be checking if you have received mail from him and that you are telling us the truth. Aiding a deserter will get you shot. If you hear from him, you are to inform your superior officer immediately. Is that understood?"

"*Jawohl, Herr Obersturmführer*!!"

Over my dead body. Christ what an utter, utter idiot to fraternise with the enemy AND desert during war time.

It was a long, long trip back to the Brandenburger unit at Düren, with his thoughts all the time on Kurt and what might have happened to him. At least he was able to get a letter written and posted to his family at home from a letter-box the SS couldn't trace. He asked if the family knew anything, but was very careful to word it so he did not worry them unduly.

When he finally got back to Düren he was met by lots of unfamiliar faces – replacements for the men lost. They all had to undergo the special Brandenburger training Martin had completed when he first joined. While they were learning their new skills, the battle-hardened men were ordered to hone their skills and ensure their fitness level was maintained.

****

"Schläfer you are to report immediately for guard duty! *Oberst* Hähling von Lanzenauer is right this moment on his way to inspect the troops, and the sergeant-major wants you to be the guard on duty to present arms when he arrives."

It didn't get much more important than an inspection from the divisional commander, and the sergeant-major thought it would be a good opportunity to show off the fact that they had first class iron-cross recipients. Martin relieved the guard on duty just in time before Colonel von Lanzenauer's arrival at the barracks. Standing to attention as the divisional commander approached he smartly presented arms. Von Lanzenauer indeed stopped and asked Martin politely how he had won his first class iron cross. One did not speak with presented arms, so Martin shouldered his rifle, quickly recounted his experiences on Ösel, then presented arms again. Von Lanzenauer nodded and disappeared into the barracks. Straightaway Martin heard a fearful bellowing from inside. "Men who have demonstrated their service to me by earning the IC 1 will NOT be put on watch! NEITHER will they be given any work duty! If I hear that has happened under your command YOU will find yourself the one on guard duty, understood?! That man will be relieved IMMEDIATELY and given the rest of the day off!" That was the shortest guard duty Martin had ever stood: almost immediately the officer in charge of the watch appeared with another man to relieve him.

The effect his first class iron cross exerted was a new experience for Martin, who had been too busy worrying about other things to really pay much attention to decorations up to then. But time and again he found the decorations indeed made him different in the eyes of the men. The next day he was sitting with his head in a western when *Unteroffizier* Weidermann was due for his daily inspection. Weidermann was a stickler for discipline and order and the men in Martin's room were afraid of him. They had agreed to keep the room in order if Martin agreed to always be the one to face Weidermann to deliver his report. "For heaven's sake Martin put your jacket and field-belt on. You know what he's like – he'll tear you apart if he sees anything out of order."

Too late! *Unteroffizier* Weidermann burst in. Martin started to get up but was not quick enough. Weidermann started screaming. "Look at the condition of this room. This is filthy, that's filthy. It's a pig-sty. The whole damn room's a mess – I'll have you all on a charge for this.

Stand to attention when an officer enters the room – why are you not wearing your jacket and belt? Outside and report in two minutes!"

Martin, always eager to avoid unnecessary trouble when possible, tried to bring himself to attention while turning round to face Weidermann and dragging on his tunic. He added the very smartest salute he could manage for good measure (that usually went down well).

"*Herr Unteroffizier*! Room number 6. Occupied by 16 men. All present and accounted for! I will have everything clean and in order immediately, *Herr Unteroffizier*!"

Inevitably, the corporal's eyes took in the brace of iron crosses on Martin's tunic.

"*Ach, Entschuldigung*. I apologise. I didn't realise. Please resume your reading. Go back to bed. Take a rest. Forget what I just said."

****

Life in the camp became humdrum, relieved only by frequent visits to the local pub. Martin, Alfred and Paul, who had recovered well from his injury, would all head there even though there was no decent beer being produced – the war effort took up all resources. The barely drinkable 'light beer' tasted more like a soft drink, but they welcomed anything when they were not working. No-one complained; it was good just to get out. Most of the pubs had pianos and there was always someone who could play the songs they all knew. Everyone would sing along and try to forget their problems for a few hours. Martin's medals were always good for a free packet of cigarettes and once in a while even some decent beer, or schnapps, kept for special occasions.

"Martin, didn't you have to go to Baden bei Wien after Riga?"

"Yes, what of it?"

"Nothing, Martin, nothing. It's just the word is we are all off there soon to join the 15th *Ergänzungskompanie*, to train the replacements for our losses. We'll help train the new recruits and there'll also be new stuff we'll have to learn. You should have stayed there. Save you making the trip again. What did they want with you there anyway?"

"Nothing in particular." As was Martin's habit, he kept his life and personal feelings to himself. He changed the topic. "Say, was there any decent stuff from the volunteers this week? For some reason I didn't get my ration."

They had started to get small packets of chocolates, cigarettes and biscuits put together by women in support of the war-effort for distribution by the army. It'd be a pity to miss out on one of those … Martin went to the orderly in charge of distribution to see if he could score a spare packet. When he explained why he had come the orderly was visibly upset.

"What's wrong? Surely the Third Reich still has some chocolate and biscuits along with the jam?"

"Yes, very funny Martin. You know I go every week to the post office to collect the packages for our group. I've got to know the post-mistress. Had quite a few nice chats. She's a lonely old biddy. Doesn't have much. Husband and sons both off fighting and she still has little ones at home to look after. Anyway, today when I went to pick up our packages she wasn't there. She's been shot – executed I mean. She was caught stealing some of the packets – that's Army property. They don't take kindly to that. God knows what her children will do. I know I can't interfere. I hope someone looks after them."

Martin went back to his bunk thinking about the old post-mistress, wondering if they could help in any way. Perhaps they could collect some money for the children? His mind was taken off the post-mistress incident however by a letter from home the next day. It was from Kurt's mum, Martha. Kurt had been captured and executed. The letter did not say when.

Martha had been notified by the SS Police that Kurt was under sentence of death for the multiple crimes of *Fahnenflucht*, *Rassenschande*, *Wehrkraftzersetzung* – desertion, racial defilement, war-effort subversion. She was allowed one last visit, to the place he was being held in Upper Silesia which many Germans were reluctant to name or pretended not to know about – Auschwitz. They even gave her directions: totally irrelevant, given how far it was from Leipzig, even if she managed to get a travel pass. It was also irrelevant for a sadder reason: Kurt had been shot one day before the letter had been sent. The very next day she got a letter giving her the grave number and warning that a cross and any mound were forbidden on the grave.

When he was alone, Martin broke down. All the things that had happened to him, to people around him, his comrades and friends, all the loss of lives he had witnessed, the lives he too had taken as part of this war. But now it had touched his family. It all welled-up. *What in God's name was it all for?*

His whole body shook with silent sobs.

Chapter 18

1942 – Partisan

Early 1942 – Hitler's invasion of Russia in the quest for *Lebensraum* in the east and the domination of the so-called sub-human Slavs had been underway for more than half a year.

Initially the invading German army liked to think that they had been welcomed by the Russians as saviours from Bolshevism. But things had changed; the people's attitude was continually worsening. This was not surprising. As they advanced, the German armies evicted Russians from their homes and took their food, leaving them to starve or perish with cold. Following in the wake of the army came the SS *Einsatzgruppen*: extermination squads specially trained to mass-murder community leaders, intellectuals and Jews. Not long after, the *Einsatzgruppen* extended their murderous brutality to women and children.

The suburbs of Moscow had been in sight but the Germany army fared no better than Napoleon well over a century before in the face of the Russian winter, and their advance had to be abandoned in tantalising view of the capital. The Russian resistance had begun to fight back, and by the late autumn of 1941, a well-planned partisan organisation had started to emerge in the occupied areas and a vicious, merciless partisan war had developed remarkably quickly behind the German lines. Very few prisoners of war here: you were captured, you were killed. Acts of sabotage by groups and individuals had become routine. Some would come over to the Germans in the guise of Russian deserters, only to wipe them out once they had gained their confidence.

It was realised that the partisans were unlikely to be stopped with conventional military might. The more you burnt down dwellings trying to flush them out, the more reprisals you took, the more people went over to the partisans. It was felt some Brandenburger cunning might be more effective, and counteracting this partisan threat was to be the next operation to involve Martin's Brandenburger unit.

****

The new recruits, who were in the top ten percent of the army both physically and mentally, were nevertheless young and had no experience. That is why the five months since the Ösel disaster had to be spent training them in Baden bei Wien. As Alfred had said, that didn't mean the experienced men were exempt – and after one operation you counted as experienced! So Martin and the others had been required to go back to training to ensure their skills remained finely honed. Martin's promotion to corporal had come through and he was now *Unteroffizier* Schläfer!

Once again the training was demanding and without compromise: that never changed. This time cross-country skiing was high on the agenda for Martin's team, to enable them to fight effectively in the frozen wastes of the northern Soviet Union. They were also shown how to sabotage their own munitions. Tinker with a whole load of German hand grenades by removing the delay on the detonator so that they would explode as soon as you withdrew the pin. Let the partisans capture the hand grenades. Encourage them to attack and watch them blow themselves up. Most important was instilling into the trainees the need for always digging a hole two shovel-blades deep to sleep in. If you slept above ground you would be likely to be hit by deliberate low-level sweeping fire from partisans. Martin felt that the edge of the obviously top-class Brandenburger training was taken off a bit by the suicide pill that was now issued to each man, along with precise instructions for use, should they fall into enemy hands.

But now they were back in Düren, 40 men assigned to help supplement what was left of the 10th Company recently returned from Russia. The 10th Company's losses were so great that their *Auffüllung* – replacement – had taken about six weeks to complete.

****

Martin and his group sat and listened. "Up to now the local inhabitants have been friendly, trustful, and entirely willing to cooperate. But now that attitude is changing fast. Russian agents disguised as civilians – well-trained propagandists – are taking advantage of the kind-heartedness of the German soldier by passing through the lines and infiltrating into army group rear areas. They are telling the people that the return of the Red Army is inevitable and there will come a day of reckoning for all those who collaborate with the Germans. *Shame and death to those who collaborate with the enemy! Save Mother Russia!* That's what you hear now. So you need to be extremely careful if you have any contact with them. Which will be very soon as you are to be sent on your next mission within two days. Any questions?

They were headed for the Russian front: *Orel*, a city located approximately 360 kilometres south-southwest of Moscow. Where the Partisan warfare was particularly fierce, they were to establish complete control to make the German retreat from Moscow easier.

It was easy to say that they were headed for Orel, but in reality, it lay some 2000 kilometres to the east. And the difference in space was more than matched by the difference in the weather. To Martin and the others, it felt during the first days as if they had stepped into another world. The intense cold made them all miserable. You could not escape it. There was just no way to keep warm. The winter that year was the severest in recorded history: northwest of Moscow in January '42 the average temperature was -32° F. Not that anyone paid attention to the precise value. They knew only that they had not experienced that kind of cold before. The fine camouflage of their uniforms – white on one side and a deep green on the other – did not make up for the fact that they were not intended for winter. Unbelievably, they had been sent into the middle of a Russian winter with inadequate protection against the elements.

They were transported in small trucks, which constantly got bogged down in the mud and had to be dug out. Complaining would not have done any good: anyway, the digging helped keep them from freezing. They also make frequent stops during their trip just to try and warm up by running around, jumping on the spot – anything to get the circulation moving.

From time to time a threatening drone would herald the approach of Russian ground-attack *Sturmovik* aircraft. The Brandenburgers adopted their usual mode of anti-aircraft attack. They lay on the ground head-to-toe in a line pointing in the direction of the planes, and discharged a volley of rifle fire as they flew over. With a lot of men – in this case about forty – there was supposedly quite a good chance of at least one hitting the target. And providing it was flying no higher than about 1000 meters, bullets from their rifles would still have sufficient velocity to penetrate and do damage. But usually the *Sturmoviks*, with larger fish to fry, continued on their way over the little convoy apparently unscathed.

The goal was to initially reinforce and hold a small village near Orel, where there were already some German troops precariously dug in. It was totally isolated on three sides by swamp and forest, and only accessible by a dirt track about three or four metres wide. They were to establish a protective perimeter and make sure the troops were not captured by any advancing Russians.

"The village has already been taken over by our troops, and we've people in some of the houses. We know the Russian soldiers or the partisans'll be coming back to try and regain the village. We'll be safe once we get in there; we can monitor the approach road without needing to worry about the swamp on the other three sides: no-one could get through that. What we need to do first is *Einigeln* – hedgehog ourselves in, spines outwards. Find tins and things – anything made of metal – which we can tie to a barbed-wire fence around the houses. Then if anyone tries to enter the area, we'll hear the tins rattle." The commander pointed to the houses on either side of the one they were in.

"We'll booby-trap the houses we're not using, so there's no shelter for any Ivans. If they try and get inside they'll be blown up. Either the booby traps'll get them or the cold. We are to dig in and hold the village until further notice."

The men had almost completed these preparations when the gun fire opened up, suddenly, from all around. They rushed to the nearest safe houses, those without booby-traps; some were shot down in the attempt.

Shit, how come? No-one could've come down the road: we had men watching it.

"They're completely around us – they must have somehow made it over the frozen swamp."

They succeeded in holding-off the first attack, but only just. Some of their attackers had entered the booby-trapped dwellings and were blown up in a blaze of burning wood. But they were still totally surrounded: trapped, with rations for only three days, and the only water was in the well out the back which they couldn't reach. But outside, of course, was *snow*. This they crawled out and retrieved with buckets in the dark. Building small fires in the house, they melted the snow into drinking water.

The siege lasted 12 days. The Brandenburgers were able to keep the enemy at bay by listening constantly for the rattle of the tins attached to the wire around the houses. Even reduced to quarter rations, their food ran out quickly. From the windows they could see, against the flames, the Russians throwing their dead into an enormous fire they had built. And not just the dead; also their screaming wounded. Even though they saw it with their own eyes, they could not believe it. It seemed mad not to always try to save your wounded. But perhaps they didn't want to leave them to the mercy of the Germans. They knew what *that* meant.

Then the loudspeakers started, in Russian-accented German, and kept up all night long:

"Brandenburgers – yes we know who you are from your uniforms! – you must be so cold and so hungry. Come out! We will feed you! We have beautiful women too. They love German men, especially you brave Brandenburgers. Think about it - three hot meals a day, three hot women a day! Come on now, what are you waiting for?"

This was too much for *Stellvertretender Gruppenführer* Irwin. A big star in the Hitler Youth, he had automatically been made second in command. Collapsing in a corner, he pulled out his pistol and started shooting into the air. They managed somehow to calm him down. Martin waited till dark and went to find their group commander.

"Irwin's shooting holes in the air. He's lost it."

"Martin, you're the most experienced in that group, I'm ordering you to take over command."

"What about Irwin?"

"Get him out of the way, somehow. He's finished. If he makes it back, which I very much doubt, he'll be shot. Hitler doesn't take kindly to cowards, Hitler Youth star or not."

On the 13th day the *Luftwaffe* started dropping provisions. Every time a plane was heard they saw the Russians taking off their coats to hail them; no longer easily recognisable as the enemy, they also succeeded in attracting a share of German provisions from on high.

That night everything went quiet. No more loudspeakers. No more gunfire. The Brandenburgers initially thought it was some kind of trick and waited and waited. Finally, they realised the Russians had pulled out. Perhaps because with warmer weather they feared the swamp would thaw leaving them no escape route.

They re-established radio contact and were given instructions to leave the village and march to Orel, 72 kilometres on the way to Moscow.

Not far from the village they suddenly heard a new noise, a whooshing-howling-screaming. Only a few recognised the sound of the weapon they would grow to hate, rushing for cover and yelling to the others "*Stalinorgel*! – Stalin-Organ! Get down!" A rushing noise overhead; missiles raining down. If you were lucky and it was summer, the missiles hit soft ground and penetrated several feet before exploding, causing the ground to bubble like boiling soup. On contact with the hard winter ground however the explosion sent shrapnel the size of a man's fist in all directions. The mobile *Stalinorgel* launchers inflicted incredible damage and delivered a devastating amount of explosives quickly and indiscriminately. Paul, right beside Martin, went down. Martin had been so busy running for cover he had not noticed. Peering out from over his bush he saw Paul lying motionless and bloody a few yards away. This time he looked in bad shape.

How come he always gets hit? Martin could see the first-aid truck well behind where the rockets were hitting, and looked in vain for a first-aid officer. He zigzagged all the way back to the truck clambering, stumbling, falling flat, getting up. He finally saw one.

"*Sanitäter*! Paramedic! I need you. My mate Paul's been hit."

The medic's sneering response was as long-winded as Martin's request was short. "I am an officer, not a *Sanitäter*. I have received special training in a medical school and have done special courses. I have responsibility for the organisation of professional medical treatment, not its implementation. I will certainly not come for you or your friend Paul. Piss off, I have things to organise."

"I am not making inquiries about your credentials, sergeant. Playing your war games, *Herr Sanitätsunterfeldwebel,* and spouting off about your qualifications and who you will and will not treat helps no-one. I may as well rid the army of you now. Your choice: you either help or ... "

The commotion brought the Medical Sergeant running over. He saw Martin draw his pistol, point it at the man's face and cock it.

"Martin, Martin, put the *Schiesseisen* down, OK? What's up? Can I do anything?"

"It's Paul. This way. You know we have to get to him before the Russians do – they don't care about the Red Cross. They'll just kill him."

Martin led the way back, bending low over rubble, beams, pot holes and mud. The approaching night gave them some welcome cover. Although Paul's upper body was more or less covered in blood, the wound was, once again! actually not as bad as it had looked. A piece of shrapnel had given him a new hair parting, taking some of his scalp with it. He was just coming around when they arrived.

"He's not bleeding any more. Let's get him back and patch him up."

"Paul, you lucky bugger! This one looks like it might be your very own personal *Heimatschuss,* the injury that will take you home."

****

"I intend to report *Unteroffizier* Schläfer, *Herr Sanitätsfeldwebel.* You were right there yesterday. You saw him threaten to shoot me. I want him court-marshalled and shot."

The medical orderly was addressing his superior officer.

"Yesterday, *Sanitätsunterfeldwebel*? Yesterday? But you are mistaken. I saw nothing that needs to be reported. I heard nothing that needs to be reported. The *Stalinorgel* took out 72 of our men in the fighting yesterday but this patient survived because you went and got him and attended to his wounds. I congratulate you on your valour!"

It was clear the medical orderly was furious. But with no eyewitness, there was nothing he could do. Martin was just glad Paul had got the treatment he needed. He also knew he would do it again if he had to, even if it meant court-martial.

They had started with 240 men; now there were only 16. Now it was no longer a case of recruiting volunteers for the Brandenburgers.

Men were simply chosen. The continual loss of his friends and colleagues was really starting to affect Martin. He wondered how long it would be before he or one of his really close friends like Alfred or Paul were killed or badly wounded. It was a numbers game, and he knew the odds – even at the outset pretty bad – were now starting to seriously stack up against them. Paul was already on his second injury and Martin and Alfred had just been incredibly lucky up until now.

Of course you were always shit-scared, but concentrating on staying alive managed to put that somehow in the back of your mind. They said that this worked, but only up until your first wound; only *after* that did the real fear come. Dreadful, incapacitating fear that could only be numbed by a lot of schnapps. He could feel the apprehension weighing heavier and heavier with each passing week. *How much longer can our luck hold out*?

The next day, Martin went to see how Paul was doing. Most of his head was now covered with bandages.

"If they don't send you home for this, at least next time for God's sake try and hang on better to your helmet. You know, for a clever person you are remarkably stupid."

On his way out of the hospital he bumped into the medical sergeant who had helped him. He was obviously in a good mood.

"Hallo Martin! Have you heard the news? General Paulus and our Sixth Army have started their attack on Stalingrad. It can't hold out long, not against that force. When Stalingrad falls it will be the beginning of the end for the Russians, and it won't be long then 'til this terrible war is over and we have our *Endsieg*. Our Final Victory, Martin!"

He paused. "If I hadn't stopped you, you wouldn't really have shot him, would you?"

"Him being dead certainly wouldn't have helped Paul any. But I don't know, *Sanitätsfeldwebel*. I don't know."

Chapter 19

1942 – Easy-peasy

OK. Gather round. There's one here for most of us to practice on. It's apparently a ZK-383. Has anyone seen one of these Czech machine-guns before? If we're going to have to use them, we'll have to know how to take them apart."

"And put them together again, Martin."

"Yes, Paul, and put them together again. Anyone know? We've got an inspection in an hour. You know what a stickler he is. We're in for it if we haven't got it down pat. So, does anyone know? I haven't seen them before."

"Easy-peasy."

The others turned towards Eric Strauss, waiting for explanation.

"I was there when we marched into Czechoslovakia. I was stationed at the arms factory in Brno. I got to know them quite well. Good weapons. They will fire single rounds or auto. It depends on trigger pull. Bit like a Tommy Sten. Fed from left."

He picked one off the bench. "Barrel comes away easy. Look, release is under the front sight. Safety is just in front of the trigger here. Bolt comes away like this, see? There's a bolt weight and if you remove it, see, it'll up your fire rate from 500 to 700. The wooden stock comes away, just … so. And the rear sight comes away with this pin. That's about it. Oh, I forgot, there's also a bipod support if you need one. It clips normally in here. But they don't seem to have given us one so don't worry about it. There you are."

They all regarded the disassembled weapon on the bench.

"Right, thanks Eric. OK. Rest of you see if you can do what Eric has just shown us with your own issues. Ask him if you get stuck. The sooner we are all familiar with it the quicker we can get back to a smoko."

The Captain came in unannounced and earlier than expected, catching them all relaxed, sitting around laughing and smoking. He was yelling before they had managed to scramble to attention. "What's this? Why are you all smoking and lounging around you lazy bastards!

Are you all crazy? Obviously none of you are in the slightest bit aware of what's going on in Stalingrad. A whole army of ours has been encircled. Looks like not even the tiniest mouse will be able to get out."

He let that sink in, then: "*Unteroffizier* Schläfer! You were specifically instructed to demonstrate to the men how to dismantle and reassemble the Czech sub-machine gun."

"Yes Sir. Correct Sir. Your instructions have been carried out, Sir. One of the men will demonstrate for *Herr Hauptmann. Gefreiter* Strauss! Step forward! You will demonstrate immediately for *Herr Hauptmann* the disassembly and reassembly of ZK-383. Exactly as I have shown you. Begin."

The sub-machine gun was expertly taken apart, laid out on the bench, and then put back together with the best military precision and not a few unnecessary flourishes. Strauss dry-fired the machine gun twice, put the reassembled weapon back on the bench and stood to attention.

"ONE CZECH ZK-383 DISSASSEMBLED AND REASSEMBLED AS ORDERED, *HERR HAUPTMANN*!!"

"So. Excellent! It seems you have instructed your men well, Schläfer. At ease, everyone. You may carry on with your cigarette break."

Normally getting one up on the Captain like this would be a cause for a bit of horse-play among the men, but the news about Stalingrad had dampened their spirits.

"Perhaps he just wanted to make us feel bad? Perhaps it's not as bad as he makes out – wasn't there an upbeat broadcast from the Stalingrad front just a short while ago saying everything was OK?"

Chapter 20

September 1943 – *Sniper*

But the captain had been right. The Germans attacking Stalingrad had indeed been encircled by a massive Red Army that had been reinforced from tank factories in the vastness of the Russian hinterland, unobtrusively and slowly built up behind the city, on the other side of the Volga. The encouraging broadcast they had heard had been a propaganda fake. In February 1943, General Paulus was finally forced to surrender and the whole of the mighty German Sixth Army was lost. Stalingrad had not fallen.

Although this crushing defeat was probably the turning point of the war, marking the start of the long Russian counter-offensive towards Berlin, it had little effect on Martin's Brandenburg unit, which was still trying to counteract Russian partisan activity. Martin was in command of small units who were mostly concerned with trying to slow down the subsequent Russian counter-offensive. Before, the Brandenburgers were active in front of their advancing army; now they often operated in their retreating rear. The men liked Martin and he was a good officer. He always led by example and never asked them to do anything he would not do himself. They blew up bridges and railway lines; reconnoitred enemy positions and activity. But they could not see it making a difference. And they lost more and more men. After each operation, they had to return to Düren to replenish numbers, train new troops. Because Paul was an experienced fighter he too was now sent to another unit, fighting partisans in northern Serbia.

****

"Four weeks without washing, so strip off. They've given you special soap and shampoo for the lice and fleas – make sure you use it especially in all the areas with hair. Chuck your clothes for incineration." They were once again back at the Düren base camp in Germany to get replacements for the killed and wounded.

Burning their uniforms was the only remedy. Lice and flea bites and infestation were indeed a major problem – almost as much as the enemy – and Martin did not have to tell them twice. Along with very bad skin conditions it caused some 'significant psychological distress' – drove the men mad in other words – and reduced the morale and fighting fitness of many of the troops. Attempts at infestation control initially succeeded, but usually not for long; they just couldn't eradicate all stages of the flea life cycle.

The Russian autumn was in the air as, temporarily deloused, they now headed for Roslavl, an important communications centre on the road to Moscow, more than 2000 kilometres from their home. In August 1941, as part of operation *Barbarossa*, the town had been swiftly captured in the first battle of Smolensk by German troops, with more than 38,000 Russian soldiers taken prisoner. Although the area had been under German occupation for two years, it was now being retaken by the Soviet Army in the second battle of Smolensk. The supporting partisans had since reclaimed the airport on the outskirts. The Germans had managed to retake it, but the partisans had not given up and were striking unpredictably, picking off the Germans at will. The Brandenburgers were to spearhead the operation to rid the area of partisans for good and hold up the Russian advance.

"It's bit nippy."

"You young'uns don't know what cold means. When our group was in Russia last year it regularly got down to minus 20, and often much lower. Everything failed – tanks, machine guns, radios – all kaput. We even saw locomotive boilers burst. It was like entering a different world, and don't forget they hadn't given us winter clothing. Fur caps, parkas, felt boots, snow hoods, you name it – we didn't have it. Frostbite! Couldn't even get your boots off. We had to fight the weather as much as the Ivans, and they're used to it; it's their friend."

"Yeah I reckon it was the forced labour back home. The people they got to pack the uniforms there sent summer ones to us in the cold and winter ones to our troops fighting in the desert in North Africa. No wonder we got pushed back, eh. Well this time it'll be different."

The new men who had been trained to replace those lost had been keen to go. They were excited at this their first mission. Martin, Alfred and Paul, now totally recovered from his injury and still fed-up that it had not amounted to a *Heimatschuss*, kept quiet. They knew they would soon get a chance to be bloodied.

The group arrived at Roslavl and set-up camp, waiting for night. Under cover of darkness they headed off for the airport to flush out the partisans and their mobile machine-gun emplacements. Finding them was not complicated: they simply threw rocks into the undergrowth. The Russians, who were clearly nervous, fired at any noise or movement.

Once located, the emplacements were easy to eliminate: they crept round to the side and opened fire. The partisans, for the most part, deserted their machine guns and ran. The Germans did not follow – that would be too risky. The partisans knew the terrain and the hiding places.

Martin and his group found the relative warmth and shelter of some sheds which faced the road leading to the airport. They started to congratulate themselves; once again they had survived a mission.

"Well, that didn't take too long, and these sheds are good, beats sleeping in tents."

"Shit!"

Mortar fire punched gaping holes in the tin shed as they all hit the ground. Martin looked up to see where a piece of shrapnel had lodged in the wooden frame just centimetres from where his head had been. Carefully, very carefully, he peered through a window. He could see the fire was coming from a small group of trees about 150 meters off to the right. *So we haven't got rid of them*. Martin could also see an anti-tank ditch lying between them and the partisans. Carefully excavated with just the right slopes so that once in the ditch a tank could neither move forwards nor backwards, it would provide the Brandenburgers with good cover for a counter attack.

"There's a *Panzergraben* we can use for cover about 20 meters away. They'd be within range of grenades from there."

"We'll use that then" master-sergeant Heine replied. "Let's go." They crept out of the shed and ran to the protection of the tank trap, from where they were able to hurl grenades and more effectively concentrate fire on the partisans. They saw them turn and run, firing as they went. "C'mon! Move! Let's get after them!" Returning fire, the Germans burst out of the ditch and this time gave chase. They had to make sure they would not be attacked again.

Martin spots flashes from the sniper's gun off to the left. He feels the air rush past his ear. He takes aim and returns fire.

"*Himmel Arsch und Zwirn!!*"

The curse comes from just to Martin's left. He turns his head to see master-sergeant Heine on his knees, holding his arm.

Heine shouts out. "Sergent Bütz! I've been shot! You take over command!"

Walter Bütz replies "*Jawohl Herr Oberfeldwebel!* Everyone, follow my orders!" Following Army protocol, he raises his hand to acknowledge the transfer and let the other men see he was now in command. Not surprisingly, his upraised arm immediately attracts a sniper bullet.

"*Scheisse.* Sergeant Bütz wounded! *Unteroffizier* Bangert take over command! You're in charge now."

The farce continues. Corporal Bangert raises his hand to acknowledge: "Everyone, follow my … ." His turn to be shot.

"Bangert wounded! *Unteroffizier* Schläfer take over command!"

There is no time to think, only to react. Martin puts up his hand to accept the command and shouts he's in charge – "*Alles hört auf mein Kommando!...*"

He feels the impact high up on his right leg. It knocks him over. The bullet enters his right thigh, exits near his groin, rips flesh off his scrotum and lodges in his left thigh. *Another sniper. Should've known there'd be more than one.*

"Heinzel Hilgardt! *Unteroffizier* Hilgardt! Take over command! Schläfer wounded."

Shit! Shit!! Shit!!! He had started to think he was invincible; he had been so lucky up until now. He sees from the blood quickly staining his groin he has been hit in more than one place. A makeshift tourniquet for each of his legs from the shirt he has ripped off appears to stop the bleeding. He is surprised that he can't feel any pain. He looks around for the first time since he was shot. Then the burning sensation hits, and his thighs and groin are on fire.

The Russians could still be seen in the distance, but the Germans in front had given up the chase and were crawling back towards their leader. The gunfire had stopped. The fire from the sniper too had ceased – perhaps he had been shot; perhaps just run off.

"What a total mess. We thought the bastards had all run off. Where did this group come from?"

"That was deliberate! They knew we'd chase them and they led us right between a couple of snipers. That's what I reckon anyway."

Not wanting to make themselves easy sniper targets again, part crawling, part hunched over, they made their way slowly and carefully back to the four Opel Blitz trucks that were waiting for them just inside the forested area out of sight of the airport. Martin found to his surprise he could still walk, just. Most of the pain came from his balls.

Paul and Alfred, who had been checking the northern fence and the plane maintenance hangars when the shooting started, came over to see what had happened. They found Martin sitting in the truck shaking his head. "Each time the command was passed on, the idiot put his hand up to accept it and got shot. I was the last idiot. Like sitting ducks for a good rifleman. They picked off four of us in as many seconds."

"Well, that's what they tell us to do – that's Army regulations."

"Well in future they know where they can stuff their regulations as far as I'm concerned."

"In future? From that wound you don't look as if you'll be doing much in future."

The truck took them back to the makeshift emergency bandaging station – just straw thrown on the ground and some canvass. They helped him in, limping. The nature of his wound made it difficult for Martin to be comfortable in any position, but eventually they managed to get him lying on the side opposite where the bullet had entered.

"Well at least you didn't get one in the arse like Arthur yesterday," Paul said. "And it means a *Verwundetenabzeichen* you know, a 'wounded decoration' to add to your iron crosses. Let's see if we can find a doctor."

"In the arse would have been better than the balls any day, Paul. And actually I'd rather have received no wound than an award for having been wounded."

Martin looked around him. Funny, he was almost relieved he had been shot. He suspected that the others might agree. It meant for a few weeks he would be away from the violence of war: its smells, its sounds, the dying, the cold, the mud and the constant fear. *How much longer is this wretched war going to last?*

It was the smell of blood, sickly sweet, that affected him most while lying there waiting for a doctor. Or perhaps he was confusing it with the smell of unwashed bodies. Whatever, he was really sick of those smells. Most of the time, when he was focusing on the job at hand, one did not notice. He looked at row after row of men, some on their stomachs, others on their sides and some with head bandages just staring into space. Bandages of all kinds, handkerchiefs, shirts, singlets – there were even some nice clean white ones. *Wonder wherever they come from?* Those who still could were scratching themselves continually. *Funny how the lice and fleas have never bitten me.*

His mind jumped to when he had first found out he had them. Paul had said "Jesus they're driving me mad these fleas or lice or whatever they are. They're worse than the cold, they just never let up."

"What do you mean? I haven't got any."

"Come on Martin, of course you've got fleas. Everyone has. When we can't wash, that's where they come from. Go on. Bet you. Have a look inside your jacket."

Intrigued, Martin took off his jacket and inspected the armpits. Sure enough, they were crawling with them. "You're right, they're everywhere. Strange, though: they've never bitten me."

"Lucky bastard. Something about your blood I guess."

After an hour or two, Paul reappeared. "It looks as if we are all going back to Mogilew. The medics say the priority is to get everyone back to the field hospital there. OK, let's get back to the trucks. They've already started loading everyone on now." Paul helped Martin into the very last of the trucks, and climbed in.

Befitzzeugnis

Dem

Oberjäger Martin   S c h l ä f e r
[Name, Dienstgrad]

10.Kompanie / 2.Regiment Brandenburg
[Truppenteil, Dienststelle]

ift auf Grund

feiner am   16. September 1943   erlittenen

einmaligen Verwundung — Befchädigung

das

Verwundetenabzeichen

in   "S c h w a r z"

verliehen worden.

O.U., den 5. November 19 43

[Unterschrift]

Lbt. u.stellv. Bl.-Führer,
[Dienstgrad und Dienststelle]

an award for having been wounded

Certificate confirming the award of Martin's *Verwundetenabzeichen*. It reads (in part): *In recognition of the single wound he received on 16th September 1943 Oberjäger Martin Schläfer is awarded the Wounded Badge (black)*. This was a Nazi badge conferred on soldiers sustaining a wound in battle. The designation black is for either a single wound or two wounds (silver and gold badges were awarded for more).

Chapter 21

September 1943 – *Little Man*

Mogilew was a smallish Russian town just under 200 kilometres from Roslavl. It took the convoy four days to get there: four days to cover terrain that is normally covered in a few hours! Mogilew could have been on another planet it seemed so far out of reach, so many things went wrong. Right from the start the partisan activity was fierce and caused constant delays. As soon as they set off every morning they were slowed down by enemy fire. All the trucks had engine trouble. Tyres had blown on three occasions. Everyone had terrible diarrhoea. Because the trucks were travelling at walking pace the men simply climbed onto the running-board, pulled down their trousers and emptied their bowels into the mud as they went along. And then there was the weather! Autumn had never felt so vicious, a cold snap with freezing temperatures at night. The morning thaw turned the ground to mud and bogged them down. At times the trucks were so stuck in the mud it was thought they would just have to abandon them and try to make it on foot. Only a mixture of sheer brute force, determination and desperation helped the men dig the tyres out of the slush. They knew it was better to have the trucks for shelter, and the cover they provided was better than being outside. Nevertheless it seemed to the men that during the time it took to cover the 200 odd kilometres to Mogilew they had spent almost as much time outside the trucks for one reason or another as inside.

On the third night they decided to start digging before the freeze; also at night there was less risk of being attacked. Everyone was ordered out; able-bodied men to excavate, wounded to make the trucks lighter.

They lay Walter Bütz down just to the side of the road. The stomach wounds he had received from the sniper after putting his hand up were bad and everyone was worried. It was touch and go – if they did not get him to a hospital soon he was finished. It took more than four hours to free the trucks from the mud, and they started to climb in.

Martin hobbled over to wake Walter. He had only managed some intermittent dozing after being shot three days ago but had finally managed to get some proper sleep. But Walter did not move, and Martin saw he was dead. He was frozen to the ground by his own blood, and they couldn't move him. He lay there, the blood from his stomach wound saturating his uniform and staining the ground around him. There was nothing to do but wrap him in a blanket and leave him.

It was difficult for Martin to avoid the thought that he would be next. He felt the heat building in his legs each day and each day the pain getting worse. Sitting down was painful; standing up only marginally better. Worst of all, the previously unnoticed lice and fleas were now driving him insane. They had gotten inside the dressings and the itching was hell, even more so since he couldn't scratch where it hurt. They were even starting to bite him at last.

But finally, somehow, on the 20th – four days after he had been shot – they made it back to Mogilew. He remembered thinking then how much it reminded him of Wiederitzsch, his own village. The same steep angle on the same layered thatched roofs so the snow couldn't lodge. Everyone poor; all the houses in need of repair. The only building that looked relatively new was *Kriegslazarett 2/521* – the field hospital that was converted from a school since the fighting for the airport had started.

Martin knew he had copped a bad infection. The bullet was still lodged in his left thigh. He watched as the medical orderly did his rounds, finally coming to him. *God, he looks like he's just out of school.* "The lice are eating me alive. For heaven's sake take the bandage off otherwise I'll go mad."

The young doctor glanced at the now filthy bandage Martin had put on five days earlier.

"There's no hurry. It can wait until tomorrow."

Anger welled-up from a place he didn't know, helping him find the strength to sit up. He leant over and retrieved his pistol from the dirty clothes bag. Pointing it, rather unsteadily, at the young doctor, he pulled back the cocking mechanism with his other hand.

"I've already waited five damn days. If you don't take the bandage off I'll put a bullet in you and you can see just what it's like to wear the same filthy damn bandage for five days!"

"What's up? What's going on here?" An older looking senior doctor in a blood-spattered white coat came hurrying over. The young doctor paled and turned very quickly.

The *Oberarzt* looked from the luger to Martin to the by now very pale young doctor. Martin offered no resistance as the senior doctor calmly took the luger, pressing its clip release button. The magazine slipped out of the grip into his hand.

"I see. Doesn't one generally need bullets in the magazine?"

"I'm not stupid, *Herr Oberarzt*. I know they remove any rounds from our weapons when we come here as a precaution against self-harm. I would not have pointed a loaded gun at him. I just wanted to get him to move his sorry arse. I was shot five days ago. The pain and the fleas are driving me mad and this little arse with ears did not even bother to look under the dressing. I know it's infected and I know I'll die if you don't treat it right now, not some time in the future."

"Did you look at this man's leg, ask when he was shot?"

"I did not think that necessary *Herr Oberarzt*."

"Continue with your rounds – and *ask*, right? Always ask. You will report to me later.'

He turned to Martin. "Right, now, let's have a look. Hmm, that's bad luck. Both legs, and your balls I see. Yes, your diagnosis was correct – everything is infected. I can't see any exit wound on this side which means the bullet is still there. It will need to come out right away. Otherwise you will lose the leg." He paused. "Well, at least you were lucky in one respect – not having any rounds in that magazine. Pointing a loaded weapon at another man means … well, you know what it means. "

"Thank you, *Herr Oberarzt*."

Martin fell back on the bed with relief, too exhausted to say more. He woke up to find the wounds dressed with two relatively clean bandages.

"I see you are awake, Schläfer. I removed the bullet and you are very very lucky – it managed to miss the arteries in both legs. Though the testicular damage means it is most unlikely you will ever be able to have children. But one leg is not good, there was a lot of puss and muck I had to scrape out and you still have a high temperature which means the infection is still probably there. So, you are not out of the woods yet, not by a long chalk. We are going to keep an eye on it. If the temperature does not go down within the next 48 hours I'm afraid we will still need to take the leg off".

There is no way I am going to lose a leg. I would rather die first.

The doctor had been right – the infection persisted and he slipped in and out of consciousness. Half the time he didn't know where he was. But he fought to stay awake for one special occasion. Every time the nurse came around and slipped a thermometer under his tongue, he watched her out of the corner of his eye until she had moved on to the next patient. Then, out came the thermometer. He held it under the bed where it was cooler, only inserting it back where it belonged when sharp steps signalled her return. Over the next two days he somehow managed to control his delirium and stop the nurses from registering his proper temperature.

Three days later he began to feel, if not exactly better, still definitely on the mend. His temperature was down and he let them put the thermometer under his tongue as much as they wanted. As the doctor said, there was no major internal tissue damage to his legs and he was soon able to get up out of bed and walk, though still with crutches.

After about a fortnight he was transferred by hospital train to a proper war hospital, arriving in Molodetschno on the 3rd November. There had been many wounded to transfer and Martin was put in the very last wagon of the very last train out. No-one looked after them and when nature called it was once again a case of pulling yourself to the side of the train, hanging on, and discharging the diarrhoea.

****

It wasn't long before he started chatting with the bloke in the bed next to him, the first topic of conversation being, of course, the nurses. One – it seemed from her accent she was Polish – had made an immediate impression. "You fancy her?" Martin asked his neighbour innocently.

"You bet!"

"Well, next time she comes round, you should say this to her: *moja matka co to jest, mój pik tak mokry jest.* That'll really set you up

129

with her. Better practice before she comes again! Remember: *moja matka co to jest, mój pik tak mokry jest.*"

"Well Martin, and how is our little man today?" The Polish nurse grabbed his willy gently but firmly and gave it a little shake before examining his testicles.

"He says he is much better now, nurse, thank you."

"You are a very lucky man. You came this close – she held up forefinger and thumb – to losing that leg. Just about the size of our little man here, in fact." She gave his willy another shake to emphasise the point.

"No way was I going to lose a leg."

Martin looked over encouragingly to his mate in the next bed, who on cue delivered the Polish message that was going to put him in the nurse's good books. She, however, picking up a wet towel, went over and gave him a very firm slap on the face. They could not see the grin she was trying unsuccessfully to suppress as she stormed off.

"Whatever was THAT for?" Then the penny dropped. "What did you make me say to her, you bastard?"

"It means *Mum, what is this? My fart is so wet!* Rhymes beautifully in Polish. You said it very convincingly I thought."

The pain from Martin's balls turned his laugh very quickly into a grimace.

Chapter 22

1943 – *All Change!*

The tram clanged and squealed slowly to a halt.

"*Alexanderplatz*! Alexander Square! End of the line! All change please! Everyone out here! It doesn't go any further. You too Dieter you handsome brute. We can't go on meeting like this you know, your wife will find out!"

The old man looked up and grinned.

"Ach Leni, but what would *your* boyfriend say?"

The conductress on the *Alexanderplatz - Stadium* route liked being in charge of the tram – at least that was how she thought of it – and enjoyed joking and flirting with the passengers. She was usually able to raise a smile with at least some of the Berliners.

"Boyfriend, Dieter? Which one? There are so many! My main one is away fighting, so you have nothing to fear from him, at least till he gets back! He writes me lots of letters, though. Would *you* write me letters, Dieter?"

All change please!

Tram conductress Leni waves amidst the Berlin tramlines.

the main one is away on the eastern front

Tram conductress Leni and one of her young beaus who, from the apparent *Totenkopf* (skull-and-crossbones) pocket badge, may well be in SS uniform. Such formally-posed, professionally-taken photos normally recorded special occasions like an engagement, or departure for, or return from, the fighting.

Chapter 23

1943 – *Blue-Eyes*

Y ou are fit for service again."
The *Wehrmacht* allowed wounded soldiers a maximum of seven weeks' recovery time. Martin still did not think his legs ready for full action. The doctors thought differently, declaring Martin's legs, and the parts between, healed. He had been shot on the 16th September. A few days before the seven weeks were up, on November 1st, he was discharged from the war hospital in Molodetschno with a short recovery leave pass. After this *Genesungsurlaub*, his orders were to report back to Düren base training camp. Since he had nowhere else to go, Martin decided simply to return to Düren. He went through delousing in Brest, and finally found his way to the second-class railway compartment he had been assigned to make the journey slightly more comfortable to his nether regions.

The elderly captain looked up, an obvious veteran of the previous war. His thick Berlin accent inquired "Well, soldier, what are we doing in second-class?"

"I have received a wound to the buttocks, Herr *Hauptmann*."

"What sort of wound?"

"The report stated: *Shot through upper-right thigh. Buttocks grazed.*"

"Well you must make yourself comfortable then!"

A little while later, as the train was pulling out, they were joined by another officer. Well, actually not a *real* officer – you could see from his epaulettes he was a *Sonderführer*: a civilian nominally accorded officer's status because he had some kind of militarily useful expertise. The real military didn't think much of these 'narrow-gauge soldiers', and this one was a particularly officious and arrogant example. Glancing disapprovingly at Martin, he asked the captain in a loud voice how come corporals were now permitted to travel second-class?

To Martin's surprise, the elderly captain's response was to start wriggling and scratching.

"Thank God we're off at last! *scratch scratch* I couldn't keep 'em *scratch* under control much longer *scratch*. They wouldn't have *scratch* let me on the train *scratch* if they knew I still had 'em."

"May one inquire what is the matter with Herr *Hauptmann*?" asked the now somewhat concerned *Sonderführer*.

"I'm surprised you have not noticed, *Sonderführer*. Lice!! I've still got lice! But at least now there's both of you in the compartment to share them with me."

The alarmed *Sonderführer* grabbed his things and disappeared. Martin hadn't seen anyone move quite so quickly for a long time, and was wondering whether he too should make a quick exit.

The captain's preoccupied expression changed into a massive grin, his scratching having miraculously ceased with the exit of the *Sonderführer*. "*Na, hab' ick dit nich juut jemacht, Landser*? Well soldier, I thought I did that rather well, don't you? Now we have plenty of room and can make ourselves comfortable without having to get an earful of nonsense from that narrow-gauge idiot." Martin joined in the laughter, relieved that he would not have to undergo another delousing.

****

Back in Düren, many new faces once again greeted him; men to take the place of those killed in Roslavl. It made him wonder if they would run out of men eventually. He had given up keeping count of those he had fought with who were now dead.

There was ten weeks of training with the new men. As *Unteroffizier*, Martin was in charge of a group of 12, the only old face being Paul. Reassuring in its way, but the rest were barely 17 – just children really. Looking at them made him feel old at 22. It was operational procedure to distribute the experienced campaigners evenly through the units and three in one unit was a luxury they could not afford. Alfred had already been placed with another unit.

"Martin, I've just caught that idiot Gary Hunder asleep on guard duty."

"You're joking Paul. No-one'd be that stupid. If he's caught asleep, as the officer in charge I'm obliged to take his weapon from him and shoot him on the spot. No trial, no nothing."

"He's very raw – one of the young ones. Only seventeen. Perhaps he doesn't know. I woke the idiot up. Must have been so exhausted from the training he couldn't stay awake. What are you going to do? You're in charge."

"Well, nothing, this time. If you catch him asleep again, come and get me first, before anyone else does."

Martin was writing to his Mum when Paul came in again. Sure enough they found the young lad leaning against the wall, sound asleep at his post, rifle between his knees. Martin took his rifle and vigorously poked him awake with it. The silence was then broken by Martin screaming at him in his best officer voice. He gave the wide-eyed youngster a thorough tongue lashing, a dressing down he would never forget. He ordered him to report immediately at the end of his guard duty, when he gave him a long list of extra duties. On the one hand, he could not let this dereliction of duty go unpunished: it endangered the lives of the whole group. On the other hand, there was quite enough killing going on without someone being shot for falling asleep, regulations or no regulations. For several weeks Martin made Hunder's life absolute hell.

Private Hunder stood to attention. "*Unteroffizier* Schläfer, may I have a word?"

"What is it, *Soldat* Hunder?"

"I just wanted to thank you. I was recently in hospital and mentioned to an older officer there about having fallen asleep on guard duty. He said 'And you're still ALIVE? If that was me I'd have shot you then and there.' I understand now. Thank you."

"Just don't do it again. Get some sleep during the day somehow. You won't get away with it next time. Dismissed."

After the training of the new recruits was completed, the company was given two weeks' leave. Arriving home, Martin found Kurt's death still hanging heavy over the family. Frieda especially was still visibly upset and was very much in mourning for her son. The circumstances of his death seemed to have made it doubly worse, and Martin realised that his elder sister would never get over her son's summary execution. He could not find any words of comfort and didn't try. They were in the middle of a war and he had witnessed first-hand what happens in war. But that didn't make it seem less unfair.

Leave was not to be wasted, though; it was time for some recreation. Where else but *Lilli's* for a beer and a meal? The war had made sure that it was a lifetime ago since their last visit, but Hanni's nice face and soft pink lips still managed to reassert themselves, for a moment at least, in Martin's memory. He recalled too that *Lilli's* was where Paul had first met Erika. Paul wasn't smiling though.

"You know I still can't believe it. I've been writing to her all this time. I was really looking forward to seeing her again. Was going to ask her to marry me even. So, I get to her house, and her mum asks me what I was doing there. She said Erika had written she'd met an officer and it was over between us."

"But she wrote you every week!"

"You know what she said when we finally met? 'Oh, hello schnucki! Didn't you get my last letter schnucki? I've met an OFFICER and he can offer me a better future than you can. He's in the SS and he's taking me to BERLIN for a holiday. You're very nice schnucki but my SS-Officer is nicer.' "

"NICE??!! After all this time?? I reckon you can thank your lucky stars you are rid of her. What a bitch."

"No, Martin. She's just looking out for herself, that's all. However can I compete with an SS-schnucki?"

"Well, never mind, plenty more fish in the sea. Tell you what, let's head back to Düren. It's pretty miserable at my place too what with Kurt's death. And you don't want to run into Erika anymore. Düren's got a decent municipal park. Lots of girls there of a Saturday afternoon. We can chat some up, see if we get lucky."

****

Martin saw them first. Blue dress with a little lace collar and lace on the sleeves. White socks stopping just above the ankle. *Hmm makes her look like a schoolgirl. Ha! Some schoolgirl – look at those boobs. Neat waist, real hourglass.* As they got closer: deep blue eyes, and smiling at him. *Yeah, OK, nose a bit on the large side but it somehow makes her look more interesting, in control. Bet she wouldn't take any nonsense from anyone.* "Hello, where are you two off to this lovely afternoon? May we accompany you?"

Blue-eyes gives their uniforms a quick up-and-down. "Suit yourselves."

"I'm Martin and this here is Paul. Would you allow us to buy you a cup of coffee?"

This addressed to blue-eyes. In fact Martin had not yet looked at the other girl.

"You've not been around here recently. Coffee's disgusting." Another quick up-and-down. "But not as bad as the beer." And as an afterthought, "My name's Maria Magdelene, but my friends call me Leni. And this is Kitty-Lisa."

Formalities dispensed with, they continued on their way through the park, breaking ice, sharing stories, happy to forget the war if only for a short time. They stuck with the coffee, and as dusk set in, Martin walked Leni home.

"So, what do you do, Leni?"

"I had to leave school at 13 and do the obligatory farm-work. Then I applied for work in a hairdressing salon but got turned down so I got a job in a delicatessen but I didn't like that and got a position in a newspaper office. That was quite good. I liked that. But then I had to do my State Labour Service. There were 300 of us in *Reichsarbeitsdienst* camp, and 300 lads too. We were up at six, exercise, breakfast, then walk an hour to the farm we had to work on. Shit-shovelling and gardening till five then back to camp. After dinner we had instruction on the merits of Hitler and his National Socialist German Workers' Party. But I mustn't complain – I was very lucky: the newspaper office where I was working got bombed just after I started Labour Service, otherwise I would have copped it along with the other nine who died."

Anyway, when my six months State Labour Service were up they told me I had to report to Berlin for War Auxilliary Service. We finished the *Kriegshilfsdienst* training, and so now I'm a tram conductress, in Berlin."

"Wow, Berlin. Long way from Düren. Have you ever been to Berlin before?"

"No. My family lives in Mariaweiler, a little village just near here, though I spent every summer holiday in Munich while I was growing up. Got an auntie there and she had no children so she and her husband asked me to spend a lot of the school holidays with them. I loved it, I guess partly because they used to spoil me. Berlin's no joke now, of course, with the continual bombing and sirens going off. We have to work long shifts too – 12 to 14 hours a day – so most of the time we're exhausted. I'm recouping here in Düren for my two-weeks' annual leave with my family.

"Your family – is that your parents?"

"Yeah. I lived with my parents before the war. It wasn't too bad. What did *you* do before the war?"

"Carpenter. I'd just finished my apprenticeship when I was sent to the Westwall for six months – you know, the fortifications against France? Then the North Sea, on the Kaiser Wilhelm Kanal, and then conscription. I'll go back to carpentry when the war is over. At least I know I'll always get work. All the bombed-out buildings. They'll all need to be built again."

"Any brothers or sisters?"

"I was the youngest of ten. My oldest sister is twenty years older than me. How about you?"

"Also the youngest. Seven brothers and sisters. Also a twenty years' gap between me and my eldest sister. My Mum had me at the same time as my sister had her son."

"So, I suppose your brothers are also in the army?"

"My nephew Kurt was, but he met a woman and went AWOL. Twice, the silly bugger. Second time they shot him."

"Oh, that is awful, Martin! I'm really sorry. My family is terribly worried the same thing'll happen to my brother Heinrich."

"Oh, why? Was he a soldier too?"

"No, but remember *Reichskristallnacht* two years ago? *Crystal Night* - I was only 16 then. After the *Brownshirts* had smashed their shop windows and trashed their stuff – and a lot of civilians did it too – all the Jews in our village were herded onto the street and they started shouting at them. Heini didn't think it was right. Wouldn't shut up about it; 18-years-old and not very clever. Dad told him to shut up but he insisted on letting them know what he thought. He just kept going on and on. 'What are you bastards doing? These people are our friends and neighbours, part of the community. They have done nothing wrong.' My Mum and Dad kept telling him to be quiet but he wouldn't stop. No sense. Nothing happened that night, but early next morning a group of SS Police came and took him away for 'questioning'. Heini was a very stubborn lad. I think he probably refused to recant, otherwise the SS Police would have slapped him around a bit and released him. After all, he wasn't a danger to anyone and was working in a munitions factory. But he didn't come back, and that's the last we've heard of him. My parents are worried sick. Dad went to ask and he was told he'd better shut up or he'd get arrested too. We are all too scared to ask again. Let's not talk about it anymore. Where do you come from? Do I hear a Saxony accent?"

"Right. I only ever lived in a place called Wiederitzsch near Leipzig, on a farm. In a house my father and brothers renovated. We were very poor, like most country folk. I'd never been outside Leipzig until the Westwall. Since then I have got around a lot. And seen a lot. A depressing lot."

A short silence, then Martin, by now pretty-much smitten, made his pitch. "Could we write to each other, do you think? I would like to meet you again, Leni. My unit comes back to Düren after every operation to train replacements for those who didn't make it. We could see each other then, when I have leave, if you can get away from Berlin too."

The answer was friendly, but non-committal. "Yes that would be nice." *Won't hurt – Bert doesn't have to know about Martin and the chances are that neither will come back anyway.* Leni was just being realistic. Düren was full of young soldiers. It seemed to be a marshalling point where large numbers were continually assembled to be sent off to fight in Russia, and to which each time many fewer returned.

"Well, here we are at my place. You can write to me at my Berlin depot."

bet she wouldn't take any nonsense from anyone
A cheeky blue-eyes at the age when she first met Martin.

We finished training

A group of war auxiliary service (*Kriegshilfsdienst*) trainee tram conductresses, with instructor, at the Berlin tram conductor school in December 1943. Leni is top row, 4th from left. The trainees wear the 'two ears of wheat and spade' badges of the State Labour Service (*Reichsarbeitsdienst*).

Chapter 24

1944 – *Hents Up!*

From mid-1943 it was not only the Russians who now had to be held back. The Allies had crossed the Mediterranean from North Africa and had fought their way up Italy to attack the Germans from the south – what Churchill had called the *soft German underbelly*. The Italians had not only surrendered but also declared war on their former *Pact of Steel* German ally. But *soft underbelly* was a serious underestimation: the Germans resisted the Allies' advance tenaciously, the fighting was cruel and bloody and their advance slow. By mid-1944 however, as the D-day landings in Normandy heralded the beginning of the end of the Third Reich, the Allies had made it to North Italy.

****

"No more cold. We're off to Italy. North Italy. Trieste. Spearhead and reconnaissance, mostly. They want us to find out how many troops the Americans have in the area, see how many partisans there are and if the locals pose a threat. We might also have to destroy communication links. Bridges, that sort of thing."

"What do you mean Martin: 'no more cold'? It's early January, in the mountains; of course it'll be cold!"

"Well yes, but not as bad as Russia. Oh yes, I almost forgot: make sure you have a red flag handy."

"What, to make them think we're Russians?"

"I meant a red-cross flag. It's not like Russia, I've been informed the Amis and Italians respect the first aid conventions for wounded, so they won't shoot at you if you carry a flag to show that you are going for a wounded soldier. Everyone will stop shooting until you carry the person to safety. At least that's what they say. Just make sure that you always keep very very close to the wounded person. Too much of a gap will mean you count as hostile again. And we will have to give them the same courtesy. Remember: no-one is to shoot if they see a red-cross flag."

"How are they getting us there?"

"They're parachuting us in at night before the main lot."

****

"If I am speaking to you today, that is for two reasons. Firstly so that you hear my voice and know that I have not been injured and am healthy." They listened to Hitler's unmistakable Austrian accent over the radio, reassuring them that, thanks to providence, he was still in charge and still committed to the good of the people and the *Vaterland*.

Well, obviously, the July plot to assassinate him had failed. What to make of it, though? Was it good news that Hitler had survived to lead them to victory? Was it bad news that someone high up – someone called von Stauffenberg apparently – had thought Hitler had to be stopped from leading them to a disaster?

For the Brandenburg Commando units it was bad news, though it made no difference to the fighting of course. Since their former head Admiral Canaris had been implicated in the plot, things now became very different very quickly. The Reich's Security Service now took over control. The task of the *Sicherheitsdienst*: to root out and neutralise all enemies of the Nazi leadership. Suspicion ran, as it will, all the way down the ranks. You had to be really careful now. Your mate might be a Reich's Security Service informant.

Worse still, they had lost their special status along with Canaris' fall from grace. In September 1944, special ops units were no longer deemed necessary, and the Brandenburg Division morphed into *Infanterie-Division Brandenburg*. Who would have guessed it – they were now an ignominious part of the ministry of transport!

Martin did not remain ignominious for long, however. For some reason that he never found out he was transferred, along with some close mates, to the *Wehrmacht*'s Alpine Division – another elite unit – for continued deployment in Italy.

****

The sneeze was muffled and stopped just in the nick of time. They could see each other's breath, as the moon was full.

"Shit Martin, so much for your warm Italy. This snow's just as bad as Russia. Three hours on our bellies and we're all freezing to death and we've not spotted one person that even remotely looks like a soldier. You'd think that now we're with the Alpine Division they would have kitted us out better."

"Ah but they're not our *Gebirgsdivision* uniforms, don't forget. I explained matters to *Leutnant* Spalt before we set out and suggested we be allowed to hang onto our old Brandenburger kit for disguise. Not being with the Brandenburgers himself he didn't know we got up to those tricks and thought it was a very good idea. I managed to wangle him a uniform for himself."

Lieutenant Spalt crept over to them. "What do you think Martin – should we move onto the next village and see what's up there? According to the map it should only be a few kilometres away." Spalt had just come from army training school. Never having led a reconnaissance patrol he had sensibly asked Martin, whom he knew as Brandenburger had lead more than fifty missions, to take over lead of the *Spähtrupp*. Martin nodded. "I know it's cold but I think it's time we do our chameleon thing now. So far we've been lucky."

They turned their uniforms inside out, morphing from snow-camouflaged German Alpine Regiment into American military. They grumbled at having the cold wet uniform next to the skin.

They located the stream shown on their map and went to fill up their water-bottles. The appalling stench hit them from a long way away. In the dusk they could make out the rotting carcasses of dogs, cats, horses, rats, all dumped into the stream. The men started to retch and turned away.

"Well at least we know there are partisans around. And I'll bet we're in some sniper's sights right now. See, Herr *Leutnant*, aren't you glad you're now American? Worth a few minutes cold wet uniform, eh? The village should be just over that ridge."

"You were right Martin! So now we know where at least some of the troops are concentrated. My god, look at all the traffic. You wouldn't have guessed it from the last village. They seem to be headed in the direction of where we've just left."

"Yeah. Looks like close on a whole battalion of allied forces, must be at least 500 men. We have to report back as soon as possible but it's too dark to go running around now, especially as they are on the move too. Need somewhere to hide and wait it out. What about that?"

Martin pointed with his binoculars at a hay stack just near the edge of the woods.

"That'll do. It's big enough for all of us. Keep us warm too. Pass it on. Follow me. And keep quiet."

Just after midnight the sound of an engine in the distance penetrated the hay. Martin peered out, broke silence. "It's a way off. From the headlights it looks like just one jeep. Everyone, listen up. Change of plan. We'll see if we can capture it. The transport'll get us back much quicker, and part of our orders was to bring in as many prisoners as possible. Even one or two might make useful intel."

They crawled out of the hay stack and ran crouching to the roadside.

The jeep's headlights picked out six American soldiers standing in the middle of the road. One was signalling frantically for them to pull over. The jeep stopped and its four occupants were surprised to find themselves the target of six sub-machine guns.

Martin took over the role of translator. "Hents up!"

One of the useful English phrases the Brandenburgers had been taught. He signalled for them to get out.

The four Americans complied, hands in air, expressions perplexed at the assault by their own. "No problem, no problem. What the hell gives?"

"Ve take you prisoner. Hent over your veapons."

The penny dropped with the accent. Martin added, rather unnecessarily, that they were Germans. The still surprised Americans were quickly patted down. A search for more weapons in the car turned up nothing else.

"Now, beck in the cheep," the machine guns indicating they were to get back in. Grabbing the windscreen with one hand Martin stepped onto the running-board and added, pleased at his increasing fluency "Now, you, drive that vay". Once again the machine gun pointed the direction.

The driver, aware of the gun a few inches from his temple, took it carefully. He did not want to hit any bumps or holes. It made it easier for the other Brandenburgers to hang on.

A burnt-out car materialised in front of them. It had been overturned, blocking the road. Martin looked questioningly at Spalt.

"*Alle 'raus, dreht den Wagen um, damit wir ihn aus'm Weg kriegen und schnell wegkommen.*"

"All out, turn the car, get him out the vay, so ve can get avay qvickly!"

As the men bent over to right the burnt-out vehicle, one of the American's tunics slid up at the back to reveal the butt of a pistol sticking out the top of his trousers. Someone had obviously missed it back there in the body search. Martin walked over and pulled it out slowly from his belt. *Which one of them missed that?* The American turned around, exchanged a meaningful look with Martin, and went back to pushing.

Why the hell hadn't the Yank used his pistol? He could have taken me and a couple of others out, perhaps even recovered the Jeep. I would have – there would have been a blood-bath – but I would have. He obviously wants to live. Smart lad.

The rest of the journey went without further incident, though they had to be very careful approaching the German camp. They were awaiting their return, to be sure, but certainly not dressed as American soldiers and not in an American jeep with more men in it than had gone out on reconnaissance the previous evening.

Leutnant Spalt decided to stop the jeep quite a way from the camp and go on foot to where he could shout out the password in his best German to the sentries. Their capture of the four Americans along with the jeep caused quite a stir. It impressed the Division Commander who happened to be present, and he wrote up an account of the incident. Martin was consequently offered a second Iron Cross Second Class. His response was rather dismissive: "I've had one of *those* for a long time."

The successful operation earned the men a couple of days' leave at the hot springs in San Martin, just south of the Austrian border. There was opportunity also for some drinking and even dancing, though the latter was no longer to Martin's taste. He preferred to keep his beer company and watch the others. The tenor of the conversation had shifted imperceptibly from available women in the bar to the odds of surviving the war. Even though they had taken their share of injuries – Martin still limped a bit from his thigh wounds – it almost felt as if someone or something had been protecting them. Now everything felt different. It was all down to luck. Not a good thought. *Don't think it then.*

Thinking of luck … Martin's gaze came around for a third time to a woman who was obviously interested. Every time he had looked she was already eyeing him up. Evidently losing patience with his lack of initiative, she walked over, pulled him onto the dance floor.

"I warn you Fräulein, I'm not a good dancer. I would be happy to buy you a drink though."

"Don't be such a wet blanket, handsome. Dance first, drinks after! So, what's Mr. Iron Cross's name?" Her voice was high, with a girlish quality to it. But her face said experienced woman.

"Martin. And yours?"

"Maria."

Blond, short and a bit dumpy, but she had a cute dimply smile. About 25, Martin guessed. Done in the fashion of the day, her hair sat low on her neck, held in place by a hairnet with sparkly bits sewn onto it. Earrings matched the sparkles.

"What would you like to drink?"

"A white wine would be nice, thank you." Martin went and ordered. One of the others walked over and chatted her up. Bit of talking; bit of laughing; a few jokes; even a dance, protecting their left-footed *Unteroffizier* as long as possible from the dangers of the dance floor. When Martin's friend left to find a woman, Martin and Maria chatted for a while, but soon Martin had had enough and made his excuses. But he did walk her out to the nearest bus stop and gave her a kiss.

"Isn't Mr. Iron Cross coming back to my place? Get to know each other better?"

The realisation that Martin did not, in fact, want to go back with her surprised him at first. Wasn't that after all what all this was about? But he recalled that his thoughts had continually turned to Leni during the night. Ah, if it had been Leni popping the question! His reluctance would have vanished, just like that.

"Maria, I think you are a lovely lady. I have enjoyed our evening and I thank you for the invitation but I fear I have to decline your offer tonight, as I have to report for duty early in the morning."

"Maybe another night then?" There was disappointment in her voice and Martin felt bad.

"That sounds wonderful! Yes, definitely."

an account of the incident

The actual report from the Commander of the Army's 5th Alpine Division dated 19th November 1944. It describes the capture, five days before, of the American jeep and its inmates. Martin's name appears six lines up from the bottom, where he is given his Alpine Division rank of *Oberjäger*, equivalent to *Unteroffizier*. It reads (in part): *I would like to express my recognition of Lieutenant Spalt and his men for their daring, decisive and successful action.* The signature is possibly of (Max-Günther) Schrank, who was commander of the 5th Alpine Division of the *Wehrmacht* in Italy between February10[th] 1944 and January 18th 1945.

Chapter 25

1944 – *Visits*

*U*nteroffizier Schläfer, I regret to inform you that we have just been notified of the death of your mother."

He clicked his heels. "*Jawohl, Herr Hauptmann.* Thank you, *Herr Hauptmann.*"

"Martin, I'll approve your leave to go back, but for heaven's sake make sure you are not caught on the Italian side of the border. They'll assume you are a deserter and you'll be shot without a trial: it's happening to many men. And there will be hell to pay for me too! And you won't have a rail pass don't forget."

"Don't worry, Sir, I will be careful. And thank you again."

As the truck approached, Martin let his binoculars drop. It seemed OK – Austrian number-plates, just the driver, some kind of fodder in the back, probably for horses. He stepped out into the road and signalled for it to stop. "Can I get a lift? I need to get across the border."

"By all means, mate. Hop in. *Wehrmacht* is always welcome, 'specially with that." He nodded at Martin's machine gun. "Good for discouraging the partisans hereabouts." Martin crawled into the hay.

There was one worrying moment when they were stopped by a German patrol. Martin whispered to the driver "Hold your tongue – you know nothing, right? If they find me you can say you had no idea I was there."

"Where are you headed? Everything alright?"

"Yes, no problems. Taking stuff back to the farm. *Alles in Ordnung!* Everything's OK!"

No passes checked. They were waved on.

The Austrian border. Encouraged by the lack of problems so far, he decided to chance it without a valid rail pass. Yes, it was a long journey, but it would be possible to get to Leipzig, and he knew that there would be a little extra charge for arranging it for him. Martin handed over the bribe. Just so long as he could get back to Wiederitzsch, and help comfort his dad. He wondered how he was holding up. Mum's death would have been a big shock for him, after fifty years of marriage. No more outstretched arm for him to proudly promenade under.

****

"Oh, my God Martin, it's you!"

"Give me a hug Martha, it is good to see you. I managed to get away for a short while to come home. Where's Father? In the fields? I'll go find him, once you let go of me!"

She paled. *He obviously doesn't know.*

"Am I too late? For the funeral, I mean. My commanding officer gave me leave but it took a while to make it back from Italy. Anyway, where's Father. Is he taking it hard?"

"Yes, for the funeral, too late. She was buried two days ago. But there's something else. Martin, you mustn't have got our first telegram. Papa's dead too."

"What?!! How?"

"Three months ago. He was bringing the horses home and fell heavily on the ice. Looked like broken ribs: it was all black and blue. He was having terrible trouble breathing and couldn't speak. We took him to the local doctor but he had nothing to kill the pain and said we should get him to the hospital in Leipzig where it would be a simple operation for them to drain the blood. It's only twenty minutes by train, as you know, but the trains are full of soldiers. We had to take him to Leipzig in the cart. We made it as comfortable as possible but it was still a horrendous journey. He was coughing up blood all the way. You can imagine. But they didn't even examine him. Took one look and said they were too full with soldiers to help. 'And he's too old for admittance anyway' was what they said. 'His lung's punctured most probably. The State can no longer help. Take him home,' they said, 'make him as comfortable as you can'. He lingered on for a few days, but he was done for, basically: he was already so frail. You know, because of the shortage of male labour he still had to be hard at work on the farm at 67. Then the government prohibited people who didn't own their own land from having livestock, and from then on they had very little food – only what he could grow in the garden. It all took its toll. We sent you a telegram but you obviously didn't get it. Perhaps it just got lost."

"Is that why mum died?"

"Luckily, Martin, by that stage mum really didn't know what was happening anymore. Her mind had gone, the doctor said. The sole thing that seemed to occupy her was getting your feather blanket to you in Russia. She would go on about Russia being so cold and you freezing over there and needing your blanket. *'Russland ist so kalt* - Russia is so cold' she'd say. *'Mein Sohn wird drüben frier'n* - my son will freeze over there. *Er braucht sein Federbett* - he needs his feather blanket. *Ich muss ihm sein Federbett bringen.* – I have to take it to him. *Ich muss ihm sein Federbett bringen!'* Once she even took it with her on the tram to Leipzig railway station. She explained to the ticket collector that no, she didn't have a ticket but she had to go to her son in Russia. He was about to call the police – people were on their way home from work and mum was holding everyone up. You know what *that* would have meant, Martin – a needle to put her to sleep, for good. Luckily our neighbour was there and convinced the man to let her bring mum back home. 'Come Mother Schläfer', she said, 'I will take you home; Martin isn't in Russia now. He's in Italy, so there is no point in trying to get to Russia. It's warm in Italy, he's not freezing. He won't need his blanket there.' Mum replied 'Really? In Italy? What is my Martin doing in Italy?' No matter how often we explained to her that you were fighting in the war, she never remembered, she just knew you were not home and therefore you needed your featherbed! But death is everywhere these days, Martin. Just look at Paul's mum."

"Why, what happened to her?"

"*Her*? Oh you don't know then? Not her – her son, Paul. You were buddies once I think. She got a telegram a week ago that he had been killed somewhere near the Caucasus. It didn't say how."

The hurt in Martin's voice became more and more obvious. "I'll try and find out what happened to him when I get back, though I'm not with the same group anymore as Paul. We actually fought together for most of the war. He … he was … a very good friend."

His brother Otto arrived later that afternoon and Martin spent the next couple of days emptying the house with him and Martha and Frieda. Room had to be made for a new family to move in. They asked Martin what he wanted to keep. 'Nothing', he said.

It wasn't until he was finally left alone in his old room that he cried. The mixture of despair and bitterness and anger would not let the thought out of his head that they would have lived longer if their life had not been made so hard by the war, and if they had operated on his Dad instead of just sending him home to die. And then there was Kurt; the pointless, stupid loss of his nephew Kurt. And the men he had trained with and fought with who had given up their lives for the glorious *Vaterland*. And now his best friend Paul. Too much death. For what?

Anger gained the upper hand. And then he felt something change inside – something about his blind obedience to authority. Up to now he had simply acquiesced to the indoctrination, without questioning. Now, for the first time in his life, he questioned. He saw how his life had been determined for him, every path he had taken since a 17-year-old on the Westwall had been decided by the State. If things went on like this, he would end up dead too. Absolutely.

His elder brother wasn't much help. "For God's sake Martin, keep your mouth shut. You'll end up in a concentration camp if you keep up this kind of talk. Remember what Father used to say."

Right, OK, so he needed to change his attitude. Radically. Orders still had to be followed, that was clear, but no more heroics. The Iron Crosses had been incidental: the result of, but not the reason for, his unreflected bravery. It was not only necessary to survive, but to be in control.

Well, one thing was under his control at least. Leni. He would go and see her. He had made it all the way from Italy to Wiederitzsch, his journey made easier by the prevailing general chaos; an onward journey to Berlin wasn't far. His positive action plan, together with the prospect of seeing Leni, brightened him up no end. She had never really left his thoughts. Her optimism shone through each letter she had written over the intervening months.

****

"Oh, Martin, what a lovely surprise!" Eyes as blue as ever, smile as wide as ever, conductress cap perched precariously on one side. *How come it doesn't fall off? Is it stuck on?* "You didn't write that you had leave. No matter, it's lovely to see you!"

"Can the Berlin Trams manage without you tonight? How about dinner? I only have one day. I made a not totally authorised detour and probably should get back to camp as soon as possible."

"That was a bit stupid. You wouldn't want the same thing to happen to you as to your nephew." She thought a bit. "Well, we could try going out, but surely you know they've been bombing Berlin at night since before Christmas. In November they pretty much destroyed the famous old Kaiser Wilhelm church. They say the bombing has killed thousands of Berliners and many, many more don't have any homes. But it doesn't seem to have demoralised anyone. It's just made them more determined to see it through. Anyway, what ARE you doing up here in Berlin when you should be down there in Italy?"

"Not good news. Look, I'm staying in a pokey little hotel nearby. We can go there and have some privacy. I'll tell you about it then."

"Martin! If you think I'm going to go to bed with you, think again! What kind of a person do you think I am? I'm not going to hop into bed with ANYONE until I'm married. Imagine if I got pregnant!"

"My God Leni, what kind of a person do you think I am? I just wanted to spend a few hours with you. I certainly don't want you to do anything you don't want. We've been writing to each other for quite a long time now. Somehow, I feel like I know you very well even though we haven't actually spent much time together. I just feel like a talk and a cuddle. Actually, I really *need* a talk and a cuddle."

"Sorry, Martin, it's just that when I go out with my girlfriends from the depo, we meet men and it's always the same. They all just want to get into my pants. I just wanted you to be different. I get really sick of fighting them off. I tell them I am saving myself for marriage and they just laugh at me. 'There is a war on. You have to live for today 'cos you could be dead tomorrow.' As if I'm not aware of that. I just need to be positive about the future and think that one day I will marry, and have children. It all needs to be … deliberate."

Martin froze; this was the first time he had actually thought about the consequences of what the doctors had told him while he was recovering from his wounds in Roslavl. 'The odds are that you will not be able to have children'. But if Leni was thinking that far ahead he had to be honest.

"Children? Children? Leni, er … you know how I got shot a while back? It was actually in my er … the er …. private parts. The doctors said they didn't think I would be able to have children. I know we have not spoken of marriage, but I really like you a lot and want you to know if children are really important to you, I will probably not be the right man for you." He bit his lip. "If that's the case, then we should probably stop writing to each other."

"Martin, I didn't know. I'm so sorry. I was just generalising, talking about the future. But the war's still far from over. And I don't think we know each other well enough to talk about marriage or babies, so how about we just spend some time together, like you had in mind. And you can tell me what you wanted to say."

But he couldn't. He knew it would upset him too much, recounting to her how he found out that that *both* his parents were dead, and how they died. And Paul. It was all still too raw. He was afraid he would end up crying in front of her, and he did not want her to remember him like that. If he survived the war there would be time then to tell her all about his loss. And if he didn't … well, then it would no longer be a problem. It also crossed his mind that Leni too might not survive. It was best to keep things light and just enjoy her company.

So when she asked the reason for his long journey back from Italy to Wiederitzsch he steered the conversation away from the topic. Of course Leni was not fooled for a moment, but realised that Martin did not want to go there. So she too played along and did not insist. They talked about little things, inconsequential things.

Although it would never have occurred to them to rationalise it thus, their attraction was one of complementation *and* reinforcement. Leni was full of mischief. She was fun to be with: it seemed she found fun in everything. Martin by nature was just the opposite. He had always been a very serious person, ready to worry about anything and everything. This was now compounded by the fact that he had already confronted enough sadness and misery for a lifetime. So perhaps it was no wonder that Leni's positive outlook and *joie de vivre* helped cheer him up (aided, of course, by her sex-appeal).

For her part, Leni found absolutely nothing *cosmetic* about Martin. She sensed that what she saw – everything about him proclaiming reliability and trustworthiness – was what she got. That was comforting in the *live now die tomorrow* superficiality of Berlin.

But deep down, where it really matters, they shared the same morality and attitude to life: the conviction that, when you had control over things, you were ultimately responsible for your actions and their consequences.

They went back to his hotel and had a simple meal and then ventured out for a walk in the park – their progression slowed down appreciably by lots of cuddles and kisses – until just before Leni's tram depo's curfew at ten o'clock. They were lucky: for once the air-raid sirens remained silent that night. Leni was rostered off the next morning, and so they met up again. But the time passed far too quickly and before they knew it she was seeing him off at the station.

This time it was really difficult to part. Martin already cared; it was dawning on Leni that she did too. The kindly railway guard interrupted their embrace with a friendly *"Na Kinder: einmal muss es sein!"*

"He's right Martin: *we've got to let go sometime*."

During Martin's long return trip he found – hey this was new! – positive thoughts linking Leni, himself and the future sporadically percolating through his mental return to the grim reality of war. His unscheduled visit to Berlin had indeed been the right one.

Chapter 26

1945 – *Effective Immediately*

If he closed his eyes he could still hear Paul's voice. "*Must say that right hook of yours is coming on nicely Martin ... C'mon Martin. I know he looks big but look how well we've done so far ... We can win this one too... Ich lieb dich, Erika...*" Now Paul Brenner was just a statistic reinforcing the Brandenburgers' unenviable record that, at best, only one in two came back.

Although he didn't relish the task, he made inquiries about Paul for his mother's sake. He never did get his *Heimatschuss*. He had been blown to pieces in a truck while reconnoitring partisan positions in the north of Serbia. The report simply stated '*Unit Meyerhofer. One Unteroffizier, two men, reconnaissance of positions near Neusatz. Own losses: one dead, one truck destroyed. Otherwise uneventful.* That was it. There was nothing of Paul left, just memories.

Martin's operations in Italy were one mission after another, and nothing had changed about the killing, the dying, the mud, the flies, the heat, the cold, the hunger, the pain, the lice, the fleas, everything; the whole heap of shit! You never got used to it, you just learnt to close your mind to it, to look away. Otherwise you'd go mad. But one thing was subtly different: not so many heroics now. To Martin it seemed everyone, not just him, was being careful, hoping quietly the war would soon be over and that they would still be alive to witness it.

Out on reconnaissance one day near the French-Italian border they came across a deserted bicycle factory. Inside a whole lot of brand new bicycles lay abandoned. Cycling beats walking any day, so, helping themselves, off they pedalled back to camp in style, like children with a new Christmas present. At the back of the group Martin felt the *bump bump bump* of a flat tyre and got off to inspect the puncture while the others disappeared down the road. Loath to abandon his new method of transport, he pushed the bike along, wondering how to mend the puncture.

He received an answer of some kind when he looked up and spotted in the distance a group of six heads making their way slowly through the long grass of the meadows towards the road. He pushed the bike hurriedly into the deep ditch on the side of the road and lay there peering over the edge. The six heads became six armed partisans. They were close enough now for him to catch their voices, but their leisurely progression indicated they had not spotted him. Martin made off down the ditch for all his life was worth, pushing the bike at the same time. Running until he judged he was safely out of sight he scrambled back onto the road and rode off as fast as he could, flat tire or no flat tire, the sweat flying off. He well knew that if they caught him, that would be that; there would be few questions asked. Coming to the outskirts of a village he grabbed a bike with inflated tires from a surprised man with an out-of-breath perfunctory "here you take this I'll take yours" and headed off again, not quite so quickly as before, back to camp. Why had he not tried to take the partisans prisoner? He had had the drop on them, after all. He realised that he had preferred discretion to valour.

****

May 1945. Once again, the small group headed towards the briefing room. The talk was all about what had happened a few weeks before in April. Mussolini had failed in an attempt to escape to the north of Italy and was captured near Lake Como by Italian partisans. They executed him and then took his body to Milan where they hung him upside down in the market place for all to see. Martin was very near Milan at the time and it confirmed the strength of the partisans and the need for the Germans to be extra careful wherever they went. The group were expecting to be briefed about another mission. However, they were surprised – almost the whole company had been summoned. The officer on duty announced in a clear voice:

"DIE HERRSCHAFTEN WERDEN GEBETEN, ANZUTRETEN!"

Martin looked quizzically at his neighbour. What kind of weird language was that? '*Would you gentlemen respectfully step forward*?!?' No-one speaks like that in the military. The captain took over the announcement:

"MEINE HERREN! AB SOFORT SEID IHR EURES FAHNENEIDES ENTHOBEN. DER FÜHRER IST … VERSTORBEN."

That got their attention: "Gentlemen. Effective immediately, you are all released from your Oath of Allegiance. The Führer has … passed away."

More followed. "For us, the war is over. We are to surrender unconditionally – to the Americans. As said, effective immediately."

Silence: the words sank in. Shock: they knew things were bad, but *that* bad? Relief: they had survived. It was over. They had survived; an end to the horror. They had survived.

They just stood there stunned.

"Pay attention. Pay attention. PAY ATTENTION! You must NOT try to return to Germany. Just because our war is over does not mean it's over everywhere, and for everyone. The Italian partisans will probably shoot you on your way out of Italy. We've already had bodies returned to us of those who tried to get out. Procedure has to be followed. The Americans will be looking after all Germans. That means at least a stay in an Ami prisoner-of-war camp until the logistics can be arranged to get us back to Germany in one piece. One more thing, we can open the cash registers now. I have money for anyone who needs it so just come and ask. Any quest…?"

The question uppermost in their minds was how quickly they could locate the nearest place to celebrate. Most, recovering quickly from their shock, were already heading out the door.

It was not far. Martin, Alfred and some of the other men in their troop arrived in the town square as American jeeps also pulled up. The GIs were offered garlands by the Italian women, which they, however, refused to accept. Martin's group watched nervously as a GI jumped out and came over to them. But all he did was thump them on the shoulder and indicate they should follow into the nearest pub.

The exaggerated revving of engines outside announced the arrival of more GIs. Then silence, enhancing the expectation. In strutted the American heroes. All of a sudden, the pub became animated. There was music, there was wine – everything became available. Normally, the Germans were frostily told there was no wine available.

It was strange – just standing there, opposite the enemy. But they're not the enemy, now, are they? Victors, more like. They could have reached over and touched them. Not that they did. They watched.

The Amis threw down several double whiskies, then handed-out packets of cigarettes to the Germans. Eager to partake of this largesse, an Italian came up behind one of the GIs, tapping him on the shoulder. The violent response shocked everyone. The GI swung round, his backhander sending the Italian sprawling. "Never from behind, buddy, NEVER! We've been warned about you." Relenting somewhat, he tossed a cigarette towards the unfortunate man. "The Germans don't creep up from behind but we know you lot can't be trusted."

The Italian landlady behind the bar respectfully handed the Captain the bill. He looked at it. He tore it up. He threw it on the floor. With a cheeky 'bye-bye!' they disappeared, engines once again revving.

"How can they not pay for their drinks?"

Martin looked seriously at Alfred. "Because they are the victors Alfred. They can do anything they like. With us too, we have to tread very very carefully despite their show of camaraderie. But they've certainly livened things up a bit in here. Let's see if we can't get a bit better service now".

Martin made a big show of slowly taking out one of the new banknotes they had been given and solemnly lighting his cigarette with it. The other two followed suit. Obviously unaware of the current inflation the woman wailed "Mama Mia! Mama Mia!" and the service the Germans got grew exponentially.

They first drank to their lost comrades.

"What about being released from our Oath of Allegiance to the Führer? Did you ever feel bound by your *Fahneneid*?"

"Absolutely! At least, at first. I took the oath in '35. Remember it well. '*I swear by God this holy oath. That I will unconditionally obey the supreme commander of the armed forces Adolf Hitler, the Führer of the German Reich and People. That I am ready as a brave soldier to lay down my life at any time for this oath*'. Back then no-one had any idea what sort of a mess he would cause. But he was stark raving mad. It's idiotic to be bound by oath to blindly obey a madman."

161

But thoughts of the past quickly turned to the future. For the first time, they could really allow themselves to think of it; discuss what they would do now the war was over. For every man had his own dream, divorced from the stark reality of how impossible a return to normality would be in an occupied country destroyed by war with no resources, no infrastructure, nothing.

As they left the pub, an American truck drove past hooting at them. Expecting the worst, they threw themselves back against the wall, but were doubly surprised to hear a voice yelling in German. "Have you guys all lost your minds! Jump in the back! The Italians have started to stone all the Krauts they can see!"

Chapter 27

May 1945 - January 1946 – *Tattoo*

It was true! In the very first village they were met by a volley of stones from Italians who had heard that German prisoners of war were approaching. They managed to hunker down but the truck's low sides meant that a couple got hit. Once outside the village, the American driver pulled-up next to a large heap of rubble for the Germans to relieve themselves. As they were climbing back in he got out, and started, in perfect German, to berate the prisoners. "What's the matter with you? Aren't you going to defend yourselves against the bloody Italians? *We* don't have the men to defend you." He nodded towards the rubble. "You have to do it yourselves!" They took the hint and loaded their pockets full. The anticipated hail of stones in the next few villages petered-out very quickly when returned with a concentrated salvo from not only theirs but also the following trucks. Peace was obviously going to be a more complicated matter than they thought.

The truck pulled up in front of what looked like a chaotic, disorganised building site. Some GIs were busy erecting a not very high fence around the perimeter. Most were watching and offering occasional advice.

The driver yelled out. "OK guys, this is where you get off."

"Hello, looks like we are prisoners of war earlier than we thought. At least, I think so – it doesn't *look* too much like a PoW camp. Wonder who we report to?"

****

Dear Leni,

Well, the fighting is over, thank God, and as you can see from the envelope I am writing to you from an American prisoner of war camp in Italy. It's near Turin. We have, rather haphazardly, became PoWs earlier than expected, with no formalities of surrender.

We spent a little time in a temporary camp down south in Naples first, and then moved back up to Pisa (yes we got to see it and it does lean quite a bit) and then back further north again to Arezzo and then on to Bologna. The reason for so many moves, they said, is because the camps have to be cleaned to make them habitable. Some have existed for some time, been badly run and are in a disgusting state. And guess who has to do the cleaning? So, life has become much more normal, well, in as much as we are no longer trying to kill each other. Some of the camps seem to be doubling up as way-stations for American soldiers headed for the war in the Pacific with Japan. We see them drilling quite a lot.

I was so sorry to hear that there is no news about your brother. It has been such a long time now since the horror of Cristal Night. *Maybe no news is good news? I will keep hoping with you.*

The logistics of getting all the prisoners back to their homeland is a major effort, and no-one seems to have much of an idea how it is to be achieved, so it will probably be some time before we get home. In the meantime, the basic human necessities have to be taken care of. All sorts of things need to be built to adequately house the enormous influx of Germans. Latrines for a start. The Italians refused to construct them, so they put us to work. You know, it is almost a pleasure to be back actually constructing things again rather than blowing them up, even if they are latrines.

Either the GIs are incredibly well looked after or their canteen management badly overestimates the amount of food they can eat. Sometimes whole steaks were getting thrown out, often still warm! The Americans agreed to give the left-overs to the Italian farmers as pig-food. Each week four of us were chosen to transport bins with the excess food to the farmers.

The Americans made it very clear to us that they would thrash us if they caught anyone lifting the lids of the bins and diving in to retrieve anything remotely edible (we have pretty meagre rations don't forget, and everyone is always hungry so you can guess how tempting those warm steaks are!). They said the Italians were deliberately throwing the freshly cooked steaks away right in front of us so that their friends could have a laugh at our humiliation when we tried to retrieve them.

The Americans came up with a good idea, though. Before they gave the Italian farmers the pig-food they stipulated that they had first to feed us Germans a hearty meal – with wine! It took some serious negotiations – the Americans drove off several times with the undelivered pig-food – before the Italians agreed. Now everyone wants to be on pig-swill-duty.

I've found a new friend. Peter Biebersheimer is one of our GI guards. He comes from a German family in the Midwest of the USA and speaks very good German. His parents migrated to America in the early 30's. Anyway he seems to feel an affinity for us Germans. He shares his cigarettes with us. Yesterday when I was having a wash – it's still not that easy given the meagre facilities and large number of prisoners – he taught me a new funny American saying about 'washing up and down as far as possible' (he calls his private area 'Possible'). Anyway I will explain it to you when I get back.

Got to go now - Peter has just arrived to 'guard' us while we work.

Love you Leni

Xoxox

****

"Hey Martin, just hold onto this for me would you, I just need to water that tree."

"Sure, Pete, Okey Dokey - no problem."

The relaxed scene was shattered in an instant. "You there – put that rifle down right now. Get over by the fence. Hands in the air. You move a single damn muscle and you're dead."

"OK! OK! OK! Don't shoot! DON'T SHOOT! I put it down! I put it down." Martin looked at the gun pointing at his chest. "There. See? Don't shoot!"

"What in Goddamn hell do you think you're doing? What's the point in trying to escape? There's no damn point. No point at all. Can't you krauts get it into your heads we are trying to get you OUT of here (the rifle waved, indicating the camp) back to your own damn country. Jesus."

"Brian, bloody hell, what are you doing? Put the damn gun down!" Peter rushed out from behind his tree, his flies still undone. "All I did was ask Martin to hold my rifle while I took a leak. He's a good guy. He's not stupid. He knows better than anyone we're trying to get him and his buddies home."

"Jesus, Peter, what got into you? Giving him your weapon!? Another moment and I would've shot him; it sure was looking as if he was gonna try and break out. "

Peter retrieved his rifle. Still trembling, Martin slowly put his hands down. For a second they eyed each other. Martin nodded towards Peter's still open fly. He did it up, remembering just in time not to hand his rifle to Martin but to balance it against his thigh. Martin retrieved his shovel. Normality was resumed.

****

Life went on, eight months of it, but by January 1946 they were informed that transport had finally been arranged. 750,000 German soldiers were on their way home. Or rather, those headed for the occupied zones in the west were on their way back: repatriation to the Russian-occupied zone in Germany's east was more complicated and was held up. Martin, of course, was domiciled in the east, but he was lucky. Because he had been conscripted in the west, in Hamburg, he did not have the extra wait. There was to be one final hold-up, however.

"Line up! Strip off! Arms above your head!"

Protocol specified one final medical before release. The camp doctors walked along the lines inspecting each one.

Suddenly one of the guards started screaming. Martin collapsed under a frenzied rain of baton blows to his ribs, head, legs, everywhere.

"You disgusting pig! Thought you could hide it from us did you?"

Martin curled up in a ball, concentrating on protecting his head as the blows continued. Kicking followed. The shock gave way to pain.

"Filthy bastard! I know who you are: damn SS murderer! You're not going anywhere buddy. Filthy fucking bastard! They'll string you up for what you've done! Don't you worry you piece of shit, you human garbage, you just wait, we'll …"

"For God's sake man, what the hell's going on? Stop it for Christ's sake." The other doctors came running up, Peter not far behind.

"This bastard's damn SS. You can see. Look under his arm, there's a scar where he's removed the tattoo showing his blood group. All SS had their blood group tattooed under their arms."

"Jesus get your fucking facts straight, buddy. It was the LEFT arm. The SS tattoo went on the underside of the LEFT arm, near the armpit! That there's a scar from a boil. I know because I took this man to get it lanced. The scar is under the WRONG arm and in the WRONG place. AND what's more it's the wrong damn size – I've seen the real McCoy and they're only a few millimeters.

"He's right, I personally lanced it. For God's sake we are responsible for these men. You and you – get him to the infirmary and I'll check nothing's been damaged. He's taken quite a beating."

Upon recovery, in January 1946, Martin was put on a train to Wissen in Germany, where he had to report for demobilisation. As suddenly as he had become one, he was now no longer a soldier. He still looked like one, though: since there were no civilian clothes – his were still in Wiederitzsch, in the Persil packet forwarded from Hamburg when he joined up – Martin's journey home from Wissen had to be made in what remained of his *Wehrmacht* uniform.

Chapter 28

1946 – *Mar-TIN Mar-TIN*

Tatty though it was, there was still enough of Martin's uniform for the young Russian border guard to pick him out straightaway.

"Вы! Вы! Куда едете? Документы! СЕЙЧАС-ЖЕ!"

Martin eyed the sub-machine gun slung purposefully over her shoulder. *A PPSh 41. How many times did we have to take that apart and put it together again!*

"Where am I going? You want my documents?" He complied quickly with the guard's orders, standing up and fishing for his documents at the same time.

Recalling what he could of his Brandenburg Russian he stuttered "Я... Я… еду... в... в… *how do you say Leipzig in Russian? Never mind, 'I'm going home' will do*: "Домой – Я еду домой."

A quick thought. *They said the Russian men have a soft spot for mothers, let's hope the women do too.* He added, lying "домой … к матерю – home … to my mother."

The guard scrutinised his travel documents. She looked up, her stare icy. "I see. You are lucky. Myself, I do not have a mother anymore to return to. You Germans starved her to death. And how old is she, this mother of yours? That you are going home to."

He started to sweat. *This is not going well.* "She … she will be 75 this year. My father died because they wouldn't let him into the hospital. I … I … I'm very sorry to hear about your mother."

The stare continued: long, hard, wordless. *God! God! How I hate uniforms.* His pass was handed back with no comment. Avoiding further eye contact, he sat down, tried to stop trembling. *So this is Russian-occupied Germany. Pity Wiederitzsch couldn't have been a bit more to the west. Well, at least I'm on the last stretch home, even without mum and dad waiting for me.*

No mum waiting, no dad, no Kurt. But his brothers and sisters were there and Martha too. And, as he entered the dilapidated old house, there was a letter on the table for him, postmarked Kiel. It had one of the new allied occupation stamps.

IRON CROSSED

****

Darling Martin,

It is some time since I have been able to write. Since the war ended I have been living near Kiel. We were lucky that we managed to get out of Berlin. It had been bombed so badly. Some of my conductress friends were also killed in the raids. Many tramlines were blown up of course, so there were few trams running and no work for us, and the company told us non-Berliners to head for Kiel where there would be work. (Easier said than done. With little fuel and hardly any transport it took nearly two weeks and we had little food to keep us going.) As soon as it was clear that the Russians were close of course all Berlin tried to get out but by then it was pretty much too late. I've heard that the conditions were terrible and they didn't allow anyone to leave. Anyway, I made it to Kiel and was able to find private accommodation in Laboe, a little town about 15 kilometres away on the coast. (I've just realised that you probably know that – didn't you work on the Kanal once?)

With its naval base and submarine building Kiel was a special target of the American and English bombers and has been flattened. But the surrounding rural areas have only been slightly affected by the bombing. There is still a shortage of food though. Well, to be exact there is no food. Me and my friends wait till dark and then go out searching for any vegetables the farmers have missed in the paddocks around the town. (It's actually the farmer's wives that do all the farming now of course.) Recently we were lucky and found some beetroot and carrots that kept us going for two weeks!

I was finally able to get away to visit my parents in Düren. The normal three hour journey took three days – there were only a few trains and they were all packed with people on top and hanging off the sides. But when I arrived of course our house was no longer there – everything was bombed flat. When the Americans started to attack in September, mum and dad had been told to take what they could carry and were evacuated into the heart of Germany along with everyone else. My sister Gretchen and I managed to locate them finally and bring them back to her place in Mariaweiler, which thankfully is still standing. They looked awful, terribly emaciated, and starving. Mum said that the local farmers had to give them a loaf of bread a week in return for work, but because she had been ill and couldn't work they were only given three-quarters of a loaf. Anyway dad managed to construct a bed from a bed-head and some wood he found in the ruins. But they still only had one blanket and this year the winter has been bitterly cold. Luckily, when I visited my brother in Lübeck, his friend, who was also in the navy, gave me a horse blanket for them. Really rough, but nice and warm!

My family did finally receive a letter from the Red Cross. It said that my younger brother Heini had been sent to the Mauthausen concentration camp near Linz. He was taken away by the SS police, remember, after complaining on Crystal Night. Nobody knows what happened to him.

[Mauthausen was a concentration camp intended specifically for 'extermination through labour' of political prisoners of the Third Reich, so Leni's brother Heini was probably worked to death there.]

I am looking forward to seeing you again soon and I hope you got home safely; one is never too sure these times.

Love you!

Deine Leni,

Thoughtfully Martin sat down to compose his reply.

****

She only needed to read the invitation once. Packing was easy – she had very few possessions anyway – and then it was off to the railway station for the train to Leipzig, and to Martin. Kiel station was a mass of people, all trying to score a ticket to somewhere. She was jostled, and jostled in return, for three days and nights. When she finally got a ticket the train was packed. Hardly even standing room. They were hanging from the steps and doors of each coach; some were clinging to the roof; some were actually on the roof. It was a teeming mass of humanity. Everyone wanted to get somewhere else.

Leni was squashed between a fat man and his equally fat daughter. *How was it possible for anyone to be FAT*? No-one had any food, and everything was rationed. It had been like that for years. *Perhaps he had owned a delicatessen or some such and still had access to food, somehow. No. Black Market more likely.* He stood out like a sore thumb; everyone stared at him and his fat daughter. You could see what people were thinking by the looks on their faces. *At least it's warm between them. And they're keeping me upright.*

Mar-tin, Mar-TIN; Mar-tin, Mar-TIN went the wheels. Leni was exhausted, hungry and strangely excited all at the same time. She had only ever seen him in his army uniform. *What'll he look like in civvies*? Hmm now there was an exciting thought! She had never liked the uniform, just his confidence and that inner strength.

And finally there he was. Out of uniform. *Oh my god! He is gorgeous! Just like a movie star.*

A restrained hug and peck from the film-star in civvies. "Shall we go back to my family's place? It's only about an hour and a half's walk."

It seemed strange: to be just walking along together holding hands after so much time just writing to each other, with only the occasional contact when Martin was on leave. He recalled their last time together after he had learnt his parents had died, and how, although he had not been able to share his grief because it was too raw, he had felt much better just being with her. And, he knew that through their letters and time together he had grown to love her. She was such a bright, happy person, full of mischief; and her spirit had not been broken by the war like so many people around him.

She asked: "Did you mean what you wrote in the letter?"

"You mean about me needing 'a little wife'?? Yes, of course. I would not have written it otherwise. Will you Leni? Be my little wife, I mean. I hope we can be happy together. You know, times are still not good, but with a bit of luck they will get better, and perhaps now that the war's over, for the first time we can have a say in our own future. What do you say? Will you share it with me? Our future, I mean."

"Why *natürlich* – naturally, Martin! You must know how I feel about you. Especially if you continue to wear those clothes." Silence. "That was a joke, Martin. A kiss would be nice though". He obliged, but being a very private person he had a quick glance around to make sure first that no-one was watching.

He grinned from ear to ear. After such a momentous decision taken so matter-of-factly: it was difficult to know what to say. Martin took refuge in family history. He pointed to an old house they were approaching.

"The first place I can remember had no water, and I had to help lugging all the cooking, washing and cleaning water up the stairs. Then one day my Dad, who had been walking past this derelict old farm house for years, asked Alfred – that's one of my elder brothers – he was a brick-layer – if he could do anything to make the place habitable. The farmer who owned it said yes, he'd pay for the material if Alfred and Dad provided the labour. This was exciting news for us. All the family, neighbours too, worked on the house every spare minute, which was necessary, because it turned out the place was indeed about ready to fall down. After they had finished work on it, it was a little less likely to collapse. I remember you still had to be a bit careful not to fall through holes in the floor though. But it was much bigger than the previous place AND even had electricity! Well, at least after Alfred organised it somehow. We had one light bulb upstairs and one downstairs. We'd just switch them on and stand there and enjoy the brightness. We had only ever had candles before, you see. Even the arrival of radio when I was eight couldn't eclipse those moments. Oh and there was running water too. INSIDE! It came from a TAP. We thought that was just wonderful!"

Leni, who had grown up in a rather prosperous household, found this confrontation with poverty a little difficult to absorb. She didn't interrupt.

"A small piece of land came with the house, but big enough to grow vegetables and fruit. And big enough to keep some animals. We had rabbits, hens, ducks, geese. AND we had four pigs! We sold two each year and we slaughtered the other two, salted them, and they kept us going for most of the year. Did they taste good! I've got some good memories of the place. Except for the plank over the open manure-pit, that is. I was always afraid I would fall in. It's not modern or fashionable, but it is home."

"So, your family was pretty self-sufficient? But how did they manage the rent?"

"The farmer was called Riegel, it was quite a big farm he owned. Dad sort of paid him in kind. He worked for him – did the ploughing, looked after the cattle, that sort of thing – but didn't get paid, in lieu of the rent. They had quite a good relationship, all in all. After mum and dad died we had to move out and make way for another family. And with the war there's been no-one taking care of the land, so there's no more food from that quarter for the new family. I'm staying with my sister Martha now, so that's where we'll both stay for the moment."

Eager to catch sight of her prospective sister-in-law, Martha had seen them coming from quite a way away. But she waited until they arrived to greet Martin's fiancée. Perfunctorily. "Pleased to meet you." Martha obviously was agitated and turned straight to Martin.

"Martin, you know what those damn Russians are doing? They're going around appropriating all the farmers' potatoes. They just dig them all up and leave them exposed to the frost for a few days so they can make their damn vodka. The farmers can't do anything about it. The Russians have threatened to shoot them if they so much as remove one spud. They're getting madder by the hour."

"Bugger the farmers. Any farms near here? If the potatoes are just lying around in the dirt we may be able to score a few when no-one's looking. Never know, we might get lucky."

****

It was difficult to make much headway against the cold head-wind, and the large hessian bags slung over the handlebars didn't help. But the three of them peddled the 30 minutes to one of the farms Martha knew had been recently visited by the Russians. Luckily there was cloud cover, with the moon shining through at intervals making it a little easier to see the way. And the bike saddles only squeaked a little.

Yes! There they were. You could just make them out; the potential vodka just lying all over the field.

"Hold on; not too quick. Let's just wait a bit. I'll go check if there's anyone guarding the field." Leni and Martha crouched down near a hedge.

When Martin got back they set to work stuffing the potatoes into the hessian sacks, trying not to take too many from any one spot. It didn't take long to fill up with as much as they could manage. They headed back towards the bikes.

"Hey! Hey! You! You there! Where do you think you're going with our potatoes? Stealing is still a crime you know!" The father and son came running towards them screaming.

Best defence is attack. Martin put down his sacks, turned and headed aggressively towards them. "Well now, that's none of your damn business." The unmistakable threat made it clear he was not one to be messed with.

"Look man, the Russians will be back soon." The farmer eyed the two sacks behind Martin. "Hell, just go, take what you've got and go; they probably won't notice anything missing. We don't like them any more than you."

Martin grunted. The three took off with their bounty, peddling a lot quicker than they came. "We need to get these out of sight right away. If the Russians see there are potatoes missing they'll threaten the farmer and he'll happily show them the direction we took off in. Then they'll come looking for us and that won't be good. Best thing is a very very deep hole. Deep enough for the Russkis not to find them and for them not to germinate. With a bit of luck we might have some nice potato soup for the next month."

Life for Martin and Leni was hard work. They never knew where the next meal was coming from and Martin took any odd jobs that he could, often doing a day's work for the farmers in the district in exchange for a little food. Mainly vegetables: it was very rare to get any meat as the Russians had confiscated all livestock for their own use.

Martin made a point of visiting Paul's parents as he knew it meant a lot to them to hear about their wonderful, intelligent son from his closest friend. Sometimes he almost made them laugh with his stories of Paul's boxing-manager enterprise.

****

"Martin, you know, I've not had my period and I've started to feel a bit sick every morning. I feel different somehow. I think I might be pregnant."

So much for those doctors saying I wouldn't have any children. "But that's fantastic news, Leni! Wonderful! First of many, I hope. So… we'd better get married as soon as we can. Then our baby will barely be even an *acht-Monats-Kind* – an eight-months-child."

"Yes, you are right, it would be best to do it before I start to show. I have always wanted children, I just … I just wish we could offer them a better future."

"Stop worrying, we have our future in our own hands now and it will be wonderful. I promise you".

Martha came in holding some cloth. "Leni, do you think you can do anything with this bit of calico? It was a table-cloth, but, you know what I'm thinking? It could be made into a very nice wedding dress. I am not very clever with sewing but you are welcome to it if you want."

"That's very kind of you Martha, thank you so much. A new dress would be SOOO nice. I'm sure I'll be able to do something with it. I'll draw some flowers on it and embroider them with some lovely bright colours."

"Here, take this to the cobbler and get him to make you some nice wedding shoes." Martin handed Leni the leather work-bag from his apprentice years.

The cobbler smiled. "Sure, Leni, I can make you some shoes from this. Quite good ones actually – it's good leather. Can Martin fix my leaking roof do you think?"

Shoes were made; roof fixed. All they needed now was the rings.

Food was more valuable than gold in those times. Two hundredweight of potatoes (courtesy of the Russians) did the trick and Martin came back from a local black-marketeer with two plain, slightly tarnished gold rings in his pocket.

The catholic priest refused to marry them. Martin was not a catholic for a start and his war experiences had long since drained any belief in a God. He put his foot down. No, he would not convert. So, it had to be a Lutheran wedding. All Martin's remaining family were there that sunny Saturday in September 1946, and Alfred too. But none of Leni's. They didn't really have the money, and they worried that, even if they were allowed to enter the Russian zone from the British zone, they just might not be allowed back again.

No such uncertainty surrounded Leni and Martin; they lived in Russian-occupied Germany and definitely were not allowed to leave.

But leave they must. Life was being made increasingly unpleasant for the Germans by the Russians there, who understandably had no love for their erstwhile enemies. There was often trouble with them, usually over German women. The Russians thought they had an automatic right to them, married or not, and more than once Martin had had to rescue his former school friends from rape. This invariably led to punch-ups and it was now so risky for him that he no longer dared go out at night. More importantly, Martin now had a family to support, and he had promised Leni a good future. He knew it would not happen here. He needed to find well-paid work; Leni needed to be closer to her family. They had to get out.

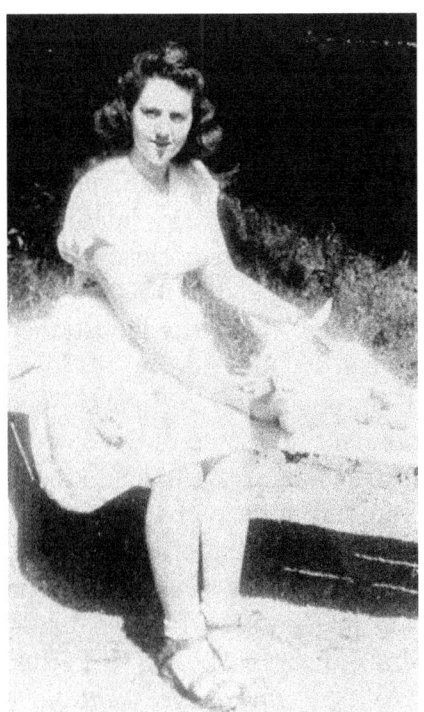

I'll draw some flowers on it and embroider them

Leni in her wedding dress with embroidered flowers on hem and belt. The goat was presumably intended to contribute bucolic atmosphere.

Chapter 29

1946 – *Yoohoo!*

A pear to share, some bread and a tiny bit of cheese. A small suitcase each. Late September 1946, just before dawn. A train took them most of the way. When the undulating countryside took on a steeper profile they knew they were close to the border in the Harz mountains. They got out at the end of the line. Martin asked a porter if he knew of any good guides. The porter looked them up and down.

"What, to get across the border? Of course. That's what everyone's after. I'll introduce you to Frantz. He's a very good guide, no problems with him. Not like some of the others you hear about: kill the customer, take their belongings. But he does cost."

"Now Frantz, you stay three steps ahead of me where I can see you. Not two. Not five. Exactly three! Understood?" The barrel of the pistol counted out the number of steps, just to make it doubly clear. The young guide nodded. They set off up the road.

Martin's well-trained eyes spotted the Russian patrol in the distance. *We must be near the border. This is going to be tricky: they're bound to be suspicious of the suitcases.*

"Leni, Frantz, stop. Patrol approaching." His voice was quiet but firm. "Just sit down facing the way we've come. I'll do the talking."

They all tried to look casual. Just taking a short rest at the side of the road. They looked up, smiling and shading their eyes in the morning sun, as the patrol approached.

The patrol leader spoke. "От куда вы? Документы!"

Here we go again. "Where are we from? We've just come from the British side." Martin handed over his *Anmeldung* showing his permit to enter the Russian zone. "On our way to see my Mum in Wiederitzsch. It's a little village near Leipzig." Martin helpfully pointed out the direction they had come. This is my wife Leni and her brother Frantz. We're just having a bit of a rest. My wife is going to have a baby. We've still got a very long way to go."

The patrol leader gave them a cursory look, and continued on his way. The rest followed, other things on their mind.

"We're not going to get away with that again. We'll give them time to get out of sight and then get a move on."

****

"Whatever's this doing in the middle of nowhere? Looks like a deserted concentration camp."

Thanking their guide for this information, they farewelled him after handing over the previously agreed-on sum of money. He seemed relieved to get away from within range of Martin's gun.

Now just the two of them, they followed the high barbed-wire fence for the length of the camp, turned a corner and there stood two border guards.

"So, two more refugees? You don't get through for nothing you know."

Paying the guide had taken a lot of his money; the rest they would need for food and shelter once they were on the other side.

"Look guys, I honestly don't have a *pfennig*. I've been fighting on the Eastern Front for the last five years and only just managed to get out alive. My wife's pregnant and wants to visit her family. Her Mum's sick. You look like a couple of decent blokes. How about giving us a break?"

"Oh for heaven's sake let 'em through, poor buggers. The next Russian patrol's due in three minutes. They'll take 'em back for sure if we don't."

Through a quarry, under a barbed wire fence, and they were out! In the 'West'!

The walking was not any easier for being there. Sometimes it was hard to see where they were going because the grass was so high. They were trudging through a field when suddenly Leni started yelling at a group of men she had seen in the distance.

"Hello! Hello! Over here! Can you help us? Are we in the right direction for Cologne? Yoohoo!! Yoohoo!!"

Martin cut her off in mid yoohoo, pulling her to the ground as gently as he could.

"Leni, those are Russian soldiers. Can't you tell from their uniforms? God knows what they're doing on this side of the border, let's hope they haven't spotted us. Stay as quiet and low as you can."

They lay like statues, giving the soldiers time to clear the vicinity. Martin raised himself, peered carefully over the long grass.

"OK they've gone, thank God. Don't do that again, Leni: you almost got us taken back. Ask before you shout. I can recognise a Russian uniform from miles away with my eyes closed."

As the day wore on they grew more tired.

"Martin, can't we find some way to manage the suitcases. I'm getting pretty exhausted."

"See that spot over there on the horizon? Looks like a farm-house. We'll head there and see what we can organise."

"Organise? Just don't get into any trouble, now that we've made it this far."

"*Guten Tag*! – Hello! I don't suppose you could spare that wheelbarrow? My wife's getting pretty tired and it would help to shift our suitcases."

"*Guten Tag*! Yes, I could certainly spare it. For two hundred marks."

"Heavens I don't have that sort of money. How about I just borrow it and get someone to return it in a day or two; my wife is pregnant."

"Sorry, need it."

Nothing for it, they trudged off again. Martin took both suitcases and they stopped more often. It took them two days to get from the border to where Leni's family was staying in Düren, sometimes hitch-hiking, sometimes walking. They were only stopped once, by a group of British soldiers. This time, Martin had his other set of papers ready from his stint on the Kiel Kanal which identified him clearly as domiciled in the West.

But there was no work for Martin in Düren, so they decided the best thing was for Leni to stay with her family there while he sought work further afield, preferably in places that the allied bombing had destroyed.

****

Martin looked up at the big sign '*Wayss and Freytag Building Contractors*'. His travels had taken him all the way to Bremen. A large harbour city on the North Sea, Bremen had received much attention from the RAF seeking to destroy the massive U-boot emplacements built there by slave-labour. He smiled. *That's a piece of luck, finding a big contractor straight off.*

"*Guten Tag*! I'm looking for work. Qualified carpenter – I actually worked for *Fricke* before the war. Did my apprenticeship there too. Had a great ... Gary Hunder!! Well I'll be blowed. So you survived Russia then! Good to see you."

"*Unteroffizier* Martin! Martin Schläfer! My God. Good to see you too! How are you? What are you doing in Bremen? Long way from your home, isn't it? It would be in the Russian zone now?"

"Yeah, we got out. Long story. I'm married now with a baby on the way. Is there any work?"

"Sure, plenty. With all the post-war rebuilding, more work than you could want. Especially for someone with your experience. Don't suppose you've got your workbook with you from before the war? Boss! Got someone here for you. Top class carpenter. Worked for *Fricke* before the war. He also saved my life once when I fell asleep on duty. If it wasn't for Martin, I'd have been shot. His group liked him so much they used to call him *Unteroffizier* Martin, not *Unteroffizier* Schläfer."

"Well, Gary, there is not much that one has control over in life, and life can be pretty shitty. Most of the time, in fact, it *is* pretty shitty. Heaven knows we've seen enough of it these past years. Most of the time, whether we survived was just a matter of luck. I remember they wanted me along as engineer once to assess whether a certain bridge would support a tank. But the lieutenant said you could tell by just looking at the bridge, so they left me behind. Minutes after they took off they were blown up by partisans. Another time we were told by a partisan we captured near Orel that they had had us in their sights and could have shot us at any time. They didn't, he said, because they'd seen we had a type 42 machine gun and they didn't want to engage with its high rate of fire. Look, what I'm trying to say is you being caught asleep on guard duty back then was one of the rare opportunities I had for evening-up the score with life – an opportunity to make a real difference. I simply took it; that's all. And that was *your* piece of luck, I guess."

The foreman told him there was immediate work on their harbour site, and Martin started right away, doing carpentry on board American ships berthed there. Gary even organised a little welcome-back party. There was even better news: accommodation for him and Leni and the coming baby. It was in the prefabricated dwellings *Wayss and Freytag* had erected for their staff in the suburb of Bremen-Farge, not far from where the massive *U-Boot* bunker was. Gary took him to look at their future home. It was a two-room corrugated iron shed with bed and not much else. There was row upon row of them. All water, toilets and washing facilities were shared. Martin had a twenty minute walk to the station, then an hour's train ride, to get to the harbour.

"I know it's not much Leni, but at least now we have a roof over our heads, and I have work."

"We're together, you've got work, we've got income. Martin, that's actually quite a lot. And there's quite a lot we can do to make it a nicer place to live in."

With scraps of wood he found in the ruins Martin built a shelf along one wall, and a tiny crib. The shelf doubled as a table they could sit at on the bed which they converted into a sofa during the day time. Leni had gone fossicking with him and found bits of material and a beautiful piece of lace in the rubble which she washed and stretched out to dry. She wondered who had owned it and whether they were still alive. Probably not. She covered one of their two pillows with the lace. The pillow normally held pride of place on the bed, helping to make the tiny room more like home.

One thing they desperately needed was lighting. The unavailability of light-bulbs made mockery of the light-bulb fixture in the middle of the ceiling. Initially, when they could afford it, they bought candles. But very quickly the shops ran out; and even if they could have afforded the black-market prices they had more pressing things to buy. So in the evenings they just sat in the dark, the only light coming from the stove. If Martin had been lucky enough to find wood for it the previous evening, that is.

They both looked up at the empty light-bulb fixture. "You know where I've seen some? Every day in fact. Bremen railway station! Be easy to just take one. From the toilets. Then we can at least see each other again once it gets dark. I know, I know: be careful! Don't worry."

What if he was caught? They were really tough on any, and all, petty theft: the police would certainly jail him, and then what would happen to the baby? The baby didn't appear to share Leni's worry. A couple of kicks seemed to admonish *don't be silly, he knows what he is doing, he'll be careful.*

a little welcome-back party

Carpenters and foreman celebrate Martin's return in front of the *Wayss & Freytag* sign in the time-honoured way, with a bottle of beer. Martin is second from right. He is wearing his traditional journeyman's waistcoat with its symbolic eight pearl buttons (see end of chapter 2).

Chapter 30

1947 – *Pressing Predicament*

She had 40 minutes to worry, in turns pacing up and down in the dark and sitting on the bed. Footsteps! Leni opened the door tentatively, half expecting to see the police. But police didn't dance little jigs with light-bulbs in their hands grinning all over their face.

A little light can make a big difference. They could see each other for a start, and read, and Leni was able to make some baby clothes from some more pieces of cloth she had found in the rubble. There was no buying baby clothes with her ration card. The woman in the shop was adamant she could not get any until after the baby had been born: "If your baby is stillborn, Frau Schläfer, the clothes will be wasted."

****

"Leni I've had a thought. You know the American ships I'm working on at the wharves? Well, *Wayss* also handle unloading supplies from them."

"Ye-es?"

"Well, it's a way we can get more food. You see, food often gets spilt from the bags they are unloading, like rice or flour. I've watched – people just walk over it and tread it in. How about you sew a little pocket into my carpenter's bag. I can scoop some of the spilt food into it. Every bit helps, we could make pancakes or bread with the flour. It would help keep the hunger at bay. You certainly could do with some more to eat, having a baby to feed as well."

"Well I wasn't going to tell you but today in the food queue I fainted I was so hungry. And the baby was kicking non-stop, poor little thing was probably hungry too. I just blacked out. I woke up in a little room at the back of the shop stretched out on a sofa with a blanket over me. First thing I thought about was whether someone had stolen my ration cards. But a lady with a lovely kind face and a very short man were both fussing over me. They gave me a tray of little sandwiches and milk. I started crying. She said she knew it was hard being pregnant, standing in a long queue, especially when you were very hungry. Oh Martin! I tried not to gobble the food down, but it was really hard. I wanted to bring a sandwich home for you but the lady said she would not leave me until I had eaten all of them. I couldn't thank her enough; it was just so nice to have a whole sandwich. I kept thanking her and thanking her. In the end she said she knew I was grateful and I did not need to say it anymore. So yes, anyway, I think your idea is really good, as long as you do not get caught. Please be careful, though: no amount of extra food is worth you being in jail. I'll sew a pocket into your work bag tonight. Seems a shame to think of that food going to waste. Rice or flour I can certainly do something with."

****

Six o'clock and no Martin. Seven, eight and nine o'clock and still no Martin. There was no point in going out this late to the worksite: no-one would be there; and there was no-one to contact, so she tried to sleep. But of course she couldn't, so she paced up and down until the light just beginning to seep into the room saw her finally collapse with exhaustion into a deep sleep. She woke. It was late morning, and still no Martin.

"Your husband, Frau Schläfer? He's in jail. They arrested him last night. Apparently he was stealing food from the Americans and they do not take that lightly. So they put him in prison." The foreman at the wharf seemed friendly enough, but not particularly worried.

"Whatever happened?"

"They said they caught him scooping flour from the ground into his workbag. Most of us have thought of doing it, believe me, but didn't want to run the risk of jail if we were caught. I'm sorry Frau Schläfer but there's nothing I can do."

"Whatever can *I* do? Can't I at least go and see him? How long will they keep him in prison do you think?"

"From my experience they won't allow visitors, even you. He's not actually *in* prison, you see. They make the prisoners labour outside somewhere. And the length of his sentence is anyone's guess. I'm sorry but I really cannot help you any further."

DAD PL COME STOP MARTIN IN PRISON STOP

After responding to her telegram, Leni's father had to ask lots of people on the wharf before someone suggested he inquire at the courts. From there it was easy: Martin Schläfer? Yes, here it is: '*two months' hard labour for stealing'*.

Leni's dad stayed for two weeks and when he went back to Düren he was relieved by her older sister and brother-in-law. They lasted two weeks: quite long, all things considered, for three in a single room with one bed. That left still one month before the baby was due. Leni became more and more depressed. It was especially tough not being able to see Martin, and the rationing meant that his absence did not double her food. But, a stroke of luck! Her neighbour had heard somewhere that enough money could buy a provisional release. Martin could be out early enough and long enough for the birth, and then go back in to serve out the remainder of his sentence. Sounded like a bribe but OK then, that's what she would do. Raise some money, find a judge, explain the situation and he might just be out in time for the baby.

First stop the local Catholic church. She explained the problem to the priest in a nice red coat borrowed for the occasion.

"But your husband's a thief, Frau Schläfer. He's committed a crime, he must pay for that crime. He needs to be punished. The church will certainly not waste its money on him. You should go away and pray for his sins."

Praying for his sins is going to be a fat lot of help. Oh well, let's see what the Lutherans have to say.

The Lutheran pastor listened kindly. Promised to make some enquiries. He came the next day, as good as his word. Three thousand *Reichsmarks* would secure the temporary release for the baby's birth. "Here you are. You'll need to pay it back of course. Now, now, Frau Schläfer, no need for tears."

****

"Young lady, thank you for explaining your predicament with respect to your husband's incarceration and the imminent birth of your child." The American judge's German was excellent, with only a slight accent. "Before I give judgement, I need to draw your attention to a rather more pressing predicament. Please pull up your underwear, it is most unbecoming in its current location around your ankles."

Leni had been so anxious in front of the judge she had not noticed her fleecy lined pink long-johns had slipped down from over her big tummy. Her dad's gift was now lying in a neat heap around her ankles.

"Quiet please. Quiet please." The giggling subsided.

"Now that decorum has been re-established, given your husband's exemplary war record I am minded to accede to your request of a premature release – but temporary mind you! – so that he can be present at the birth and help you during this period. Your husband is accordingly granted temporary release from tomorrow for a period of no longer than four weeks. If your calculations are correct that should coincide with the birth of the baby. Of the 3,000 *Reichmarks* fine, I am furthermore returning 500 to you so you can invest in some underwear with more efficient elastic. It could actually be dangerous if you trip in your current condition."

"Thank you so much your gratefulness, I am most honoured!"

The giggling reasserted itself.

"Sorry, I meant thank you so much your honour. I am most …"

"Yes, yes, I understand. Off you go now and good luck with the baby."

So Martin would be home for the birth of their baby after all. Waddling home, Leni recalled in her elation when Martin had told her the doctor's pessimistic prognosis about his having children. And she remembered her reply back then that it wasn't an issue for her. But my oh my! Things were certainly different now! And at least some of those five hundred *Reichsmarks* could go towards baby clothes – once it was born.

The baby, unfortunately, must not have been paying much attention to the judge. Martin came; the baby didn't. After his four weeks at home, Martin had to go back to prison for another month, thereby missing the baby by a fortnight.

Considering the preceding shenanigans, it all went off rather problem-free. Sunday 11th May 1947 the labour pains started. Leni's neighbour fetched the local midwife. The baby was born at ten minutes to one in the afternoon. Now the baby had come, but Martin hadn't.

The little one had in fact to wait another ten days for her dad to come home.

****

Martin just lay on their bed and stared at his daughter, little arms and legs working ten to the dozen. He was captivated with her tiny face, her lovely skin, her bald head, her tiny weeny fingers and toes. And why not? He had seen so much death; it was amazing to see a new life he had helped create. A smile came back to his face.

"You know what, Leni? I think she looks just like a *Renate*."

Chapter 31

1950 – Two fingers

B oss, would it be possible to get a couple of weeks' leave? Our second baby's due in the next two weeks and it'd be great if I was there for this one. I missed the birth of the first."

"Sure Martin, no problem. We've got enough men around at the moment to cover for you. How old is your first now? How come you missed the birth?

"It's a long story boss, and Renate's just turned three. But I'm really grateful for the couple of weeks."

Leni grinned. "Two weeks off, eh? That's good news Martin. Perhaps you and the baby can synchronise it better this time. Things are very different."

"Hmm Leni, *are* things really all that different? I'm not so sure. We've been here for three years. We're still in the same old shed with no indoor plumbing or heat and it doesn't look as if things'll be changing in a hurry, except that rationing has gotten even tighter since the war ended. We're still short of basic food and heating. We're still only just making ends meet. I was thinking the other day there must be a better way of living than this. Hello, look, it's my foreman coming up the path. Wonder what he wants."

"Martin, sorry about this. I know you've only had two days off, but would it be possible for you to come back just for a couple of days? We need to sink some pylons with one of those *Bummelrammen* – you know, the fairly small 500-pound hammers. The bloke we thought could do it – turns out he can't. So there's no-one else but you who's got the experience. The boss said he'd give you your time off as soon as the pylons are in and we can continue with the building. Shouldn't take too long."

To be specially asked by the foreman: that was a real compliment! "Don't see why not. We were at the doctor's today and they said baby is still not quite ready yet. So we still have few days. And I'll have more time with him after he's born."

"*Him*, Martin?"

****

The sand gave way from under him and he slipped forwards, his head directly beneath the pile-driver. Instinctively he pushed himself away as 500 pounds of steel took off the tops of his middle two fingers instead of his head. He grasped what was left of them to staunch the bleeding and called out. His mates came running to Martin's second near-death experience with a pile-driver.

"The debris and mangled flesh will have to be removed. That means an operation."

Martin just nodded. At least there was no call for a luger this time to encourage the doctor toward a decision.

All Martin could think about was how long he'd be off work. He soon found out. According to the doctor at least a month. A month! How were they going to survive that long without any income from work?

As soon as he was released he went to see his foreman. He explained he would have to be off work for about a month but had used up all his savings. He was about to say how worried this made him with one child to support and one on the way when the foreman interrupted.

"Nothing to worry about, Martin. The firm'll keep paying you your wages while you're off work. That's what insurance is for. I must admit I thought you were coming to ask for compensation for the loss of your fingers."

"Really? Can I get compensation for that? How much?"

"A hand: perhaps. An arm: definitely. The tops of two fingers: no chance. You'll find the stumps'll hurt all the time because you'll keep on bumping them at work. But that won't affect your skill as a carpenter."

Two weeks later Leni asked him to go for the midwife. He insisted on staying despite the midwife's disapproval. Not that he hadn't seen birth before – there had been all sorts on the farm – but this was special and he wasn't going to miss it this time. His painful fingers were the last thing on his mind when little Erika arrived. She fitted snugly into Renate's crib, who had meanwhile graduated to a home-made bed of her own. A month later he was back at work.

Erika was only a few weeks old when Martin was promised a house on the building site in Hamburg where he first did his military training. Even after six years the well-nigh obliterated city was still being rebuilt and *Wayss* was heavily involved. They had set up a housing scheme there for their workers.

Eighteen months later, however, and Martin was still in Bremen. One of his new workmates, fresh from his wedding the previous Saturday, came onto the site waving keys to the new Hamburg home he had been given by the firm.

"How come Horst has landed one of the firm's homes? He's only worked here for a few weeks. I've been here for over three years, with two children, and I'm still waiting. Tell me how that's fair!"

The foreman was surprised to see the normally unflappable Martin so riled.

"Martin, didn't you know? Horst is the boss's nephew. That's it, plain and simple."

Martin turned away. *Well that makes the decision easier then.* The foreman wasn't quite sure whether he heard the word *arsehole* as a disgruntled Martin slammed the door.

****

"Leni, how would you like to live in America? They've been recruiting workers on-site for overseas – America, Canada, even Australia! They're all supposed to be crying out for carpenters. Quite a lot of the blokes have been filling in application forms on the quiet. What do you reckon?"

That night they both sat down to fill out the forms. Martin put them in the mail the next day.

Chapter 32

1951 – *News!*

Leni, playing in the dust out back with Renate and Erika, heard the tinny squeak of their shed's front door.

"Leni! Leni! Where are you? I've got some fantastic news! LENI!!"

Martin emerged with an enormous grin. "Guess what! I've been accepted! We're going to Australia. We can start a new life in a new country! Isn't that wonderful?"

Little one-year-old Erika was sitting on a dirty old rug. He picked her up and threw her into the air.

"Erika, we're going to Australia! We're going to Australia, and you're coming too! We're all going to have a new life, we're all going to have a new life, and you're coming too!" He sang to her as she fell back into his arms. Whirling her around he did a little jig, keeping his movements in rhythm with his song.

"Me too Dad, can I come too?" Four year old Renate picked up on her dad's excitement.

"Of course you can darling. You are our *Grosse* – our Big Girl – we can't go anywhere without you. We are *all* going. It will be a whole new life, in a new country."

"Australia, Martin? AUSTRALIA?? I thought it was going to be America or Canada."

Her voice managed to simultaneously convey surprise, dismay, fear and shock. "But Australia was an afterthought! I can see you are really happy, but I think we should wait for a reply from the American or Canadian immigration people first. What do we know about *Australia*? It's the other side of the world! At least America and Canada are just on the other side of the ocean."

He felt his conviction and excitement drain but reminded himself of why he wanted this so badly. "Well, that's one thing we know about it: that it's on the other side of the world! Leni, this is a wonderful opportunity. It is a new country. They need carpenters *now*, for something called *The Snowy Mountains Scheme*. America or Canada may take another three, four or five more years. Don't you want to start our new life as soon as possible!"

"I see. Well, you may be starting a new life without us then! I need some time to think about such a huge move to a country I know nothing about. I'll have to see if I can get used to the idea of going to the other side of the world. When would we have to leave?"

Martin evaded the question. "Well, the letter I got has asked me to sign up for two years. Here, look, it says *'The period of employment shall be a minimum period of two years but the period may be extended if I am considered satisfactory by the Authority'*. But you can read it yourself, they've attached a translation. It reminds me of the apprenticeship contract with *Fricke* I signed all those years ago. See, it says *'the period of employment is subject to efficiency, proper conduct and character and in respect of which the decisions of the Authority shall be binding and final.'* "

Leni took the document and scanned down the page. She got to the part where it said salary would commence on the date of arrival in Australia and that the applicant had to repay the cost of travel. Then she read the next lines and froze. The colour drained from her face and she had to sit down.

"Martin how can you do this to us? *'When accommodation in Australia is available to the employee for his family, BUT NOT BEFORE A PERIOD OF SIX MONTHS FRM ORIGINGAL DATE OF EMPLOYMENT, the Authority will if required advance money to the employee for the payment of the cost of travel of his wife and dependent children'*. Can you really go for six months and leave me and the girls here in this shed on our own? How am I supposed to manage? What if it all takes longer than six months?"

Martin felt sick. This was a much worse reaction than he'd anticipated. Normally she was so positive about such things. He knew they absolutely needed to make this move, to start a new life. It would be hard enough being without them for six months. *But I can't go if it means leaving Leni and the girls behind for good.*

Chapter 33

1951 – *Positive*

Martin tried to summon up his most convincing tone.

"Leni, we'll write to each other every week – just like we did during the war, remember? The time will go quickly. We'll only be separated for six months. My contract is only for two years, so if we really hate it we can always come back to Germany. It's a work-contract, not emigration! But, honestly, look around you…" His hand executed a broad sweep starting from the grime of their back yard, moving to their corrugated shed, then taking in the row of sheds, and the devastation of the bombed-out city background. "It would have to be better than this!"

"I know, I know, but wouldn't it be better to wait for one of the other countries so we can all go together? I'm scared Martin. We'll be on our own. We won't have any family to support us. I'll have to cope without you for such a long time. It's all a bit overwhelming, happening so suddenly like this.

"Who's to say that America and Canada won't ALSO require me to go alone first? Leni, please don't cry, I want you to be happy. The girls want you to be happy. We've been on our own before, we've overcome problems – much bigger ones than this! Think about what it will be like to have some control over our future and the children's future. Please try to look past the difficulties and think about how … Oh Leni, don't cry, it will be great! Honestly, trust me: have I ever let you down?"

Leni stopped crying, wiped her eyes on the back of her sleeve and sat there with some residual sniffles. She hated the thought of being without him for six months. Leaving him permanently really was not a choice she could or would seriously consider, even though she had blurted it out when she first heard his news. In truth, her uncustomary pessimistic reaction was compounded by the suddenness of the news, the unexpected destination and the fact that she would be left behind to cope on her own. Also her ties with her family ran deep and she realised that this would mean they would now be broken, probably for ever.

Gradually, though, Leni's positive side started to reaffirm itself and she was pleased to find herself becoming more receptive to the idea. She asked around about Australia. One of her neighbours told her about a little library which had just reopened for the first time after the war. It was not far from where she lived and she went and borrowed as many books on Australia as she could. Many people congratulated her on the move. Some said she was very brave going so far away to a country no one knew much about. She did not feel brave but it gave her courage to hear the stories people told of the funny animals, the vastness of the country, and the sun (which seemed to be the main things people mentioned when the topic of Australia was brought up).

The weeks were speeding past and correspondence from her family intensified. It was as if they felt they had to get as much contact with her as they could before she went out of their lives and could no longer be reached so easily. Leni also wrote more often, sharing with her Mum and Dad, brothers and sisters, all the exciting things she was learning about Australia and of course telling them about her preparations for going to their new life. She knew they worried about her and she wanted to make things as easy for them as she could.

It was only two weeks before Martin was due to leave and Leni was sitting on the back step of the shed with the two girls playing in the dirt when the mail man came on his squeaky bicycle. Renate heard him first. She ran around the tin shed and was back with the mailman in just a few seconds. He was holding a telegram.

LENI SORRY BAD NEWS STOP MUM DIED SUDDENLY LAST NIGHT STOP KEPT ASKING FOR YOU STOP MADE US PROMISE TELL YOU SHE LOVED YOU STOP CAN YOU COME FUNERAL SATURDAY STOP

Leni started crying so the girls started crying too. Seeing this, she summoned all her self-control and stopped. She told them about her lovely Mum and tried to explain what it meant that she had died.

Renate offered some consoling words. "Don't cry Mummy, she will be in heaven with God. Are you going to see them put her into the ground?"

"I can't honey, I would love to go but my family know how much it costs to go on a train from here and until Daddy starts working in Australia we do not have any money left over for our train tickets. Once Daddy is making more money he will send us enough to buy tickets. We will try and visit then."

Leni sent a telegram saying she could not go home for the funeral and it broke her heart. She then sat down and wrote about anything she could think of. She needed to feel she was connecting with them, that she was still part of their lives. The many return letters from her siblings told the same story. Her Mum had not been well and she had been diagnosed with cancer. By the time it was diagnosed it was only a few short weeks before she died. They said her Mum had asked them not to tell her how sick she was, as she knew Leni would get upset if she could not visit to say goodbye. They said she never complained and told no-one of the pain she was in until it was near the end.

She promised her sisters and brothers she would try and get home once Martin had started to send money to her from Australia. That she would see them at least once before she left to join him. In June 1951 Martin embarked on the *M.S. Skaubryn*, for Australia.

Chapter 34

1951 – *Overboard*

MS Skaubryn, July 1951

Hello my darling,

It was so hard to say goodbye. I miss you and the girls already. But you'll never guess who I met on board ship! Alfred Stepke! I am sure you would remember him. I first met him when I started my carpentry apprenticeship; we were together on the Westwall and in the Brandenburg Commandos. I could not believe it when I heard his sniff behind me at the card table. At first I thought I had imagined it, but then realised there can only be one sniff that sounds like that. I still questioned my own reaction until I turned around and saw him.

We have spent hours catching up. He had quite a story to tell. They surrendered in Hamburg, but he was told he had to march with the rest of his company to central Germany where they could be formally freed. The British Army actually had to issue rifles to the PoWs so that they could defend themselves on the way! (That reminds me a bit of that American guard asking me to hold his rifle while he had a pee!). On the way Alfred was able to get out of the holding camps at night, go to dances and cafes, and do a bit of black-marketeering in cigarettes and booze, not to mention liaise with all the good-looking women in the vicinity. It's amazing: it all seems to come quite naturally to him. He made a lot of money. But he lost it all when the currency was changed from Reichsmarks to Deutschmarks. He was very philosophical about it all – 'easy come, easy go' he said.

Alfred is also going to work on the Snowy Mountains Scheme. His wife will come over to Australia as soon as she can.

[As Alfred was still single, this was a little bit of a white lie on Martin's part intended to make Leni feel better that she was not the only wife left behind.]

We talked and talked about all the experiences we shared and how we first became friends when I started my carpentry apprenticeship in 1935. He is still an incredibly good looking man. Naturally the conversation led to Paul and how we wished he could have been with us on this adventure too. I am sure academics would have been very welcome in Australia, especially those who could manage boxers!

The meals seem to have improved slightly since my last letter and although they are a bit repetitious they taste fairly fresh. There is a lot of prejudice against us Germans. It is shown in many ways, one being we cannot get any beer. The other nationalities have no problem, but when we ask we are always told there is none.

There are about 1200 men aboard. I have not seen any women. There are about 150 carpenters from Germany and we share a large area with about fifty of them. There are a lot of other nationalities on board as well, I often hear many different languages being spoken. Some I recognise, like Polish, Italian and Greek, others I am not sure. The mixture of nationalities has caused all sorts of problems. I will tell you about it another day.

Be good, love you and the girls

Love Martin

****

MS Skaubryn, July 1951

Liebe Leni,

Do you remember, before I was accepted to go to Australia I had to do a carpentry test? I complained at the time that I could not understand why my German Carpenter's Guild membership was not sufficient. Well, I have been told I will need to pass ANOTHER test when I get to

Australia! Apparently the unions there do not acknowledge either my guild membership or the test I already did for their Government officials! Seems a bit odd that they are not in sync with the Government: very different to Germany! Can you imagine anything being out of sync with the German Government? I am not worried though. If the Snowy Mountains Authority wants me to prove I am a carpenter yet again, I am happy to do so.

I got into a fight for the first time since the war. One of the Polish men on board kept hassling me. He riled me up so much I just hit him on the chin and he went down. I told him that was just a warning and if he came near me again I would do for him properly. It seems he has been really harassing other Germans too. Last night I went up on deck for a cigarette. A big bloke was just picking him up off the deck where he had knocked him out. He threw him overboard.

There had obviously been a fight between them as there was a crowd and it was bedlam, everyone was screaming. The ship slowed down to look for him but they couldn't find him. One of the men I know said "bloody good riddance. He's been asking for it." The people who organised this trip have obviously not put enough thought into which nationalities they were going to mix together in the relatively confined space of a boat. It's pretty damn obvious that there is going to be no love lost between Poles and Germans, given what happened. The whole episode left a bad taste in my mouth though – the bugger was probably just as keen to start a new life as we all are. A shame he could not control his big mouth.

I have met a few men on board who like to play chess as much as I do, so most days we have at least two games. Some last for hours and it is keeping my brain working overtime to beat the best of them. The best chess player is a man called Willi Bachus; I can beat him sometimes. He's a carpenter too, going to work in the Snowy Mountains. If we end up in the same area at least I will have someone to play chess with.

The days are a bit long and I also read a lot. They have put on a few concerts for us, and debates and choirs, and games of deck quoits. But to be honest I would rather read, play chess or just stroll around the

200

ship. I have played a few games of skat and poker – don't worry, not for money! – just because it fills in the time.

Well 'my little wife', I think writing letters is not my forte. So I will close for now. As soon as I get there I expect a letter to be waiting as I have given you the address of the office in the Snowy Mountains. I will write again as soon as I get there, I promise.

Lots of kisses from your Martin.

Don't forget to give the girls lots of love and kisses from their Dad.

****

Bremerhaven, August 1951

My darling Martin,

I was so happy to get your letter; it just means so much to know you are OK. I felt sick when I read you had been in a fight. It's terrible that someone has actually got thrown overboard. How awful, please please do not get in any more fights or they might do it to you and I would just die!

I am happy about your chess; you always enjoyed a good game.

Guess who came to see me and the girls on Sunday. Rudi Köster! I could not believe it - your old boss coming to see how we were. He heard you had already left and the girls and I are on our own, so he came to see if there was anything he could do to help us. He has a beautiful car and of course the girls wanted to go for a ride so he took us to the Zoo Hagenbeck near Stellingen. It's a lovely drive from where we live.

Rudi told me that the zoo had to be closed for two years after the war, because the original one was destroyed when Hamburg was bombed. The girls loved the elephants the most; they are so big and so smart. It was a wonderful day. Rudi was just marvellous and the girls loved him.

I did talk about you a lot and in the end, I think Rudi felt as if he knew you better than when you were working together. He has offered to come again next weekend and take us somewhere nice. I think he is lonely, as his wife left him for another man during the war and he has not found anyone else.

Apart from that our news is not very interesting. I have been busy with the girls and Mrs Steiner our new neighbour has been marvellous. She did ask me the other day if it was true that you had been in prison while I was pregnant with Renate and I told her the whole story. She thought it was terrible that they put you in prison for such a minor offence.

She did laugh when I described the scene in front of the judge with my undies down around my knees though. She has a few interesting stories of her own to tell and I will share them with you when we are together again. It's too long to try and write it all down. I was even told about the temperature in her village on the day that the war broke out, can you believe it? Of all things to remember!

Speaking of remembering, I can imagine how much you and Alfred Stepke had to talk about. It must have been wonderful to catch up and exchange memories. Hard to believe he still has that dreadful sniff!

It is already six weeks since you left, I keep telling myself it is only a few more months and we will be together again. I feel like a part of me is missing. But I have to be strong, I know that we will be together soon and our new life will be good.

Well my darling, I better go. I look forward to hearing from you again.

Yours and only yours with all my heart

Your Leni xoxoxoxo

Chapter 35

August 1951 – *Primitive*

I knew it! I should have warned her about that Rudi. He had a reputation with the women, always skiting about his conquests. It sounds as if he has her wrapped around his finger. I bet having a flash car impressed her and the girls. Him and his smooth mouth. I have to get her here as soon as possible or I will end up losing them."

"Calm down Martin, what's got you so upset? What's your wife written?"

"Here Willi, read it for yourself. That smooth-talking ladies' man, just oozes charm. I saw him use it lots of times on different woman while I worked with him. He is such an arsehole. Now he's using it on my Leni. You hear so many stories about men's wives who end up not coming to Australia cos they had found other men. Aren't you worried about your wife?"

"Martin, for God's sake write to her and tell her how you feel. Of course she'd never leave you for someone else. Just warn her about arsehole-Rudi and his reputation."

****

Island Bend, Snowy Mountain Scheme.

Darling Leni,

I was both sad and happy today. I got your letter. It was so lovely to hear from you and know that my three girls are well. But I am really concerned that Rudi has appeared in your life, I know from work that he has a reputation as a ladies' man. Leni, he is after only one thing, please do not be fooled by his smooth talk. A man does not spend time with someone else's wife and children unless he has an ulterior motive. Yes, I know I am jealous, I admit it. I love you so much and do not want to lose you. Promise me you will not fall for his charm.

I am glad that you seem to be coping OK. Sometimes I feel as if we have been apart for years and then I realise that it has only been two months.

Let me tell you what has happened to me since I last wrote. We have arrived, obviously, and are at a place called Island Bend.

On arrival in Melbourne they made us do another test, just as we had been forewarned. It was very easy: make a trestle. One of the chaps could not do it so I gave him a hand. I am not too sure how he passed the first test they gave us in Germany if he could not make a simple trestle, but anyway. We all got through in the end.

We went by train to a town called Cooma – you say it like 'Kuhma'. It took almost a whole day. They call it the 'Gateway to the Snowies'. ('Snowies' means Snowy Mountains. The Australians seem to end a lot of their words in 'ie', bit like the Swiss.) Then we went by bus to Island Bend, which is the real Snowies. It took another couple of hours. It was freezing all the way – not so bad as Russia to be sure but easily as cold as Germany. We thought Australia was hot and sunny! But it is August, and their winter, and we are quite high up and there is snow everywhere. Our work contracts clearly stipulated we would be working below the snow-line, but they are obviously not keeping to that.

When we arrived and stepped out of the bus we were up to our shins in mud, it was awful. Cold, miserable and smelly! We were shown to our tents, which was pretty much all there was there: it's in the middle of nowhere.

TENTS! Can you believe it? Well, they <u>did</u> tell us, but I don't think we believed it would be quite as primitive as that. I share a tent with another German. I mentioned him in my last letter – Willi Bachus. He is a good chess player. He is from Cologne (so at least I can understand some of what he says). Leni, he never washes and he hangs his socks on the foot of his bed every night so they can dry out and the next day he puts them on again. The smell is awful!! Sometimes I think *it's a strategy to win at chess – you spend all your time holding your nose and can't concentrate on the moves!*

You know, it's just like the Westwall again! Our job as carpenters is to build barracks for the people who will be constructing the Snowy Mountain Scheme dams. They will be mostly Norwegians, I think. But all WE are thinking of is building huts so we can get out of the tents!

Like I said, at first there was nothing there, but bulldozers were trucked up and they started to clear away a flat area for us to build on. While they were doing that we had to go and cut down and shape the timber for the floors and foundations. That's no joke, Leni – we have to use proper hardwood, which blunts the saws very quickly. We drive piles into the ground and then lay the floorboards on top. Then the sides go up, and then the roof. It's pretty simple work for men of our expertise. Amazingly the sides are sent prefabricated from England by ship. It makes our job easier of course but heavens knows why they would want to do that, as there is enough timber, and we have the expertise, to build the sides from scratch.

Oh! I have just thought of one thing here that is not as bad as Wehrmacht *training! Hot water to shower with! Mind you, we have to heat the water up with an enormous wood fire because there's no actual running tap water. And so far, no-one has drowned.*

Let me tell you about the food. It's very simple to describe. It's revolting. We have baa-aa! for breakfast, baa-aa! for lunch and baa-aa! for dinner. You guessed it – mutton, usually tough and cooked in dripping, with just a few chips and eggs in all permutations of fried and greasy. Well it takes some of the uncertainty out of life to know what will be on the menu on Monday, on Tuesday, on Wednesday etc. Alfred has given up eating the food and just exists on chocolate he buys from a little provision store they have set up on-site.

We play a lot of poker and skat, but just for fun. Alfred and me are not going to lose our 12 pounds per fortnight cash-in-hand. Labourers get less – 8 pounds – which they can afford to lose even less than us carpenters and electricians. A lot of men gamble on a dice game they call 'in-out'. It's often run by gamblers who come up from Cooma together with their standover men (their enforcers need to be pretty tough because the men here certainly are!) We also get men coming up trying to sell us suits and clothes. Strip-heaters are very popular, even though we are supposed not to use them.

Many of the men get drunk most nights and we hear a lot of fighting. The noise is hard not to hear as everything is otherwise so quiet at night, especially when the men go off to a dance, which also usually ends up in a fight, and usually about women. At the last one, even the local policeman – they call them 'coppers' – got involved too! They said they had a great time.

During the day though there are a lot of bird sounds that are very different to what we are used to and there is a bird that sounds like it is laughing. It is called a Kookaburra. You say it like 'Kuckabahrer'.

I have been told I will be going to a place called Guthega when we have finished putting up the barracks here. It is about six kilometres away from Island Bend and word has it the food there is much better. It's interesting – they say Island Bend will not exist in years to come as it is a construction town we are building just for the Snowy Mountains Scheme. They say it might even be under water when the area is finally flooded.

Australia is such a big country. There's so much land that has no one living on it – no fences, no fields – it is hard for me to come to grips with.

I have just realised I haven't really told you about the Snowy Mountains Scheme *itself, so you can tell the girls and your family. It's basically an enormous engineering project to use the water in the Snowy Mountains, where there are several big lakes, to generate electricity for New South Wales and Victoria (two of the Australian States), and for the Australian Capital Territory, which is where the Australian capital city, Canberra, is. The water is also going to be used to irrigate the land to the west, where there is often drought. To do all this they have to stop it flowing away down the Snowy River and divert it into the Murrumbidgee river (what a name!) and the Murray river. Of course they will have to build lots of dams and power stations (they are planning 16 dams and seven power stations). And also many kilometres of tunnels and aqueducts. As I said, our job is to build the places where the builders will live.*

I thought the Westwall was big but the Snowy is enormous! They say it will be the most complex reservoir-hydro scheme in the world. It is certainly the biggest project I have ever seen. And we only get to see a bit of it! They say it will cover more than three thousand square miles. I guess that might not mean much to you but I hope I can bring you here when you come to Australia. You will have to see it with your own eyes so you can see the enormity of it.

Can you believe the name "Murrumbidgee"? Isn't that a funny name? They say it's aboriginal. I've already heard lots of funny aboriginal names in Australia. We will have to find out what they mean. I asked one of the Australian men on site what Murrumbidgee means and he said he thought it was the aboriginal word for 'big water' in the Wiradjuri language. Well, it certainly is BIG!

Well 'my little wife', I love you. Do not forget that ever! It is so hard not having you to hold in my arms but I keep telling myself not long now. I do not have much more news.

Yours forever Martin xoxox Give the girls lots of hugs and kisses for me too.

P.S. Remember what I told you about Rudi!

they started to clear away a flat space for us to build on

Snowies bulldozers clearing and grading ground for the barracks.

places where the builders will live

Outside one of the *Snowy Mountain Scheme* huts they constructed, Martin and his mates demonstrate why they're called *the Snowy Mountains*. Martin is second from left, Rolf third.

Chapter 36

1951 – *Aqueduct*

A nd guess what? The Snowy Mountains Scheme is SOOO BIIIG. Daddy says it covers thousands and thousands of miles and will have 80 kilometres of aqueducts."

"What is an agwa duck Mummy?" Renate was puzzled at this new creature.

"Well, it is a very special Australian duck that says *agwa! agwa! agwa!*"

The ducks had fired Renate's imagination. "How come they have so many ducks in one place where Daddy is? How do they agwa with their heads under water? Can we see the agwa ducks too?"

"We'll look really hard when we get to Australia to find them, OK? I know what! Let's sing the agwa duck song!

The new version of the old German nursery rhyme sounded much more fun:

> *Alle meine Agwa-Entchen schwimmen auf dem See,*
> All my agwa ducklings are swimming in the pond …

> *Schwimmen auf dem See,*
> Swimming in the pond …

> *Köpfchen in das Wasser,*
> Tiny heads into the water …

> *Schwänzchen in die Höh'.*
> Tiny tails into the air.

> Agwa! Agwa! Agwa!

After a couple more choruses, they got back to the letter. Leni's fingers were all thumbs as she opened the letter again. She read it out excitedly, like a story.

"Daddy says he is missing you all so much. I know! Why don't you sit down and draw him a lovely picture and I will put it in with my letter to him. It will make him very happy." Of course the picture's subject was a foregone conclusion.

"I will draw Daddy a picture of an agwa duck."

****

My darling wonderful husband who I love and miss so so so much,

Thank you for your lovely letter. I read it to the girls and Renate wanted to know what an agwa duck was (she meant 'aqueduct') so we had a bit of fun with that. She has drawn you a lovely picture which is on the piece of paper enclosed. This is to help you with your agwa duck spotting! Of course Erika had to draw one too. Not sure the resemblance to a duck is very clear, especially the six legs, but anyway.

Renate is growing up so quickly and seems to be developing an interesting sense of humour. I am busting to tell you what she got up to last week, I can still hardly believe it. She was outside Frau Schneider's house when a man selling cheap tools came by wanting to see Herr Schneider. He thought Renate was one of their children and he asked "Is your Dad home?" She said "Yes he's around the back, I'll get him for you, but you will have to yell at him because he is really deaf." Then she ran around the back and said to Herr Schneider "There's a man out front who wants to see you but he's very deaf, so you will have to yell at him to make him understand you."

Renate and the Schneider children killed themselves laughing as they watched the two men screaming at each other. I went out to see what all the commotion was about and so did Frau Schneider, and when she asked her husband why he was screaming he told her the man was deaf and the man said no, you are deaf, and they both looked at Renate who was very sheepish by this time. I did not know if I should laugh or cry, and then everyone saw the joke and started to laugh so it was OK.

Please do not worry about Rudi – he is just a lovely man. He has not tried anything funny and he has been great for the girls and me. Every

210

weekend since he first started coming around we have been somewhere different with him in his lovely car. He is so good to the girls and they just love having him come to visit. I told you about the zoo visit in my last letter. We have been on picnics and drives to the countryside with lovely lunches. It is really nice for me and the girls.

I received mail from Mariaweiler and my three sisters there are hoping I will spend at least a fortnight with each of them before I leave for Australia.

It is now three months since you left and I have not heard anything about our trip over. Have you heard any news? Your letter said we would be allowed to come over after about six months, so wouldn't they have to give us at least three weeks to a month's notice? Can you ask? I miss you so much. Sorry, darling, I am not trying to make it harder for you; I just want to be with you as soon as possible.

I love you

Yours as always Leni xoxoxo

PS don't tread on any agwa ducks.

PPS second thoughts – an agwa duck or two might make a nice change from mutton for breakfast.

Chapter 37

November 1951 – *Short 'n Curly*

Goot Day Bob. I wass wondering when can I bring my vife to Aushtralia? She asks in her latest letter how much longer it vill be so I thought I would come and ask you, seeing ass how you're the foreman."

G'day Martin. Mate, how long have you been here now? It usually takes at least six months and then they will write to her and give her all the details. I can ask for you if you like. How long is it now since you arrived?"

"Four months almost."

"No mate, it is pointless me asking anyone until you have been here at least six months. Those are the rules!"

"Oh, so, I cannot expect them any time before six months?"

"'S right mate. Some blokes are here for more than a year before their family gets out to join them. You gotta be patient. Ask me again in another three months if you haven't heard anything by then."

"OK, Bob, I vill do that."

"Whoopeeeee!!!" Something flashed by the window. They rushed outside to catch a glimpse of a wildly gesticulating Rolf Stelzer careening down the snowy slope behind the hut on a piece of cladding serving as a primitive snowboard.

There was a brief pause before a loud *splash*! indicating that Stelzer and snowboard had hit the river at the bottom of the slope. Martin and Bob thought they had never seen anyone move quite so fast, as Rolf scrambled out of the water and raced back up the hill grinning all over his face.

"Couldn't resist having a go – next time I'll put some brakes or steering on it!"

"Better dry off mate, before you catch your death", Martin advised before turning back to Bob. "By the way, I was going to ask you. You know how Phil reads the papers to us – it seems there's been a lot recently about us Snowy Mountain Scheme workers. It seems three Germans have made a real fuss about the working conditions at

Perisher. It was written that one felt they had better conditions during the war in Russia than they have here in Australia. They were told to go to Perisher and apparently told the bosses where they can stuff it. All three of them are saying that they would rather work their passage back to Germany than go to Perisher."

"That's probably not a wise move, given the contract they signed. They might very well soon find themselves on the way back to Germany."

"Yes, that's another thing he read out to us. Some people are questioning whether the contracts foreign workers signed are legal. I think they were saying that contracts should have said what the wage and employment conditions were. Some of the men reckon it's not fair we have to pay back our travel costs from Germany to Australia as well – it means we're actually getting paid too little for the work we do. And is it true our employment can be cancelled whenever the bosses feel like it, but not the other way round? They say there's nothing in the agreement that stops them from doing that. The blokes were wondering whether it would be a good idea to go and see the Chief Magistrate, Mr. Dawkins. You know, the man who has been criticising the contracts a lot in the papers."

"Martin, be careful. My advice would be for you to pull your horns in a bit. At the moment, they have you by the short and curlies."

"What curly horns? Is this your Ozzie shlang again?"

"It means you don't have much of a choice in the matter. The contracts are harsh, yes, but you wouldn't have got the jobs if you hadn't signed them in the first place. You can't win. And don't forget it's all too easy for the Government to suddenly remember whose side you were on in the war."

Martin heard again in Bob's words his dad's advice before he went to the Westwall: keep your counsel in matters you disagree with. He had always done so. He knew he had a reputation among his workmates of being a closed book: no-one ever knew what he was really thinking and that was how he preferred it. Thoughtfully, he turned to go back to his hut.

The phone suddenly rang from inside Bob's hut and he called Martin back. "That was the Cooma Police Station. They've just arrested Willi Schmitz for using indecent language to the lady in the hardware store. Strange, cos I wouldn't have thought his English was good enough for that. Your English is pretty good Martin – can you go down and do some translating? Perhaps sort things out?

****

Dear Leni,

I miss you so much but we are more than half way through our separation now and will be together soon. I did go and speak to my 'mate' Bob (everyone is a 'mate' in Australia), and asked if he could find out how much longer it will be before they have accommodation for you and the girls. He promised me he would find out, so I will write as soon as I hear anything.

People are getting really upset by the fact that our contracts do not mention anything regarding the treatment of married employees. They say that some sort of financial arrangements should have been made for the maintenance of the families staying in Germany. And there's the journey back to Germany too, if anyone decides they want to return. That has to be paid by the employee. How wonderful it would be if we did not have to pay for our fares over. I am keeping my fingers crossed. That money would give us a lovely little nest-egg to start our new life here once the contract runs out.

Well, we are all interested to see what happens of course. I will tell you next time I write, especially about the complaints we are hearing from some of the men about the living conditions here. I think they are probably a bit on the soft side and have not experienced the war in Russia without adequate winter protection like I have. It is now getting very cold, especially at night, and we are only allowed kerosene heaters in the huts. They are not desperately effective, so most of us still sleep in our day clothes. As I wrote before, some of us use strip-heaters, which we are legally not supposed to as they are considered a fire hazard. But actually the kero heaters can also be dangerous. Just last week an Irish bloke had one on all night in his hut after he had closed all the windows and filled-in all the gaps in the walls with snow to keep warm. They found him the next morning dead and coloured all yellow, poisoned by the fumes after his heater had gone out.

214

Speaking of heaters, one of the men has just heard from Germany that he has become a father and so last night they were celebrating in the usual way. They were so drunk that they forgot to turn their heaters off and during the night the heaters went out and covered everything in soot. Rolf Stelzer said that when he woke up the next morning he got the shock of his life to see this frightening black face staring at him from the bunk opposite! Not just that, but when he got up and put his foot in his shoe he found something else warm and squishy deposited in it. His mate had been so drunk that he had apparently mistaken it for a toilet and shat in it. Rolf didn't see the funny side of it, but when he told me I nearly doubled up. It took them the whole of the day to get a fire built to warm up enough water to get themselves and all their belongings free of soot, and shit. And they were docked that day's pay.

The plan is to move us around depending on where the work is most urgent. I have been told I am going to Guthega once I finish here at Island Bend. Guthega is supposed to be really, really cold. Listen to me! I seem to have gotten a bit soft myself. It's still nowhere near like the cold the Brandenburgers experienced in Russia.

Leni, your letter has once again caused me great concern. I wish you would not see Rudi anymore. I know you enjoy his company but I cannot help worrying that he may come between us. The girls will start to think he is their Daddy if he keeps coming around all the time. Leni, I know it is selfish of me but I am here so we can all have a new life. I hate the thought that Rudi may take that away from us. I hope I am worrying needlessly.

Your letter did make me laugh about Renate and the agwa ducks and the deaf story. I told all the men I work with about the story of the screaming men. Some of them nearly wet themselves. I still chuckle about it when I think about it. I can just see them yelling at each other and the kids having a good laugh.

Do the girls still remember me? I think Renate will, but I think little Erika might not anymore. At her age they forget so quickly. Do you show them photos of me?

I am still playing chess with Willi, although it is getting harder and harder to live with him as the smell from his socks gets worse and wafts all over the chess-board. Like I said, perhaps it is part of his strategy. In the four months since our arrival he has washed the one pair of socks four times!! Hard to believe. There are now brothels and pubs being established for all the single men but I must admit at the end of a hard day I am happy just to relax and read or play chess or cards with the others.

What I wouldn't give now even for a weekly bath like we had on the farm when I was growing up. Remember I told you how every Saturday we took our tin bath to the wash house? Each of the four families in the house got one hour. Everyone filled the tin bath with their own hot water heated in their own big copper and carried it the 30 meters to the washhouse. As youngest member of the family I got to go first, then more water was added, then it was the second youngest's turn. Mum and Dad came last. I don't think they would have got all that clean in the dirty water that was left, but I can still remember how lovely it was to sit in a warm bath. On second thoughts I do not think I would want to take turns in a bath with Willi Bachus. Maybe one day we will have our own bath. Now that is something to aim for!

I have a few good friends here. As well as Alfred who I met on the ship, there is Rolf Stelzer of course, and Willi Schmitz. I had to go and get Willi out of jail the other day. Turns out he had gone into town to buy a new three-edged file. His English isn't so good so he asked the lady in the hardware store for it in German – you know: 'Dreikantfeile'. Well, 'Feile' is the same as the English word 'file', but 'drei' sounds like 'dry' and 'kant' sounds unfortunately like a very rude English word 'cunt'. So anyway she thought he was asking her whether she had desiccated private parts, and called the police. I explained it all to them and they let him go. Willi now has an extra word in his vocabulary.

Anyway, my good friends have all been in the war and they are all waiting for their families to come to Australia. Maybe we can become friends with them and you will have some German wives to talk to until you learn to speak Australian. They are all nice people so I am sure their wives would be nice too.

I love you. Look after yourself and the girls.

Yours always, Martin.

xoxoxo

Chapter 38

1952 – *Roof*

My darling Martin,

I hope you are well and still missing us as much as we miss you. I thought it best not to wait for your letter, but get something off to you to let you know what is happening at home. I have some news!!

On Tuesday last week after we had all gone to bed the wind got up something dreadful and started to howl, then the shed started to shake and rattle. We had a terrible storm, like a tornado. The thunder was so loud it made the girls scream. Then came the hail stones – as big as plums. The shed roof was torn off. Just like that – gone! And the hail came in of course. I grabbed the girls and their feather-beds and we ran next door to Mrs Schneider, whose roof must have been more secure. It felt like she lived miles away with the wind howling and tearing at us. I had to carry Erika and hung onto Renate's hand to make sure the wind did not blow her away too. I was so scared, it was awful.

We were soaked to the skin but Mrs Schneider helped me dry the girls and dress them in some of her children's clothes. As you know there is not much room in their shed either, so we just sat on the floor waiting for daylight. The next day I went to see the foreman on the building site and he said they would replace the roof as soon as they could, but in the meantime he would find some temporary housing for us – though it's difficult to think of something more temporary than what we have, or rather had, at the moment.

Rudi met me on the way to see your foreman and as he is the boss he said he would organise something as soon as humanly possible. He offered to move us into his house until that happened but I said no! I don't think that would be right, and anyway I have decided to go home to Düren and see my sisters before we depart for Australia. Then we will only need to stay in the shed for a few days before the boat leaves.

The girls are slowly getting over the shock; I think they were scared more than anything. Renate kept crying "I want my Daddy, I want my Daddy!" Australia must be better than this.

Do you have any news on a date for our departure yet?

Well Martin, my darling, I will write from Düren and let you know how we are and how the family is.

Lots and lots of love

Yours always and forever,

Leni xoxoxoxox

****

When Leni got back with the girls from her family visit to Düren she found Rudi had organised the repair of their shed. Finally – finally! – Rudi tried it on, suggesting a sexual reward from Leni for all his kindness. That made her very annoyed.

"Look, Rudi, I've always been honest and upfront with you. I hoped you understood I love Martin – I've never given you any reason to think otherwise, have I? I really enjoy your company, and you must know the girls do too. But I've never ever led you to believe that there was a romantic element to our relationship. So please stop."

"I'm sorry Leni. Your Martin is a very lucky man." That was the last they ever saw of Rudi.

****

My darling Martin,

Guess what? We'll soon be seeing each other again. I am so excited. So are the girls of course. The letter came this morning. They've arranged accommodation for us in a place called Bonegilla. *I can't find it on the map, but I'm hoping you'll be meeting us at the*

219

Melbourne harbour when the ship comes in, and we can travel there together, wherever it is. I can hardly wait.

Our ship's called the Anna Salen. They say we will be among 1500 European immigrants bound for Australia on that one ship. Can you believe it? But the important thing is when we are getting there: 30th March is the day! What a day that will be for us all! 1952 will always be an important year for us to look back on.

We are only allowed one medium-sized suitcase per person. That doesn't seem very much for such a big change in one's life. But on the other hand we don't have much anyway. I think that the most important thing to pack will be our down quilts and a few clothes and such. Oh and I will have to bring my mum's cooking pot. I know you think that's silly but that is the only thing I have of hers. And it does cook well!

Renate has developed pneumonia. You would have thought she would have picked it up in the storm, but it must have been sometime during our visit to the family in Düren. The doctor told me to wrap her very tightly like in a cocoon and then pour cold water on her back to make her take a deep breath. I have done it a few times but she is so uncomfortable. Even with her hands tied tightly at her side she manages to manoeuvre herself up a bit and crane her neck to look out the window at the other kids playing. But it makes her so angry and frustrated and she gets so upset and cries that I have stopped. The doctor did say that I could take her on the ship even if she is still a bit unwell, so I am hoping she will be alright.

Your last letter really worried me. Please do not do anything rash by questioning the validity of your contract. I thought if you complain now about a contract you signed almost twelve months ago they may say "well, bugger-off home then if you are not happy!" The girls and I already have one foot on the boat and I do not want things to go wrong now. We have started down this path and I think we should keep going. So please don't go to see that Mr Dawkins. It is fine for him to make comments and complain – it is not his life that he is putting in jeopardy.

I have lots of news about the family and our friends and neighbours but I will save it until I see you. No more letter-writing!

You were right about Rudi. The man did feel I owed him a 'reward' for fixing our roof shed! And he didn't mean extra potatoes. In the end I told him I would prefer it if he did not come around anymore. He has not been here since.

I love you Martin and am really excited about seeing you and holding you in my arms again.

Yours always and forever,

Leni xoxoxo

Chapter 39

April - May 1952 – *Anna Salen*

The *Anna Salen*, out of Tasmania, had been plagued with problems throughout her various war-time transformations from cargo vessel to aircraft carrier to transport ship. But Leni, embarking in Bremerhaven on April 29th 1952, was prepared to be optimistic standing in front of the old rust-bucket. At least, she observed, there was no shortage of life-boats. Hold on, though – wasn't the excessive number of lifeboats something to worry about?

The deteriorating situation in Egypt – the British garrison at Suez was under attack and there was rioting in Cairo – meant they were unable to take the short cut through the Suez canal. So the journey was to last six weeks, around Africa via Cape Town. Life on board was hectic with two small children to look after on her own. There was very little time to chat and make friends. Most of their days were filled with meals, washing clothes, ensuring the girls didn't fall overboard (the railings were so tempting to climb!), and trying to keep them amused.

One day Renate came to the cabin from playing with the other children. She was struggling to carry a beautiful doll with long shiny black hair that was almost as tall as her.

"Renate, wherever did you get that? You must take it back at once."

"No Mummy, it's all right. The nice officer called Pierre gave it to me. Her name's Princess. Look how beautiful and blue her eyes are and they close when she lies down to sleep and she can walk!! Look you hold one hand and I'll hold her other. See! She walks!! And … and … He said I can keep it. He said you just have to go to his cabin tonight."

"Right. We're taking it straight back right now." The devastation showed on poor little Renate's face.

"But Pierre said I can have Princess. That's not fair Mummy!"

"That's enough of that. You stay here with Erika and I'll take it back. I know which one he is. I'll find him and tell him it is a lovely doll but you cannot keep it and I am certainly not going to meet him in his cabin. End of story, understood?" The door closed firmly behind her.

"Look Erika! Look what I've found! It's mummy's baby-powder tin. Let's pretend it's snowing. I'll go first. Let's surprise Mum. She's always saying how she doesn't like how hot it is. We can tell her it's snowed in our cabin and she will be really happy. Let's make it snow over everything, nice and deep."

"Yaaah!! Loooooooooook! It's snowwwwiiinnnng!! Atchoo! Atchoo!!"

Leni opened the cabin door on a blizzard of baby powder. "Mum! Mum! Look! We've made it snow in the cabin. Mum! Mum! … Don't cry Mum."

Leni sat on the bed contemplating through her sobs the mountains of baby powder. The children had done a thorough job. It had been a very big tin. It was over everything. The girls hugged her, not understanding her sudden tears. But there was nothing for it. The mess had to be cleaned up. She pulled herself together, got up, and went to fetch a shovel, broom, bucket and scrubbing brush.

The powder hung in the air. Renate coughed all night.

"Come on, I am taking you to the doctor. Maybe your pneumonia has come back. Cough, cough, cough, all night long. I can't cope with another night like this!"

"Now Renate, open your little mouth nice and wide, so I can have a look at your throat".

Renate, previous experience still fresh in mind of being prodded and poked and wrapped up like a cocoon with cold water poured on her back, didn't like doctors. She eyed the finger approaching her mouth, computing the right moment. It arrived. Lunging forward she bit down hard. It had the desired effect.

Leni was on the receiving end of the doctor's fury, who found himself in the novel position of having to stitch himself up. The chances were now slim that this family could hope for any more medical treatment on board. The baby powder and finger biting had combined to make *sparing the rod* a non-existent part of Leni's philosophy, and, back in the cabin, Renate received a real thrashing with a wooden coat hanger. Sitting-down was painful for several days.

In the end, Leni could hardly wait to leave the ship; the trip had rather quickly turned into a nightmare. While others called out enthusiastically about seeing whales and dolphins, all Leni saw were two little girls and all the unending worries associated with them.

no shortage of life-boats

Stacks of life boats on the *Anna Salen* providing initial reassurance against the heavy rusting at its waterline.

all Leni saw

All eyes in the prow of the *Anna Salen* scan the horizon, perhaps for the first view of Australia. All eyes, that is, except Leni's. Standing on the right, she holds Erika and doll, and looks determinedly in the opposite direction, perhaps towards Germany and home. The little girl grinning cheekily at top right is Renate.

Chapter 40

March 1952 – *Confiscation*

But all bad things also come to an end, and, on March 30th 1952, Melbourne at last came into sight. The ship slowly docked and people finally started to get off. Leni struggled down the gangway with two of the suitcases and Renate dragged the other. So this was it! The New Country! Everywhere there were men, woman and children greeting each other, hugging, kissing, and squeals of delight and crying. The noise and the energy made Leni think all it needed was balloons and streamers. It felt like a gigantic party. That is until she could not find Martin anywhere.

She scanned the crowd but he was not there. She and the girls stood beside their three suitcases in the sun and waited and waited as the crowds started to leave the wharf.

"Renate you wait here with our suitcases and keep an eye on Erika. Make sure she doesn't wander off. I'm going to see if I can find your dad. He should have been here by now. He's probably been held up somewhere. This is such a biiiiiig place isn't it!" After what seemed a long time to Renate, she came back, but still with no Martin. She put on a brave face.

"Right, I think it's best we go through customs. Dad might be waiting on the other side. Can't think why, though, as the others seem to have been allowed through to meet their relatives."

The customs officer made a gesture for them to open their suitcases.

"What are these?" He held up one of the eiderdown quilts.

"*Ja, Ich versteh' nicht – Das is' mein Federbett, das ich mitgebracht hab' aus Deutschland. Mein Mann hat gesagt, es wird kalt hier im Winter.*"

"Hey, Wolf, what's she going on about?" He called to the translator nearby.

"She's saying she doesn't understand you. That's her doona. It's filled with eiderdown. She's brought it with her to keep warm in winter."

"I see. Sorry love, you are not allowed to bring anything into Australia that has animal products in it. I will have to confiscate them. You will have to use blankets like all us other Australians."

His mate translated: "*Er sagt, man darf solche Federbetter nicht reinbringen. Er muss sie beschlagnehmen.*"

Leni burst into tears again. She could not believe it. It wasn't as if they had been able to bring lots with them. They were the three things – apart from her cooking pot of course – that they had especially chosen to bring. They were so snug and warm in winter. However would they sleep without one?

They dejectedly carried the by now rather redundant empty suitcases towards the exit. But wait! There was Martin in the distance running towards them! As he saw them he started waving madly. He gave her a biiiig looooong squeeze. He saw she was crying.

"Leni, I am so sorry. I had to hitch-hike to Goulburn to get the Melbourne train. I thought I left plenty of time but not one bastard picked me up for hours. I feel as if I've walked to Melbourne. Hey, please don't cry, we are all together again now."

"But the customs guards have taken our feather beds! You know how much I love my feather bed. All we had in the world was in those three suitcases, and now two are empty. All I have left is a few clothes and mum's cooking pot. And how will we cope in the cold weather without a feather bed? You said it got very cold where we are going."

"Leni this is the land of the sheep! They have lovely woollen blankets here, so don't be upset. We'll soon get some more stuff. We are all together again, that's the main thing."

"Well I hope you're right. You know those last six weeks on the ship have just drained all my energy and I am exhausted. The girls have been such a handful on my own. Well, OK, OK. We will be OK now."

"I've booked a nice hotel room for tonight. It's not far from here, we can walk. Tomorrow morning we catch the train to Bonegilla!"

"Where?"

"Boo-nee-gill-laah. It's a camp where all the new migrants stay until they find somewhere more permanent. You'll learn English there and all sorts of things."

Erika took one look at the hotel room, and Martin, and burst into tears.

"Tell uncle to leave our room. I don't want uncle in our room. Mummy tell uncle to leave our room, I don't want uncle in our room." She became hysterical. Martin became upset.

"What's with this uncle thing? I guess she thinks Rudi is her real dad? I knew this would happen. I *knew* this would happen. The thought of it happening has made me almost sick."

"For heaven's sake Martin! Erika's not seen you for nearly a year. She's only two years old. She's lived half her life without you – every man is an uncle to her. If you say one more word, I will pack up and find a hotel to stay in until I can get a return fare to Germany! What a miserable way to start our new life together!"

Martin set his mouth in a tight line that said he would not open it again, but she could see he was not happy. Nothing they did or said would stop Erika from crying. What with the feather beds it had not altogether been the start she had hoped for.

Finally Erika fell into an exhausted sleep, broken only by regular little hiccoughs. The three of them followed.

When Martin woke he just looked at Leni and the children. It was wonderful to have them with him at last; this is what he had been thinking of in the cold of the Snowies, all the time he was separated from them. Leni woke to see him watching her.

"Sorry for the miserable start to our new life, but I promise it will get better."

They discovered that they were not too exhausted to make love. Then they talked, made love again, slept a little, and the Australian sun had risen on a new Melbourne day.

It was not a long walk back to the pier from which the train would leave, where they found many migrants already waiting (their battered suitcases were a giveaway). Martin, who had to get back to work, found places for them on the train. After he had waived a teary Leni off, he walked to Flinders Street Station to get the train back to Goulburn, after which there was the long hitch south again down to the Snowies. He couldn't afford to be late; they might send him back and make him repay all the fares.

One night together after ten months apart, and now apart again for God knows how long. Well, perhaps only for a few weeks. Perhaps we can find a place for them closer to me in the Snowy Mountains.

Chapter 41

April 1952 – *Middle of Nowhere*

The journey to Bonegilla took all day. It was soooooooo slow. They stopped in the middle of the country for half an hour at a time where they were offered, at the side of the track and on tables taken from the train, a strange repast of baked beans on toast. Each time they knew they had *not* arrived because they could see no station, no houses. The fifth stop, towards dusk, at first seemed no different. Again no houses, no station; just a paddock with long grass. But then suddenly a German voice over a loudspeaker announced their arrival and told them to get off and board the busses waiting for them. So, they had arrived! They were given a piece of cord and a name tag to hang around their necks. A brief drive through more scrub saw them at the camp.

No-one said it, but everyone was thinking it. *My God, this place is in the middle of nowhere. There is not a tree, not a flower, no greenery of any kind. It's all grey. It looks just like army barracks in an empty, hot, dusty place.* There was even barbed wire all around it reminding Leni of the wire fence they had crawled under when they escaped from Russia-occupied Germany. Near panic set in. *We've come so far to THIS?*

But some assurance then came from the loudspeaker voice telling them to go to a big hut for a welcoming speech and the allocation of their living quarters. That didn't sound quite as bad, and Leni and the kids followed the others to the big hut. Here they were issued eating utensils, crockery and blankets, and then shown by a friendly woman – lots of smiles and encouraging gestures – to the hut they would be staying in for the duration of their 'visit'.

The hut was very long with bunks down both sides for twenty women and children – they had been segregated from the men after their welcome speech. It was very basic: timber-framed, without lining, but with corrugated iron cladding and a low-pitched, gabled roof like the sheds they had left in Germany. Leni spotted a gap between the top of the wall and the roof through which some kind of insects were buzzing in and out. It had now become freezing cold, but

Leni could also imagine how hot it would get in the summer without any insulation. Looking outside through the window next to her bunk, she could just make out the other huts arranged in blocks. She wondered where the toilets and canteen were that they had been told about. She sat down on her bunk, a primitive army affair with a thin straw mattress and springs that squeaked at the slightest movement. Erika and Renate joined her, producing another bout of squeaking.

The Department of Immigration told us Bonegilla was a 'centre' and not a 'camp'. But this is no 'centre'! She tried not to think about the primitive surroundings and focus on what Martin would say. "*You are always so positive Leni! Remember it is only for a short time. Just concentrate on learning English. That will enable you to get a job so that we can be together.*"

Feeling a bit better, and aided by exhaustion, Leni put aside her disappointment. She gave the kids a big hug and told them it was time for bed. No undressing though, as it was cold even with the blanket. Tomorrow was, after all, another day.

****

The train from Melbourne was again desperately slow. Sitting there he kept thinking about leaving Leni and the girls, but also his dreams for their new life together. He knew she was not happy now, but that would surely change once they were together and could find a place of their own. He thought about the optimism he felt now regarding the future and compared the feelings he had when he had been conscripted into Hitler's army. Then everything was out of his control and he did not know if he would survive the war. Now it was different. It depended on him, on them.

Martin managed the hitch-hike from Goulburn to Cooma much easier than the way down, and was able to get a bus to the Snowy. He hit his bunk and fell asleep.

it was very basic

An early photograph capturing the *ennui* around hut 5
at the Bonegilla migrant centre.

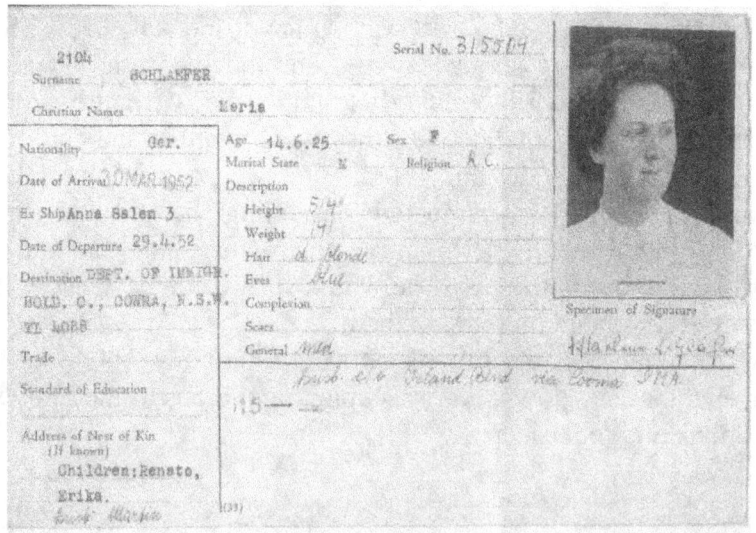

they had arrived

Leni's Bonegilla registration card, with 'blue eyes' officially recorded. However, her
full name – Maria Magdelene – is given as just *Maria*.

Chapter 42

1952 – *Three Blind Mice*

The locals called their village *BONEgilla*, and still do. To the migrants the name was, and still is, *BonnyGILLa*.

By the time Leni arrived at the camp, on April 2nd 1952, Bonegilla had been in existence as a *migrant reception and training centre* for five years. Heeding the post-war imperative of 'populate or perish', the Australian government had originally hoped to replenish male stocks depleted by the recent war by resettling eugenically acceptable Baltic migrants with their impressive 'bearing, physique and industrious character'. For there was still a *White Australia* policy, don't forget. The new influx of '*Beautiful Balts'* would also guard against the perceived threat of the yellow peril to the north.

Bonegilla was where they were all to be turned into true-blue Aussies, well versed in British monarchs and Don Bradman. An optimistic goal, and a naïve one. In the end, of course, from culinary delights to the massive constructions of the Snowy Mountain Scheme, it was the migrants who transformed Australia; not vice versa.

Bonegilla had been taken over, with minimal upgrade, from the army barracks there. By the time Leni arrived though it was no longer a camp but almost a little town, with its own cinema, hospital and hairdresser. But it remained rudimentary – very basic, very … barracky. It would only be years later that trees would provide enough shade from the *So Much Sky* that made such an unforgettable impression on the new European arrivals.

The migrants either regarded it favourably, as the first stage in their new life, or they hated it as worse than the life they thought they had escaped. Leni belonged to the second category. Unlike most of the migrants, she was on her own; two children to care for and no support. Meals were scheduled at 11.30 for babies, 12.00 for toddlers, and 12.30 for adults. Often she missed the 12 o'clock feed and had to give Renate and Erika some of her meal. Another thing she missed was Martin – terribly – but, although letters home to her sister said she would come back if she could, she realised she just had to get on with life with its outdoor latrine pits, communal eating and sleeping, and above all the aggressive, and mostly dangerous, Australian fauna. Spiders, bull-ants, mozzies (she soon learnt that Australian word), snakes, the Kookaburra's demented laugh and oh ... those ... FLIES! All things she and the kids had to get used to.

Heeding the ubiquitous camp slogan, *No English, No Job!* she concentrated her energies on learning English. The teaching was actually not at all bad. Focus was on oral skills and it mixed traditional repetition with role-playing methods of second language teaching that would not appear in Australian schools for some time. It wasn't immediately obvious to the migrants how chanting *Three Blind Mice* to one's prospective employer would help them land a job. But, strangely, it seemed to work, especially the buddy system which paired each *new chum* with a more fluent Australian. Leni gradually found herself able to read and understand a little more of the newspaper they distributed every day. What she could not make out she sought help with. But, as will always be the case, the language was picked up quicker by the children, who found themselves in a strange position of power as primary translators between their parents and the camp officials.

Most of her reading was in the *Positions Vacant* section of the paper, which she scoured for anything she might be able to apply for. Any job that would get her and the girls out of Bonegilla!

****

The advertisement was written in German - that was probably why it had caught her eye. A house keeper in Sydney was wanted. One of the ladies in her hut helped her to reply immediately and she was excited when a train ticket arrived for an interview in Sydney. A one-way ticket: the return was to be given when she showed up. The communal presence of so many women and children together made it easy for Leni to find someone to look after Renate and Erika, and she headed off, full of hope, for Sydney.

It was a big house on Sydney's North Shore. Only a short ride after changing at Sydney Central, across the magnificent harbour bridge, but then still several miles' walk to the house.

"What do you want, go away, I am not buying anything."

The body odour reached her at about the same time as the voice, quickly followed by the sight of the enormous nose as its owner looked up from his stooped posture.

Slow and deliberate now: *three ... blind ... mice ...* as she had been taught. And polite: *don't forget to smile.*

"Hello. My name iss Maria Magdelene Schläfer. I haff come for my interview for the position off housekeeper you advertise-ed in the paper."

"Hmm! Come closer. Come closer. Let me look at you. Do you eat garlic? All you wogs eat too much garlic. Let's have a look at your tits."

Leni was unprepared by the Bonegilla English lessons for quite such a barrage, but his attempts to pull up her blouse helped make his intentions perfectly clear.

"*Du Ferkel. Hände weg*! You pig, hands away!"

"Bloody Kraut. Piss off. No tits no job."

Leni turned around and walked off, tucking in her blouse. No job, obviously, and this time not because of lack of English. And no return ticket to Bonegilla. No money for one either. She allowed herself just a little cry as she walked. She had really set her hopes on this job. She just wanted to get away from Bonegilla. God how she hated it! The girls were bored, there was nothing for them to do. The constant fighting between the different nationalities drove her nuts. Every day there was a screaming match between the women over some silly, petty issue. She couldn't take it much longer.

But someone who had made it halfway across the world on their own is not going to be over upset by a big-nosed malodourous arsehole with wandering fingers (she thought that in German of course, not English). Now, wasn't that a police station she passed on the way here?

"Never mind love, we know who you're talking about. You're not the first woman he's tried this on with. Tho' usually he waits till they've been there a few days. You're actually quite lucky you didn't accept the job and bring your kids, come to think of it. Do you want to press charges?"

Leni looked perplexed, unable to understand what exactly in the circumstances needed pressing.

The policeman saw the problem. "Never mind". "We ... give ... you ... ticket ... Bonegilla. Leave ... tomorrow. Tonight ... you ... stay ... hotel ... near ... station. We ... pay. OK?"

almost a little town

Aerial view of *Bonny-GILL-a*, ca.1952

Chapter 43

1952 – *Cobweb-free*

As it turned out, Leni's dislike of Bonegilla was soon remedied. She was only back a few days when she was summoned to the administration office. They told her she and the children had been there for over a month, so they would have to be relocated to a place called Cowra. People were not allowed to stay too long in Bonegilla. So Leni took the two children and a lot of relief on a train heading north, for a new camp in Cowra.

Cowra was an improvement on Bonegilla; much smaller, with only 150 women and their children. Still the same old huts freezing from their generous ventilation, but what was this? A room for themselves! A small space with just two beds and a cot, much smaller than the Bremen shed. Leni's determination to find a job made the surroundings feel temporary. She started scanning the papers the day after their arrival.

"Muswellbrook. Household help wanted on farm. General cleaning and cooking."

The reply came too quickly for her to dwell on her culinary shortcomings, asking her to go for a job interview. It wasn't a very long way from Cowra to the Upper Hunter Region of New South Wales – about four hours – but after her last experience, Leni did not want to go alone. She telegrammed Martin, who hitch-hiked up from Cooma, and they took the bus to Muswellbrook to be interviewed by the farmer's wife. They left the two girls with a woman Leni had befriended.

They had no trouble finding the place. It looked like a hotel or boarding house it was so big. A short, round lady with an apron opened the door, her grey hair tied in a ponytail, wisps of which had escaped and framed her face. Her soft grey eyes looked tired, the bags under them emphasising the tiredness.

"Hello, can I help you?"

"Yes, Goot dai. My name iss Leni and this iss my husband Martin. I haff come for the job interview."

"Oh, g'day love, come in. I'm Mary. I hope you found my little guest house without too much trouble. Would yous like a cuppa?"

"Sorry, what iss a cubba please?"

Mary laughed and explained, then went to get the tea.

The room had a comfortable feel about it, very calming and homely. Water-colour pictures hung on the wall. Soft lovely subdued hues – in one, horses foaming at the mouth raced through a green field; in the other a river bordered with willows – both picked up the dark green colour of the heavy curtains. A velveteen sofa, two one-seater lounge chairs of a floral material exploding in green leaves and white, pink and black flowers. In all, more sumptuous than they had experienced since before the war. But there was nothing personal. Not one picture of family.

The silver tray, silver teapot, silver sugar and milk containers enhanced the feeling of luxury. Leni noticed the little net on the milk container, held in place by coloured beads at its edge. No flies would penetrate there. In the delicate bone china she recognised the kind of crockery her mum reserved for visitors.

"It's like this. I live here in town and run the guest house. My husband lives in Muswellbrook and runs the farm. We need someone who can clean and cook for all the farm hands. It's a pretty big farm, though. Wool mostly, but we breed horses too. You'll have your own room, of course. Interested? I'll drive you out and show you the farm if you are."

"Triffic!" Leni smiled at being able to put a recently learned word to good use. It was lost on Martin.

"I really need to find work. I'm at the migration camp in Cowra with my two daughters. Martin here's working on the Snowy Mountains Scheme, you know? Near Cooma, and he still hass to work there for some time."

The drive in the jeep took them about 30 minutes along a dusty track. Mary had to get out three times to unlock and open big gates. Martin got out after the first one and shut it after Mary had driven through. A clump of trees became visible, revealing yet another large house. This one had three dogs tied to stakes guarding the entrance. They barked furiously until Mary yelled "Shuddup you bloody mongrels!"

The farm eclipsed anything Martin had seen during his childhood. Vast, fenced-off fields as far as the eye could see full of horses, and separate paddocks full of sheep. There were many sheds – huge sheds – which must be where the shearing was done. But the lasting impression for both was of one huge dust bowl. The roads were dirt; the grounds around the farm were dirt; and any disturbance by people or vehicles created great clouds of dust. And this was in Autumn.

Mary led them inside and went to find 'hubby'. They stood in the furnitureless vestibule, and Leni had a glimpse into what looked like a lounge room on their right. Unbelievably, given the temperature, several large logs were burning away in a big fireplace. The occasional crack, and the smoky smell, reminded them of fires back home. Furniture was sparse and to Leni's eye the plain wooden floor looked like it could do with a really really good wash.

Hubby turned out to be Bill. Informal introductions were followed by a move to a huge kitchen. Forgetting for the moment that her culinary skills were somewhat limited, Leni let herself be inspired by its size. *This looks pretty good. I can see myself cooking some nice meals here*. She turned encouragingly to Martin, for whom the kitchen's size appeared to make no difference one way or the other.

"I've told hubby I think you'll do just fine. How soon can you start?"

So it was now only a case of how long it would take to retrieve the children from Cowra. Elated to be finally free of camps, she saw Martin off on his hitch back to the Snowy.

Two days later, Leni was shown her room by the farmer. Bill's taciturnity made her nervous, especially in contrast to his wife's former garrulousness. But not as much as his looks. His face reminded her of something made of leather, tanned and wrinkled. You couldn't see his eyes, his eyelids drooped so much. And when he did speak to you he never looked at you. An occasional glimpse of nicotine-stained teeth from the cigarettes which always dangled from his lips. Above all, Leni couldn't take her eyes off his nose, which, perpetually sunburnt, shone a bright red colour like a light-bulb.

Their room was very, very basic. No tables, no chairs; the sole furnishings a double-bed, and a cot for Erika in the corner. So Leni and Renate would sleep together. No wall-paper to mention; just old, yellowed, fly-stained paint. You looked out through the dirty hessian curtains of a single dirty window onto the driveway that led towards town. Looking closer, it wasn't dirt but cobwebs.

But at least it wasn't the camp and at least she would be earning some money.

Leni set the suitcases down to unpack, then realised that there was nothing to unpack them into. Well, they would have to live out of the suitcases.

She gave the girls some tasks to occupy them while she set to washing the floor and cleaning those awful filthy cobweb-encrusted windows. They had in fact been the first thing she noticed on being shown the farm. She would start with the front room; it would make Bill very happy to come home from work and behold all those lovely gleaming cobweb-free windows!

Bill did indeed notice them immediately.

"What in all the fuck have you done? You stupid bitch! We never, ever, clean the fuckin windows. That's how we keep the bloody flies down. It'll take bloody weeks for the spiders to cover them again with their webs. We'll be inundated with bloody flies now. You stupid cow! Never EVER fuckin do that again, you hear me?"

Shocked and more than a little upset, she realised she still had a lot to learn about this new life, this new land. Without the webs she came to understand very quickly the compromise between good old-fashioned cleanliness and physical comfort. Heavens those damned flies were a nuisance. You couldn't keep them out of anything. She kept on looking hopefully at the windows for signs that the spiders had begun their activities again.

Chapter 44

1952 – Ready to Run

Friday night. Dinner had been cooked, washing up done, the girls put to bed. Since Bill had come in from work he seemed to have drunk an awful lot, the bottles piling up during and after dinner. She left him to the booze and went back to her room. Finally she had the time to sit on the bed and write to Martin. Tell him about the flies and the windows.

The voice erupted right from outside her door in a drunken slur. "You fuckin Nazi bitch, cleaning all my fuckin windows! What else did you clean back in Germany? Were you in those concentration camps, cleaning Germany of all its Jews, eh? Maybe I should clean the world of people like you, what d'yer think about that idea, you fuckin Nazi bitch. Bloody Mary, makin you the cook! She doesn't have to eat that slop you serve up. Who ever heard of fuckin soup with raw fuckin eggs! Bloody disgustin! Bloody Mary'll be sending me a fuckin slant eye Nippo next. Let me tell you if you come up with any of that fucking sauerkraut stuff you bloody kraut I'll fuckin stuff it down your throat you bloody Nazi bitch. I'll fuckin kill you, you hear me?"

The prolonged abuse woke the girls. Scared stiff, they both started crying.

"Stop crying now, it's all right. He can't get in, there's a lock on the door. Get up quickly and get dressed – your clothes are all in the suitcase. I'll open the window and if he tries to unlock the door we'll climb out the window and run. OK?"

"Why is he so angry Mummy? Is it because you cleaned the windows?"

"Maybe that's it honey. Don't worry, he'll get tired and stop soon."

A poor estimate. He kept it up, with breaks for alcohol to fuel his anger, for another two hours, the abuse alternating between the Germans, the Japanese, and Mary. Finally the pauses between the swearing got longer and longer. Then silence descended on the house, followed by loud snores coming from the lounge room interspersed with just the occasional inarticulate, but still angry, mutter.

The next morning Leni was exhausted from trying to stay awake all night listening for any noise that might suggest Bill had woken up and was once more coming to direct his rage at her. But in the kitchen it was as if nothing had happened. He ate his breakfast with typical surliness and with a "see yous lunch time" left for the fields. His amnesia encouraged her to imagine that it was a once off.

But it wasn't. Saturday night was an exact repeat with threats and shouting and abuse; Sunday morning again the amnesia. Once – well twice, actually – was enough. Leni described it all in a letter to Martin, asking him with some urgency to help her find somewhere else to stay. She feared for herself and more importantly for the girls.

It turned out to be a weekly thing. The following Friday Bill took her into town to do the shopping and she posted the letter. That night again the abuse, and the threats, followed finally by the snores.

Martin's reply did not raise her spirits. Bill seemed like a hardworking man to him and he could not imagine him hurting a woman and her two children. Leni was probably worrying needlessly. Perhaps she could look for another job if she was not happy? There was still twelve months of his contract to run, and he was a long way away. Basically, there was nothing he could do.

But the suitcases were kept packed and ready to leave at a moment's notice. This might be the night he makes good his threats. Friday night and Saturday night were the nights you sat under the window, hand on the latch, eyes on the door, ready to run.

The threats never materialised. For nine months Leni and the girls held out. During the day it wasn't so bad. She had the cooking and the cleaning to do, and sometimes the girls were allowed to feed the lambs with a bottle. But in the absence of a school the girls usually just played around and often got both in the way and dirty, usually at the same time. Some spare moments were given over to reading to the girls from a couple of old German children's books Leni had brought with her describing in horrendous detail all the bad things that happen to little German children who do not listen to their parents. But two books do not go a long way and the girls soon knew their grisly contents by heart. So well in fact that she started believing they could read. Open any page and Renate would look at it and repeat the text word for word. When Martin came down she proudly showed off Renate's skill. Ever the sceptic, Martin tested his daughter with some of the text he wrote on a separate piece of paper, with predictable results. Everyone had a laugh.

But the weekend nightmares never diminished, and Martin came down only three times. Each time she begged him to take them back with him. An impossibility, he said. The men no longer lived in tents and had been allocated barracks, but they were men-only, with nowhere for a woman to stay, let alone two children.

At last, she made up her mind. She couldn't take it anymore; she would have to pack up, borrow money and take the girls back to Germany. She had become a nervous wreck, and it was not good for the girls to be scared out of their wits each week. As often, the woman's lot had been much the tougher. She had drawn the short straw. She had had to stay behind looking after two little children, then sheppard them half way across the world, and *then* put up with all the subsequent difficulties while Martin had blithely carried on with none of the responsibilities she had to shoulder. Martin's third visit degenerated very quickly into a fight when Leni told him her intentions. She was unreasonable; he an arsehole. UNREASONABLE. ARSEHOLE. Then a third hysterical voice joined the crescendo.

"Mama, Papa! Renate's in the paddock with the horses, the wild ones Uncle Bill said we mustn't go near."

Unreasonable arseholes forgotten, Martin and Leni rushed out to the brumby paddock. Frightened at her parents' screaming, Renate had sought shelter with the horses, specifically in the dirt, between the sturdy legs of a big powerful-looking chestnut stallion.

"Don't scream Leni, that'll frighten the horse. If he rears up she'll get kicked and that will be the end of her. Renate, honey, we were all going to have some lemonade. Now, don't frighten the horsey, just crawl out very slowly from under him and then we can go for that lemonade. Nice and slowly mind, nice and slowly!"

"No Papa, you and Mama are fighting. I want to stay here. He is a nice horsey." By way of demonstration she reached up and tickled the brumby's tummy. His shiny coat shivered and his muscles rippled but he appeared to like it. So she did it again. This time he started shifting his legs.

"Please Renate, I promise we won't fight any more; just come out really slowly for Mama."

Perhaps convinced by the tears of fright streaming down her mum's face, Renate started crawling out from under the horse, giggling when a couple of other horses helped her on the way with a nuzzle on the back.

Martin picked her up and gave her a bear-hug, his guilt helping suppress the urge to yell at her for going into the paddock.

"*Meine Grosse,* my big girl, what would we do if something happened to my big girl?"

Then he had a thought.

"You know there is a story in that book about what happened to the little, sorry BIG girl who disobeyed her parents and went into the horse paddock?"

She had always been his big girl ever since she was born and was in fact rather little; she snuggled up to him and wished her Dad could stay with them. She hated that he only stayed with them sometimes.

"No there isn't Papa. You don't know ANYthing!"

Leni picked Erika up, full of praise for coming to get them and saving Renate.

Back in the small room, thirst was quenched with lemonade. And time for some adult reappraisal.

"Look, I'm sorry, I should never have left you here for so long. And I guess I didn't really appreciate the danger. Yes I promise we'll get you away from here and nearer the Snowy. When I get back to camp I'll ask every man I know if they have any idea how we can find a room for you closer to the Snowy. My contract will be finished soon now and then I'll try and find work near you."

"Mama, Erika wants to have a turn sitting under the horsey."

Chapter 45

1953 – *Turnaround*

It was not a hollow threat: this, at least, he understood. It had taken a great deal of courage for Leni to come alone with the girls to Australia and hold out for nine months on the farm. But the same willpower would also take her back.

A lot of asking around turned up a small room for rent in a strangely named place near Canberra called Queanbeyan, only about three hours' drive from the Snowy. Martin took it on the spot. One week later they stood in front of their new home – or at least the house with their room in it – full of hope and glad to be away from farm, flies, spiders, and xenophobic drunks.

But it was not total escape. The Polish man on one side of the house screamed at his wife, and the Italian woman on the other screamed at her husband, her screaming usually accompanied by the sound of hurled cooking utensils. All too reminiscent of the farm, the screaming lasted well after midnight, keeping them awake. The Italian man having an affair with the Polish woman did not contribute to the international entente, and Leni had to gloss the odd unavoidable glimpse of copulation to the girls as 'the man is trying to help the lady feel better'.

One night the fighting seemed worse than usual, with a lot of yelling, banging, and crying. Suddenly, quiet. What a relief! Not for long. Loud sirens, lights flashing outside, running feet, screaming and banging on doors. Her doors too, with policemen doing the banging. Somehow, they got her to understand that the Pole had killed the Italian. Leni told them what she and the girls had seen only the afternoon before. That people could kill out of jealousy was new to her. That pretty much did it. She could not get away fast enough.

It wasn't so difficult to find alternative lodging. From easily struck-up conversations and scouring the papers, Leni quickly found two rooms in a house just a few streets away. This time though she had spent several hours with the girls walking up and down the street to make sure they could hear no screaming neighbours before moving.

The first time he came to view the new lodgings, Martin was straightaway introduced to the neighbours. Hardly neighbours – they shared the same house – Hilda and Frederick Zovko (everyone calls him Fred) also had two daughters. It was not long before the girls were playing with each other, undaunted as kids will be by their linguistic differences.

Hilda suggested "Why don't you leave the girls here with me for a little, whilst you go and have a look at the lodgings? Mine are clearly having a great time. I'll bring them to you in about an hour, OK?"

It was a new experience, being able to leave the kids playing happily with someone else.

They were not to know it then, but the innocent games marked a turnaround in their fortunes. Life was still tough, very tough; but it turned out that that was the end of the life-threatening events.

Martin's inspection revealed a single smallish room with a double-bed, which cushions and a blanket cunningly disguised during the day as a sofa. To the left of the sofa-bed was a door leading into a second room not much bigger than a cupboard, offering little space to manoeuvre between its single bed and cot. A small window was framed by a curtain with little red flowers to the right of the main door. You pulled the curtains aside and could look out onto the main street – McQuoid Street (yet another strange name!) There you saw a small shop that sold all the basics like milk and bread. Just under the window a small shelf on which stood their stove – a single gas-powered hotplate. So, meat first, then potatoes, then veggies.

In a flash-back to Bremen, there was no inside water or tap of any kind. You needed to wash or cook? You had to leave the front door, bucket in hand, walk about ten metres down the main road, turn left, go up the driveway about twenty metres and there, at last, was your tap! A small laundry stood next to the tap with a copper tub the families shared according to a roster system. A bit further away, sensibly, was located the dunny, and yes, the dunny-man was a reality, visiting every Thursday to remove the human waste.

For the first time in she couldn't remember when, Leni was happy. Despite its size, this was clearly the best place they had lived in since the war. Not a tin shed; part of a proper house; no roof blowing off. Most importantly no screaming neighbours or angry drunken men.

Leni started to transform the room into something homelier. The milk crates that served as chairs received embroidered floral covers more reminiscent of an exclusive ladies' boudoir. She took an old sheet, cut it into squares, drew on it the little pictures that were to become brightly coloured flowers. Some lace around the edges and voila! She enjoyed that. The embroidery was done every night when the girls were asleep and Martin away.

The embroidery appeared to have little effect on the local rodents, however. On more than one occasion Leni looked up from her handiwork to see another big rat making off with an item of cutlery (whatever would a rat want with a carving knife?). Recalling an effective remedy from the vermin-infested farm of his childhood, Martin broke a glass bottle and stuffed the glass fragments into the various ratholes. The rats disappeared.

It was now time to see to the schooling of Renate, who had turned five back on the Musswellbrook farm. The headmistress looked her up and down.

"Gosh, you're a tall girl for five! I think because of your size we should skip kindergarten and pre-school: you'd look out of place with all the little ones. We'll put you straight into first class, how does that sound?"

Not wanting her daughter to be embarrassed by being the biggest in the class, Leni consented, although size was not so much of an issue as the teasing about Renate's sandwiches made from finest German black bread, and her outlandish German hairdo, with its braids and sausage-like creation on the top.

Some German habits *were* changed, however: Leni's name, for example. According to her new Australian neighbour Marg it sounded a bit unusual. Hearing that *Leni* was an abbreviation from an even more formidable *Maria Magdelene*, Marg suggested a change to the more acceptable *Marlene*. Marg was unaware of the famous precedent, but Leni wasn't: Marlene Dietrich had also derived her stage-name *Marlene* from Marie Magdelene! So that settled it. Leni thereupon became Marlene (though she was happy to remain *Leni* for Martin).

Now they were living closer to his work, Martin hitched up from the Snowies more often. One of the predictable results was another baby. He was happy: he loved babies. Leni was not too sure, wondering how to manage on her own with three.

But soon his turn to look after them came while Leni was in hospital. The immediate neighbours couldn't be more helpful, one taking her to the hospital and one looking after the girls pending Martin's arrival. But not everyone! An offer to take over the washing and ironing was rather spoiled by a request for payment.

"Ten pounds!?" Martin swallowed the Australian building-site response that had formed unbidden in his brain.

"You must be joking, I only get 12 pounds a veek in my pay packet and you vant me to pay you ten pounds to do our laundry?! I vass for six years a soldier and so I am very able of doing my own vashing. I vill manage on my own, thank you."

The door closed.

"*Die spinnt! So was gib's doch gar nich'* – She's got rocks in her head! Would you believe it!"

Yeah, that felt better. Nothing beats venting in one's own language.

The new baby was Marlene Judith. Everyone agreed she was the most beautiful baby they had ever seen, and her parents could see the objectivity of the judgement. Like a doll, her skin a velvet coloured peach; her eyes big and wide and her eyelashes so long they touched her eyebrows (well, almost). She had the cutest little nose; in every way perfect. Except some musical beds was now in order. Baby Marlene into the cot vacated by Erika; Erika and Renate at opposite ends of the same bed.

****

"Marg, I don't know what to do. I'm pregnant again. I haven't told Martin yet. He's coming up this weekend, so I guess I'll tell him then. But heaven knows where we'll put another baby. Marlene is still only nine months. I have her in the room here with me and there'll be even less space with Martin too. There's just no more room for another child."

"Of course there is you silly sausage! What about that little sideboard? Its drawers are just made to fit a baby in. You can embroider a pillow for HIM that will fit in the drawer too. It will be a him this time, right?"

Leni was impressed by Marg's laterally-thought furniture reclassification but was still not sure what sausages had to do with it. "Oh, Marg, Martin wants a son so badly, it is crazy. I am not having any more children after this; I will refuse to have any more. Though that might be a bit difficult as his two years on the Snowies are up and he'll be moving in for good soon. At least he won't be in any more danger of being killed. You read about it in the papers all the time how people are being killed on the roads during the weekend. I often wondered why there are so many murders in Australia."

"*Killed* doesn't mean *murdered*, Marlene; maybe in German it means the same thing but in English it just refers to people who've had accidents, usually car accidents. But anyway you know one thing is clear. It's time he lived with you. There's no way you'll be able to manage four children on your own in these two rooms. You know how even just fetching water is a task. And then heating it on one primus for their baths, that's crazy. Marlene, you must insist he gets a job in Canberra. Queanbeyan would be even better eh?"

"Oh Marg, I thought I told you. He *has* found work in Canberra, with a firm called *Jennings*. They have a lot of Germans working for them, apparently. This'll actually be the last time he'll be hitching up to stay for the weekend."

"Wonderful, I hope he is here for the new baby this time."

Martin was indeed working in Canberra when Peter was born in August 1955. Just as Leni had said, he was predictably thrilled to have a son, although she could not understand why a boy was so different to their three beautiful girls. But she enjoyed his enthusiasm all the same. Except for its extension to a German name.

"No Martin, absolutely not. We are in Australia now. He has to have an *Australian* name, just like I changed mine to an Australian one. You can make *Manfred* his second name if you want."

One member of the family, though, was not happy.

"Mum, please promise me you will not have any more babies. I do not want any more babies Mum. I hate their screaming and I have to look after them all the time. Will you please stop having any more babies, please Mum?"

Surprised a little by the request, Leni gave Renate a big hug. "Honey, I didn't realise you felt like that. Yes, you are right. Four is already too many (don't tell Papa I said so!). I will do what I can not to have any more babies. They will not *always* be babies, you know. You'll see, they'll grow up really soon and you will have lots of fun with them. You know, once upon a time the doctors in Germany said Papa would not be able to make *any* babies *at all!*" *They sure got it wrong about that.*

****

Their first Christmas all together in Australia! A special, expensive, meal to celebrate: pork! (Martin loved pork). It needed a long time to cook on the primus so Leni cooked it the day before. That way, too, they could enjoy it cold in the hot Canberra summer. She covered it well with a tea-towel, leaving it under one of the milk crates overnight to additionally protect it from any wandering hungry fingers.

"Tears? Whatever's wrong now Leni? It's Christmas!"

Leni lifted the milk crate to reveal the beautifully cooked pork crawling with maggots. Not for the first time the Australian flies had spoiled an occasion.

"OK so we've learnt the hard way again. We'll just have to get a fridge. We simply can't leave cooked food out in the open. Let's just have the veggies now with some dry bread and butter and I'll eat you later, how about that?"

Five pounds deposit – close to half a week's wages – secured a second-hand fridge. It was so big that all the other families also took the opportunity to pack their perishables inside. The only problem was, it was turned up so high that everything froze. When they tried to turn it down it didn't work: the next day everything inside had thawed. The vendor assured Martin that all he needed to do was to turn it upside down for the night – that would do the trick.

"Shall ve see whether you would work better upside down? What do you think?" The vendor could see that Martin was not joking. A fully functioning replacement appeared.

Not long after came another acquisition. It was thanks to a big increase in wages from 12 pounds to 20, following a new job with the Canberra concrete construction firm *Civil & Civic*.

There was Martin again, executing a little jig, waving keys in the air, the biggest grin on his face Lenihad seen since the evening of the light-bulbs from the Bremen railway station toilets.

"It's not brand new but it's in really good … knock. Come on let's all go for a drive!"

"It's *nick*, Martin – *really good nick*, but how lovely to have a real car. We can go on picnics, or away on the weekend."

"I never said anything to you Leni, but I was so sick of riding my bike to work or trying to get a lift off someone. I hate having to rely on others, it was embarrassing. Now I can drive myself, thanks to the pay rise. And you know what? When I asked how much it was the dealer said I could pay in instalments. It's called higher purchase. I'll have it paid off in three years."

A car was a big deal. But an even bigger deal than the big brown shiny Oldsmobile – and Martin kept it gleaming – happened about twelve months later. One of Martin's colleagues had just turned down the offer of a two bedroom government house because he had four children. But, it was a *proper* house. It had an inside, fully flushing toilet, a bathroom – with a bath! – a kitchen – with a stove! – a lounge room, and two (count 'em!) separate bedrooms.

"A proper house? With *two* bedrooms? Any way I can put my name up for it?"

"Sure, Martin. I don't see any reason why you shouldn't have it. Come to the office and sign some papers and I'll give you the keys. You're lucky mate. It's yours."

"How can you give Government house to people?"

"Easy mate. *Civil and Civic* get ten percent of the govvies for their contractors as a way of enticing people to come and work in Canberra."

Now this really WAS fantastic news, and triggered an even more exuberant heel-clicking jig when he got home. Leni eyed the keys he was holding above his head suspiciously. A certain degree of concern entered her voice.

"Whatever's up, Martin? I've never seen you this excited. Not *another* new car?"

Chapter 46

1956 – *Cook Pussy!*

No.18 presented a compact, camel-colour face to the quiet street, nestling behind a little front garden through which a cement pathway lead to three steps before the front door. Leni guessed the two mission-brown front windows were bedrooms. Between the metal fences on either side of the house they glimpsed a large back garden, big enough to grow their own vegetables! But most importantly No.18 was a house! Their house. They all tumbled excitedly out of the car eager to explore their new home.

It didn't take long to settle into their new life. In those days the end of the street marked the extent of the northern Canberra suburbs. Immediately beyond lay the Australian bush. Trees to climb, dams to swim in, sheep grazing in-between. Life was pretty idyllic. Fresh air, good food, lots of children for the girls to play with, comfy beds and two happy parents.

One of their favourite outings was when Leni and her new neighbour Thelma took their children clambering up nearby Mount Ainslie to enjoy a picnic lunch, the slowly burgeoning Canberra spread out at their feet.

It turned out that Thelma, to the children's delight, had a new cat. Squealing with excitement they rushed to have a pat, calling out to their mum.

"Mum! Mum! Cook Pussy! Cook Pussy!"

Puss was immediately swept up protectively into Thelma's arms, unsure about the exotic culinary habits of her foreign neighbours.

"You're not cooking my bloody cat!"

A pause of incomprehension, then Leni erupted with laughter.

"No Thelma, it's all right, pussy is safe. They were speaking German: *cook* is just German for *look*. Anyway, Germans do not eat cats. At least not when they are as small as yours."

A second pause of incomprehension while Thelma struggled to interpret the German sense of humour. Then they both laughed, setting off up the mountain.

****

Despite the occasional linguistic hiccoughs, and inevitably helped by their already assimilated children, Martin and Leni had acclimatised rather quickly to the Australian way of life. Truth to tell, this was not difficult for anyone who had known the hardships of their generation, and they were part of the emerging multicultural Australia well before they stood in their best clothes at its citizenship ritual taking an oath to the Queen – the same Queen who was much later to send them her best wishes on their 60th wedding anniversary. Indeed, since one of the roots of modern Australian multiculturalism was the disparate origins of the Snowy Mountain Scheme workforce, it can be said that Martin and Leni were not just a part of New Australia, but a prototype.

To be sure, with four children there never seemed to be enough money to go around and they still had to work hard. Martin was usually employed up to seven days a week helping to build Canberra. Leni worked six out of seven nights, first waitressing and then in a drive-in bottle shop. The two were an effective tag-team, one might say. Later, when her language skills allowed her to pass the necessary language and IQ test, Leni worked in the public service as a clerical assistant (which she loved). Good weather, good food, good schools, a closely-knit family – it made life, well … good.

The next two acquisitions that were to bless Australian families in the late fifties – telephone and television – followed in due course. Mesmerised by the novelty, families gathered just to watch the black-and-white test pattern on the first box in the street. Later, from the front room could often be heard "C'mon ref he hass been doing that all day!" or "No way vass that LBW! The ball pitched outside the leg shtump!" It was Martin venting his displeasure in German-accented Australian at the cricket or footy on the TV. In other words, a typical Ozzie.

****

"This is the RSPCA Canberra, what's the problem?"

"Hallo my name iss Martin Schläfer und there iss a fairy in my garten. He just came into the garten and chased my vife up the stairs, so I put a bucket over him. And some bricks on the bucket. And then a chair on the bricks. Can you come and get him?"

"Sorry mate, what've you got? A fairy??"

"Yess, he hass a long tail and iss hairy. He iss in my garten, under the bucket. It hass frightend my vife. Can you come and get him? Hallo? … Hallo??"

Barely suppressed laughter could be heard at the RSPCA end.

"Sounds like you've been hitting the booze a bit there, mate. This is the *Royal Society for the Prevention of Cruelty to Animals*. We don't handle fairies, hairy or otherwise."

One of Martin's grandsons, Adam, took the phone, also trying very hard not to laugh. Waiting until the RSPCA man had regained some composure, he explained that his grandfather was German and it was actually a ferret rather than a fairy currently held captive under the bucket, bricks and chair.

"OK, NO probs. Actually, yesterday someone rang up to report they had lost a fairy. Put your grandad back on the phone and I'll get his addre … er, second thoughts perhaps you better tell me where he lives."

****

Martin eyed the rooster. The rooster eyed Martin. He held its neck down on the block and slowly lifted up the chopper. The pet rooster had recently become hyper-aggressive, starting to chase Leni around the back-yard and peck her when she wanted to hang up the washing. So, termination time. Only, he couldn't do it, not when it was looking so accusingly at him with those little beady brown eyes. He let it go and went to have a smoke and a think – for the tenth time – about alternative solutions for converting the back-yard pest into an ex-rooster.

Leni stuck her head around the corner. "Heavens Martin – you *still* haven't cut the thing's head off? What's the matter with you? Never mind, I'll get old Grandma Summers down the road to do it and then I'll cook it for dinner." The pensioner-executioner duly appeared, caught the rooster, and deftly broke its neck with one abrupt jerk. Martin was relieved. *We could have done with Grandma Summers in the Brandenburgers.* The rooster had its revenge, kindof: no-one had the heart to eat it when it was served up for dinner. No-one, that is, except Grandma Summers.

****

Leni and Martin did miss the families they had left behind in Germany – of course they did! So they were thrilled to receive – out of the blue and twenty years since they left – two return tickets to Germany paid for by Leni's relatives. They had saved up over the years to pay for the visit.

Martin was even able to return to Wiederitzsch in East Germany to see his remaining brother. He was moved to tears to note that nothing whatsoever had changed: same furniture, same carpets, same table-cloth and cups even! For the stagnation of the East German economy under its soviet-style socialism meant that they had known none of the prosperity of West Germany's rapid post-war *Economic Miracle*.

****

The rest of their story is quickly told. The final stage in their assimilation was an upgrade to a three-bedroom house they brought from the Government – the so-called Australian Dream of home-ownership – together with the regular family barbecues made possible, nay obligatory, by its spacious back yard. On such occasions Martin was usually to be found in shorts and singlet surrounded by the aroma of sausages, onions, steak and prawns, dispensing them to the by now several generations of his family. Sometimes they were even joined by Alfred, who had driven up from the coast with his current wife – but not his sniff, which had strangely disappeared.

It was during one of these gatherings – with Martin using his BBQ tongs to depict how he had stabbed the Ösel sand with his bayonet to search for hidden mines – it occurred to Renate that her dad had started to talk a lot more about his war experiences.

"You know what Dad, I've been thinking. It'd be really good to record all those war experiences you keep on telling us about. And Mum's story too. And what it was really like to migrate here, and the Snowies, and everything. Sure, I can handle another sausage. I could get you both on my cassette recorder. You never know, other people might be interested in hearing the stories too."

Martin gazed for a moment at a place Renate could not see. "Hmm. Goot idea. Go easy on the mustard. Yes, vell, you know the first thing that comes to mind? Walking home from work in Bremen wondering however I vass going to tell your Mum we were off to Australia ..."

their 60th wedding anniversary

Also the time the intrepid couple were interviewed for this book.

Chapter 47

2012 – *Time and Chance*

It was mostly at night, late at night, that he got really agitated. He had to get home. Had to pack his clothes. Pack them neatly on the bed. All ready to go home. It wasn't far to Wiederitzsch. Just down the corridor. Had to be careful of the partisans though. Look out! There was one, behind the sofa! He made a gun with his hand and shot him. Up and down, up and down the deserted corridor, going home … watching out …

****

The old man's face lit up as his wife came in. He did not recognise her, though he knew she was special, somehow.

"Hello Martin. Still that lovely smile. They gave you a nice shave this morning, I see, and you've got your new trousers on! It's good to see they are looking after you."

"Ja. Look at the new light-bulb I got from the toilets at Bremen railway station. Much better than those old candles. I've been thinking, there iss enough space in my room here for a bigger bed and then we can be together again – just until the firm gets us a bigger house. And I can easily build a new table too, and a crib for the baby. What do you think?"

"Martin, what are you going on about? We're not in Bremen now. We're in Canberra. The staff tell me you have been shooting partisans again. And you really must try to remember to speak to the nurses in English. You've been in Australia for sixty years now. They don't understand German here."

The exasperation in her voice upset him and his smile vanished. Who was this woman? He knew, though, that he had to fix that table and the shelf. He struggled painfully to his feet, and wobbled for a minute trying to get his balance. He did remember one foot needed to move first; he just couldn't work out which one it should be. Now, where were his carpenter's tools?

"Martin what are you doing with your walking frame? You know it doesn't go on the table. Sit down again and I'll get you a beer, or a coffee. What do you want?"

A moment of lucidity. "Home. I vant to go home. I don't like it here."

"Yes, Martin, I know. But I can't look after you any more when you go wandering all over the neighbourhood at night in your pyjamas and the police have to bring you home. It's too dangerous for you they said and they're right. And I don't like it here either. Everything's wrong: the bed, the heating, the food … everything. My room here is not nice either, I would much rather go home too."

A lucidity short-lived. "*Ich muss gehen, dem Mann helfen mit dem Ding* – I haff to go and help the man with the thing. He vants me to put in another two things for them over there."

"Hi Marlene! Hi Martin! How's it going?"

"Oh, hello Dawn. I'm glad you've looked in. He does need a change of underwear. He's got a bit smelly again."

"OK. No problems. We'll soon get him clean. Isn't he amazing – ninety-one!!"

The nurse held her breath as she struggled to get him out of his clothes.

"Up with your arm now Martin!" She took hold gently and raised it for him. It was so difficult to do anything for him when he did not seem to understand what she was saying. With the other hand, she removed the intercom from her belt.

"Julie, I can't get Martin to sit down while I remove his soiled undies and pants, he is such a big man still. If I push him onto the seat I am worried he might fall. Any chance of giving a hand? I'm with him in the dementia wing."

The help was there within a couple of minutes and they started again.

"Honesty Julie I do wonder at times how a person can smell so bad." The incontinence nappy and pants were removed, off came shoes and socks, and Martin was positioned on a stool in the shower, not a part of what was happening to him. The only way to remove the smell was water, though even that was hard at times because he kept wanting to get up and get on with those building jobs he said he had to do.

"*Das reicht jetzt. Ich muss gehen, dem Mann helfen mit dem Ding.*"

"What's Martin saying, Marlene?"

"That that's enough, because he's got to go and help the man with the thing. Martin, you really must speak English; they don't understand German. They can't guess what you want. Or point to those lovely translating cards Renate wrote for you with English and German on them. His English was so good once, Julie."

"And how are *you* going Marlene?" Julie looked up from dousing Martin down. "You look quite good – cheeks all nice and rosy!"

"That's because it's always too hot in here, Julie, and most of the time I don't feel well – always out of breath. I wish they'd let me die when I had my last heart attack. You know once we made it on foot over the mountains all the way out of East Germany. Now I can hardly make it to the bathroom."

"Oh Marlene at least you're alive and (nodding at Martin) know what's going on around you."

Tears welled up. "I'm so unhappy. So unhappy. It was OK till two years ago, but it was such a strain living with Martin and his dementia – he sometimes didn't even recognise me. He just sat and stared into space and I had to do everything and I was always so buggered after my heart-attack. Eventually I couldn't even go for a little swim. And then there was the problems with his night-time walkabouts – always 'trying to get home' he said. You know he would walk miles before the police picked him up – yet during the day he couldn't make it even to the letter box! I was beginning to hate him. I was relieved when the doctors said it was too dangerous for him to stay at home any more. When they took him away."

A pause to wipe away the tears. "And the four children don't understand either. Each of them at different times offered to let me stay with them and I did try. But, to be honest, nothing makes me happy anymore. Also none of them could afford to give up work to be with me all day. My quality of life is terrible. I can't do the most basic things for myself. All my life I was so independent, now I need to have help with everything. That's how come I ended up here in the same nursing home as Martin. You know, my room here's smaller than the one we once shared in Germany, just after the war, when we started our life together in just a little tin shed. It's tough to go back to living in just one room, knowing that I'll never go back to my lovely home."

The now clean and dry Martin heard all this, but didn't register it. *Who was this woman? Why was she crying?* He looked at her strangely. Then he gave her a kiss. "*Kommst Du* tomorrow Leni?

"Sure, I'll come tomorrow, Martin."

She waddled off slowly, panting, the pain from her bunions taking her mind briefly off her shortness of breath.

****

The official death certificate nominated heart failure and hospital-induced pneumonia. It had all happened quite quickly, quite unexpectedly: the nurses had assured everyone that day the patient was strong as an ox.

She had died in Renate's arms. Suddenly, after a visit to the bathroom, she had felt faint and leant against the wall gasping "I'm going, I'm going."

The children had taken Martin to see her in the hospital when she was declared dead. They thought he would continually ask after her if he had not seen her for himself – he might wonder why she no longer came to visit him in his room. But within days he had forgotten her death. He would to be sure sometimes ask about 'Mum'. But it was clear he meant his own mum. She used to write such lovely letters to him when he was in Russia.

****

"When did you find him?"

"I didn't. I was watching him on his way up the corridor like he always does, holding on tightly to his walking frame. He just collapsed. He was ninety-one you know. He'll be happy now he's re-united with his wife. Well, wouldn't it be nice if all that religious stuff was true! They say he was a bit of a war hero. Difficult to believe, isn't it, seeing him lying there so frail. I wonder what his life was really like. Anyway, come along, the family needs to be informed."

Chapter 48

2018 – *Final Reckoning*

Martin died in 2012. His wife Leni had died a year before. You will probably have already realised from their photos that their story, *Iron Crossed,* is based solidly in fact.

It is seldom nowadays that one has access to first-hand accounts of dramatic historical incidents by people who actually took part in them, but that is precisely the oral history from which *Iron Crossed* originated. For it derives from extensive tape-recorded interviews with the main characters of Martin and Leni (*aka* Marlene) made by their daughter Renata during 2000. In these recordings Martin and Leni tell their stories, spanning their lives from pre-WWII Hitlerite Germany to post-war multicultural Australia, where, as you have read, they had to face hardships of a different kind – the tough migrant experience of forging a life in a new country.

If you want, you can actually listen to some of the interviews. We have posted several excerpts, with accompanying translation, on the 'Iron Crossed' section of the second author's website: http://philjohnrose.net. There you can hear Martin describing the events leading up to the failed Brandenburger attack on the Estonian Island of Ösel in 1941, where the gliders are forced to circle the island and thus forfeit the element of surprise over the Russians (chapters 13 & 14). You can also hear him describe how he got shot by a Russian sniper in 1943 when adhering to army protocol after the attack on Roslavl airfield (chapter 20). And you can hear him talking about the surrender to the Americans in 1945, where Martin's Alpine Division is told in formal language that they are free of their oath of allegiance to Hitler (chapter 26).

****

We never get to know our parents properly, do we, most of us? Get to understand everything that made them … well, them? They too were young once; they too had hopes. They succeeded, failed; were frustrated, happy, sad. They fell in love – or lust – and out. Did bad things; did good things.

The past is a foreign country where people do things differently (as *The Go-Between* famously begins), and by the time we are old enough to realise that there is more to *mum n dad* than just *mum n dad* it may be too late to ask them "what was it like when …?" and discover their stories.

But, there are foreign countries and there are foreign countries. The gap separating the war generation from those that came after is not just one of increasing time, which might still permit, perhaps, some understanding; it is also a qualitative discontinuity. The experiences of the war generation were so utterly different from our own that we cannot possibly comprehend, even with the help of oral histories like the present book, what the war generation really went through.

For a start, it would be naïve in the extreme to believe that we have, in Martin's and Leni's narratives, a balanced sample of all their experiences. There were several times during the recordings that Martin hesitated and then, with a "I don't want to talk about that", ceased talking. Clearly, some experiences remained too painful to remember or narrate. These they have taken with them to their graves.

There are other indications that the sampling is unbalanced. Martin's narrative, for example, is not short of the odd amusing anecdote. The reader should be aware that this is regarded as a common mechanism for helping the recollection of a traumatic past. We hope it is abundantly clear that Martin's story was anything but fun and games. Never, ever, forget that Leni and Martin belonged to a generation that was cheated, lied to, abused and violently coerced by a brutal, and brutalising, system that brought death to millions. Try not to judge, therefore. Very few of us are Sophie Scholls. You probably have all too good an idea of how *you* would have coped under such a system.

If you are looking for a moral, perhaps the book's real message is an existentialist one. It tells how, once allowed to take responsibility for themselves, Leni and Martin were able to live a full and valuable life, working hard to give their children a future in freedom, in a much better world than they had been born into. That is a kind of heroism, is it not?

****

The fact that this book is anchored in Martin's and Leni's narrative makes it, we think, incumbent upon us to specify the main areas where we have deviated from the content of that narrative. Our main principle was to include stories which we were able to tie-down reasonably well historically, for example Ösel (chapters 13-16), the siege near Orel (chapter 18), the fight with partisans near the Roslavl airfield (chapter 20) or the capture of the American jeep in Italy (chapter 24). Thus we have had to omit a few parts of the narrative, the time and location of which we were not able to determine with sufficient accuracy. For example, Martin's war record which we obtained from the military personnel archives of the government agency in Berlin (*Wehrmachtsauskunftsstelle* http://www.dd-wast.de/en/home.html) is extremely sketchy. It provides information on the units he was assigned to and where his injury was treated, but the dates and localities of his deployment are vague (e.g. 'middle Russia'), and do not allow one to determine exactly where he was and when. His record does not specifically mention his Ösel deployment at all, for example, possibly for reasons of secrecy. According to Martin, following retraining after the Ösel assault he was deployed first to the south of Russia before heading northwards; but we have not been able to ascertain where in the south. Therefore we have described the Orel siege as his first 'Russian' incident. Another episode we have omitted is Martin's participation in the battle around the Velikiye Luki encirclement. (Velikiye Luki is a town about 550 kilometers west of Moscow. The Germans had occupied it in mid-1941, as part of their invasion of Russia. The Russians retook it after an encirclement that took place in the winter of 42-43, but we have no exact dates for Martin's involvement in this.) In April 1943 Martin was awarded an infantry assault badge (*Sturmabzeichen*) which may have related to the Velikiye Luki battle (this award is another thing we have omitted). It is from the Velikiye Luki part of his narrative that we took his description of being fired on by the *Starlinorgel* which we included in the Orel siege story.

The primary oral history source recordings have been checked, and augmented a little, with material from additional research. Of particular use among the voluminous literature on WWII were:

Stephan Zweig's chapter 'Incipit Hitler' in his *Die Welt von Gestern* (1942), Ian Buruma's (2013) *Year Zero*, and Richard Evan's (2003 – 2008) *Third Reich* trilogy. We found two descriptions, both without references, of the first attempted glider landing on Ösel narrated by Martin. The much more detailed one, with a map, is in Tim Lynch's (1988) *Silent Skies – Gliders at War* (pp. 153-155). It agrees well with Martin's narrative except it states that the landing occurred without loss of life. You can hear on the web that Martin contradicts this when he says "Haben wir schon in der Luft Verluste gehabt - we sustained losses even while we were still in the air". Franz Kurovski's (1997) *The Brandenburger Commandos – Germany's Elite Warrior Spies in WWII* also has a short paragraph, but no new information, on the failed Ösel mission (p.116).

Among the historical-fictive literature on the Brandenburgers (so-called *Romane nach Tatsachen*), we found Herbert Kriegsheim's (1958) *Getarnt Getäuscht and doch Getreu* very useful. It is a battalion commander's very readable fact-based account, in the form of a novel, of Brandenburg operations in several theatres, with also a brief paragraph (p.309) on the Ösel failure. We have plundered the book here and there for ideas that obviously preoccupied the writer – for example the moral question of donning your enemy's uniform – and for some details in our narrative, especially the Brandenburger recruiting scene in chapter 11. Will Berthold's (1977) *Division Brandenburg* is another fact-based novel which covers similar ground.

The web also of course has much information on the Brandenburgers (try googling: *Wikipedia Brandenburgers* https://en.wikipedia.org/wiki/Brandenburgers). Apart from the inevitable mystique surrounding their covert 'warrior-spy' operations they have also attracted attention because of accusations of war atrocities (google for example https://de.wikipedia.org/wiki/Brandenburg_(Spezialeinheit)#Kriegsver brechen or https://camp59survivors.wordpress.com/2014/04/20/the-brandenburgers-war-crimes-investigations/. Some of these crimes are associated with the war against the Russian and, later, the Italian partisans, and involved the execution of prisoners: a fact of partisan war practiced by both sides. Martin acknowledges that he did not expect any mercy from the Italian partisans. In narrating his encounter with the partisan group in Italy (chapter 26), where he pedalled for his life on punctured tyres, he said "*wenn sie mich geschappt hätten, die hätten mich ... finished. Die hätten nicht viel gefragt* – if they'd caught me they'd have … end of story. There would have been few questions asked."

On the *Westwall*, where Martin worked as a carpenter to build the *dragon teeth*, we found *Germany's West Wall*, by Neil Short and Chris Taylor (2004), very informative. You can easily find more information by googling *Siegfried Line* or *Westwall*.

The *Bonegilla Reception and Training Centre* described by Marlene is an important part of modern Australia's migrant past (google it on Wikipedia or *Bonegilla Migrant Experience*). Bruce Pennay's (2012) *Sharing Bonegilla Stories* contains some more positive accounts of the place, to balance Leni's; and the current centre's pamphlet *So Much Sky* also repays a read. A small part of the centre is preserved and can still be visited. It's worth it.

Most of the photos for *Iron Crossed* – and also the documents, including the original awards of Martin's 1st and 2nd class Iron Crosses – come from the personal collections of Martin and Leni and their relatives. We have reproduced some photos with permission from the *Bundesarchiv* (German Federal Archives) – who were very quick and efficient in answering our inquiries – and others from the web. We have made every effort to source the other photographs properly, but will be glad to rectify any omissions if notified! Of course, although we have received help from many sources, we alone remain responsible for the content of the book.

As is often the case with oral histories, the amount of recorded material was too great to include every single thing Martin and Leni talked about, and we had to decide what to include and what to leave out. Martin quite often recalled things in considerable detail. For example, he had a lot to say about the *Oberfeldwebel* who led the platoon supposed to take the glider assault troops off Ösel (chapter 14); or the old captain who had a sudden attack of lice on the train (chapter 23); or specific incidents during training; or the logistics of how the company was kept fed. He also expatiated on perhaps the slightly less engaging details of potato and turnip cultivation in Saxony when he was a child. We left such things out because we did not think they ultimately contributed to the story. (If for any reason the reader wants to know more, we will of course be delighted to hear from you!)

So, perhaps the best way to treat this book is not as unadorned historical fact. It was never meant as that, and the notion of *historical fact* probably only exists on the macro level of historical narrative anyway. Treat the book rather as a personal story: the story of Leni and Martin, as they told it to their daughter.

Also, although Martin and Leni of course are true names, most other names are best treated as fictitious, with the usual caveat of *coincidental reference to individuals living or dead.*

And, yes, Ellie is true.

Befitzeugnis

Dem .... Gefreiten ....
(Dienstgrad)

Martin S c h l a f e r
(Bor- und Zuname)

lo./ 3. Regiment Brandenburg
(Truppenteil)

verleihe ich das

Infanterie-Sturmabzeichen

— Silber —

O.J.,den 19.4.43
(Ort und Datum)

Jacobi
(Unterschrift)

Oberstlt. u. Rgt.-Kdr.
(Dienstgrad und Dienststellung)

he was awarded an infantry assault badge

Certificate for *Sturmabzeichen Silber* awarded Martin in April 1943, possibly for participation in the 42-43 Velikiye Luki battle. The designation *silver* indicates an award for various types of engagement with the enemy, including three infantry assaults, or hand-to-hand combat. The signature is of lieutenant-colonel (Fritz) Jacobi, commander of the 3rd Brandenburger Regiment.

****

We have received much help in writing this book.

We first have to thank two German friends for an astonishing amount of advice and information on a wide range of relevant matters, including writing many letters of inquiry on our behalf to German federal and local archival agencies and a very careful aural check of the recording excerpts on the web. They have indicated, for professional reasons, their wish for anonymity, which is a pity because we have so much to personally thank them for. Well, *they* at least know who they are!

We have also benefitted from the still vividly detailed and often humorous recollections of Rolf Stelzer on what it was like in post-war Germany immediately after surrender; and what it was like to work on the *Snowy Mountain Scheme* way back in the early fifties. Rolf, who has just celebrated his 90th birthday, was also a German carpenter and the baby of the group working on the Snowies. He met Martin on board the MS *Skaubryn* to Australia, where he became, and remained, his close friend.

We would like to acknowledge the help of Frau Foth-Müller of the Berlin Federal Archives. She spent considerable time retrieving very useful dates from the meagre information available in what is left of Martin's military record.

Thanks also to Michael Weaver for critiquing an early version of the book and offering his professional journalistic advice – and not least for suggesting our title!

****

We believe personal histories like *Iron Crossed* are valuable, not only for their individual, but also their vicarious significance. Many, many others of the Australian war-and-immigrant generation will have shared experiences similar to those described in this book, and thus a single history like this can become representative of many. Oral histories have an immediacy lacking in generalised historical accounts. They are how History's *grand narratives* are fleshed out. They are important also because, of course, they recount where YOU came from. Indeed, one of the reasons we wrote the book was for Martin and

Leni's grandchildren, great-grandchildren and great-great grandchildren.

We hope you have enjoyed *Iron Crossed* – perhaps it will encourage you to make your *own* recordings, and recount your *own* histories, for future generations!

Renata Rose & Phil Rose
Canberra, Australia, 2018.